BEYOND
THE
CHURNING
TIDES

Anastasia Arellano
Stevi Lynn
S.B. Barrett
Jennifer L Linn
Emily R Bellas
AJ Braun
Taylor Lust

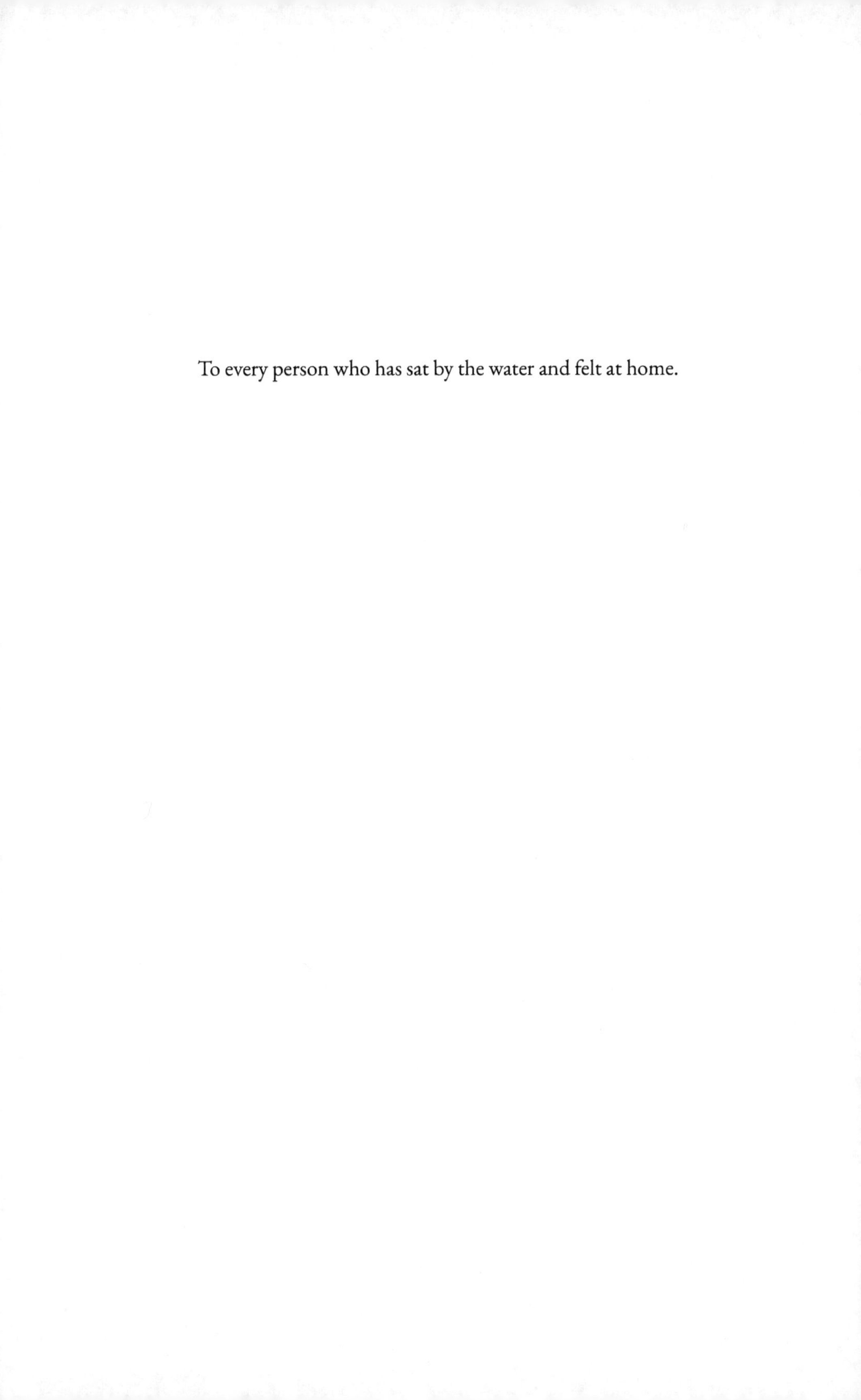

To every person who has sat by the water and felt at home.

Chapter 1

The breaking of the waves across the rocks below keeps me awake for the third night in a row. I know she's there, though I can't see her in the lantern's light. But her song, her song is constant – a quiet whisper on the gusts of wind pounding the shores as she calls my name. even as I write this, I hear it. Clara...

I snap the notebook shut.

"Emily, honey? Can you come here a second," Theo's voice booms from the small kitchen next to the living room. I get up, padding barefoot across the tiny hallway. The wooden floors groan ancient sounds, even though the Airbnb boasted all updated interiors. "What?" I reply, his eyebrow raising.

"Sorry, just eager to get started on the book. What's up?" I try to sound as light as possible.

"Just wanted to check that you like leeks, right?"

I nod.

"Good." He says, unpacking the last of the groceries we bought at the farmer's market on the way up before he clears a counterspace and starts prepping for dinner. I should offer to help, but he's more than capable in the kitchen.

"Hey, check this out," I stand in the doorway with the notebook, making conversation. "It's someone's diary."

"Like a guest left it behind?"

I shake my head, thumbing to the first page. It's a slim, water-warped thing, its cover bowed as if it's been soaked and dried off a few times.

"No, someone named Clara Hayes. Think she lived here in the early 1900s when it was still a functioning lighthouse."

"Really?"

"Yeah." I continue looking through with fascination. "Most of her entries are mundane, day-to-day records of life. Interesting stuff, I'm not even being sarcastic." Theo barely glances up from slicing carrots so thin, they'll barely survive the stewing process. "Anything spicy written in it?"

"We'll see. Doubtful though." I go back to flipping through.

"Shouldn't you be writing instead of reading?"

I prickle at his tone. "It's called inspiration. Besides, you didn't have to come."

"And miss out on a week in a New England lighthouse? Never."

I watch him carrying on with his cooking. I'm lucky he loves to cook, saves me so much time. But sometimes I wonder if I'd have been better off following Tess back home to California. I shake off the thought. We were young and silly, though sometimes I can't help the what ifs. "Stew will be ready in an hour."

I nod, "Cool. I'm going to flip through this a bit more beforehand. Can't believe they left this woman's diary behind."

"Mm," he grunts out in response. "Maybe your story will finally come to you."

"Maybe."

Dinner is a quiet affair, Theo doing the majority of the talking for the both of us. I've got too many pre-occupying thoughts as we sit around the coffee table in the living room playing cards.

The publisher wanted the new manuscript weeks ago and I've got squat – less than that, I've got squat's crippling anxiety. When Theo suggested I spend a week in a lighthouse – because nothing screams gothic romance like a lighthouse – I thought he meant alone.

"Got any 4s?" he interrupts my racing mind.

"Go fish."

I scowl at him from across the small table. Only one of us is enjoying themselves so far. One day down, six to go. At least the sunset is pretty.

"Em, honey?"

I whip my head back. "Yes?"

"It's your turn."

"Right," I look down at the cards in my hand. "Got any 4s?"

"I just asked you that."

"My bad," I apologize, noting the annoyance in his voice before folding my stack. "Do you mind if I take a walk? Feeling a little distracted."

"Yeah sure, no problem."

"I meant alone?" I quickly add when he rises to get his coat.

"Oh. Sure." His face resembles a kicked puppy. "Guess I'll just hang back and clean up." I watch as he starts collecting our bowls.

"Sorry, it's just, I might have something, and I want to think about it." His smile returns and he pounces, placing a kiss on my lips. "Glad to hear it. I knew that sea air was the cure for writer's block."

I chuckle. "We'll see. I'll be back in an hour. If not, assume I've been lured into the sea by a mermaid."

He laughs, kissing me again before I pull on my thick coat, wrapping up with a hat and scarf as best I can to combat the cold.

Outside, the Maine coastline is taking a beating by the winds rolling in off the Atlantic. Large, white-crested waves crash against dark, silt-covered rocks, sending spouts of seafoam skyward. Definitely a perfect backdrop for a gothic romance. I wander further from the lighthouse, past the little welcome sign, and towards the well-worn path that meanders the rocky coast. I glance back, the little red cottage at the back of the white lighthouse growing smaller with each step. My thoughts return to gothic romance, mulling over what's needed. A despondent FMC, check. The perfect partner on paper, check. And a raging, passionate romance that can never be, double check. Because like clockwork, my phone vibrates in my pocket, her name flashing across the screen like a curse.

Tess.

How's the book going?

I feel a wave of guilt as I move to open the message. One innocent DM after a viral video of my debut novel, and here we are, a year later, conducting clandestine affairs.

Not great, I write back. *I'm actually in Maine right now, hoping for some inspo.*

Really? Where?

Little lighthouse I found on Airbnb. I don't dare say Theo found it. That was the first rule we agreed to when reconnecting. I never mention my husband and she doesn't name drop the wife.

Well, if you still need some help with inspiration, next month I'll be in NYC for 3 nights. Hoping I can see you then.

I inhale sharply, the cold air stinging my lungs.

I'd love that.

Great! Free for a quick FaceTime?

I don't even bother to reply, immediately hitting the call button before I have a chance to hesitate.

It rings twice and then her grinning face fills the screen, long red locks bouncing in the air, matching her flushed cheeks. Behind her, the LA skyline is waking up.

"Hi!" she says, breathless from her morning run.

"Hi," I echo, the audio crackling a bit.

"Let's see where you're at." She says between breaths.

"I've just found this charming little cove," I flip the camera, watching her reaction to the view. A stretch of rugged coastline fills her screen. Dark cliffs rise unevenly from the water, their faces worked down into jagged lines from centuries of waves breaking on their surface. Below them, waves crash hard and white, cresting against black rock before pulling back in long, foamy stretches.

"What's that down there?"

I look further down the path between the cliffs. There's a narrow beach tucked between it all. Pale, smoothed pebbles and rough slabs of slate scatter together, glistening under a blue-grey sky. The tide is half in, curling around the edges of the shore.

"Looks like I found the perfect little hidden beach," I say, turning the camera back towards me.

She's slowed to a walk, the camera no longer jerking with her motions. "It looks so..." "Untamable?" I offer.

"I was going to say pretty but yeah, untamable. This is why you're the writer." I smirk, looking down as I find a large stone to take a seat on. It's only slightly damp. "You always liked places like this."

"Places like what?"

"The kind of place that feels slightly out of reach."

She smiles faintly, her gaze lingering on me through the screen. "I remember liking the idea of them."

"I miss you," I say as a gust of wind cuts across the mic. "I wish you could be here with me, seeing all this."

"Like our coastal fall road trip junior year?"

"Yeah."

"I can't wait to see you."

"Me too," I say. "Too bad you can't come out this week."

"A bit far to go from LA."

"Not really," I joke. "Just a flight, a drive, and a questionable life choice." "Tempting," she chuckles.

"Good," I reply. "It's supposed to be."

Chapter 2

"How was the walk?"

"Very inspiring," I avoid eye contact with Theo as I hang up my forest green coat, draping the yellow scarf over it on the peg.

"Glad to hear it," he pulls off the matching yellow beanie from my head. He smiles so innocently I can't help but hate myself after only feeling exhilarated minutes ago. I lean in, giving him a quick peck on the cheek.

"I'm going to write a bit," I warn, running a hand through my dark, amber bob. I catch a reflection of myself in the mirror. When did I become this woman who lies without flinching? "Good luck," he nods. "Do you want the bedroom or the living room?"

I hate how considerate he is sometimes.

"Bedroom please," I say, picking up a notebook and pen to make it look legit. Instead, as soon as I shut the door behind me, I rummage through my small travel case, searching for my vibrator. Talking to Tess always leaves me with a desperate tingle. I think about her touch, the way her lips caress every inch of my skin with her kisses, her soft moans of my name in the middle of...I sigh, cumming hard at the thought.

"You okay in there, babe?" Theo knocks on the door.

"Yeah, just frustrated!" I shove the vibrator under the pillow before pulling up my pants. Thankfully he doesn't come in, his footsteps creaking away back down the hall. I roll over on the bed, sighing again. The diary from earlier sits on the bedside table where I left it. Seems as good a time as any to do a little bit of reading. Maybe I will find some inspiration in it. *I saw her, for the first time after hearing her call for nearly a fortnight. She was beautiful, her skin a pale opalescent like the inside of a mollusk shell, with long silver strands flowing down her back. They shined in the morning light. She made no move to abandon the rock on which she sat. A true to life mermaid. And when she spoke, a calm came over me, the likes of which I'd never felt.*

I pause, rereading that sentence. *A true to life mermaid.*

"You got to be fucking kidding," I scoff. Just some bored lighthouse keeper's work of fiction. I sigh, shutting the diary and sticking it in the drawer. I was really hoping for something salacious. Something I could potentially spin into a bestseller. Instead, I've been reading someone's 20th century Hans Christian Andersen fanfic. The bed springs groan as I move around. I go in search of my laptop, but nearly throw it against the wall in frustration when the wifi signal is too weak to stream anything. With no ideas in my mind, I end up just staring at the original wood-beamed ceiling for an hour. This is going to be a long week.

I don't crawl into bed until almost midnight. Despite the weighted feeling of tiredness, it takes me almost half an hour to settle and find a comfortable position. Theo radiates heat like a furnace. I get up and quietly slip out the bedroom towards the living room. The Airbnb feels different at night. I shake off the spooky vibes. I've been letting that silly diary get into my head. Outside, the solar-powered lanterns in the grass line the perimeter of the lighthouse's yard. Their glow is barely enough to penetrate the night, giving off a ghostly ambience. The living room window reflects nothing but a smear of blackness where the sea should be just beyond the edge of the cliffs. For a moment, I stand there, listening to the crash of the waves matching my own heartbeat.

Looking down to the coffee table, I notice the outline of the diary, right where I left it after my bedtime cup of tea. I pick it up, reaching for my phone in the pocket of my hoodie, turning on the flashlight to get a better look. The light pools over the page as I open it, the thin pages near transparent. No more mention of a mermaid, just back to moody descriptions of the weather and the mundane tasks carried out in her day-to-day. But then something from the 4th of June, 1901 catches my eye. I lean in, brows knitting together as I read the passage. *She doesn't keep one face. She will watch first. Listen. And then the sea will sing back your wants, your grief, your name.*

"Shit," I hiss, my phone tumbling to the ground making a soft thud as it lands on my toes. I really need to get it together. I'm a grown woman, I can't be flinching at the vibration of an incoming text.

It's Tess again. I bite back a smile, quickly opening her message.

Are you awake?

Before I can start a reply, another message follows.

Can't stop thinking about that pretty mouth of yours.

A cacophony of butterflies erupts in the pit of my stomach. I start to type back. *Oh yeah? What about it can't you stop thinking about?*

Outside, the wind rises, sharp against the windows. It slips through the seams of the cottage with a thin whistle. I pause. There's something in it. Something hypnotically melodic. My pulse picks up speed.

"Emily..."

Chapter 3

"Emily!" I jolt awake to Theo's urgent shaking. I shiver, my back and neck stiff, suddenly aware that I'm laying in a patch of tall grass, only a few steps from the cliff's edge. The surging water below roars in the wake of screeching gulls.

"What are you doing out here like this?" Theo wraps his giant green parka around me. "You could've frozen to death. Let's get you back inside."

I don't say anything. A pit forms in my stomach as I follow him, the fuzzy socks I wore to bed soggy and offering little protection against the uneven ground. God, I hope I don't lose a toe over this.

"What happened?" Theo asks the moment we've crossed the threshold. "I don't know," I take a seat on the living room sofa, fully aware we'll probably have to pay a cleaning fee for the mud and grass stains on the white linen couch. "I couldn't sleep, so I came out here for a bit to write. Then, I must've fallen asleep. Last thing I can remember was singing."

Singing. The pit in my stomach widens. Maybe there is something to this notebook phenomenon. I strike the thought from my head.

Be realistic, Em.

Theo looks at me with a wary gaze. "You, came out here to write?" "Yes."

"Then why were your notebook and laptop left in the room?"

"I wrote bits in my notes app on my phone."

He nods, not saying anything. I know he's been growing suspicious of me in the last few months.

I watch him go into the kitchen, putting the kettle to boil. Withing minutes he's back, placing a grey ceramic mug in front of me on the coffee table. The cup of tea is dwarfed by the ornately large wooden piece of sanded driftwood. I reach forward, the warming scent of peppermint overtakes my senses as I bring the tea towards my lips.

"I'm going to go shower," I say, feeling a sudden chill taking root.

"Don't forget this," Theo pulls my phone from his pocket.

"Where was it?" I take it in hand.

"You left it on the sofa."

"Thanks," I slip it into the parka pocket, heading to the bathroom. The Airbnb boasts a beautifully spacious bathroom with stunning views of the Atlantic coast. The reality is more a micro-room with a comically large claw-footed bathtub that leaves little room to navigate around the sink and toilet. The window is small and frosted, blocking out any trace of the outside. Not that there would be much to see on such a grey, moody morning. I climb into the tub, rinsing off before filling it up with piping hot water. Sinking down into the bath, I generously add the provided bath salts and oils for a luxurious start to the day. Sitting in the bubbles, inhaling pleasant scents of peony and lavender, puts me at ease. I let my mind wander, trying to figure out what happened. I allow my brain to go, step by step, drawing me back into the events of the previous night.

Slowly, it starts coming back. I remember sitting downstairs on the couch. The text message. The diary. The voice. Despite the warmth of the bath, a shiver crawls up my spine. Tess's voice was outside, I'm sure of it. She was calling me, like casting a spell of enchantment that propelled me through the door and out into the cold of the night, dressed in nothing but an oversized hoodie and pink, fuzzy bed socks.

She learns your voice...

My eyes fly open and I sit up, scented water sloshing over the sides of the tub onto the floor. The notebook.

As carefully as I can manage, I get out, wiping the suds off myself with a towel before racing to the living room. I spot the little diary on the corner of the couch and grab it, rushing back to the bedroom.

"Em?" Theo's voice follows me down the hall. "What's wrong? Did you get inspired?"

"Yeah!" I call out, hoping he doesn't come after me. I rush to my side of the bed, plopping onto the creaky mattress and getting as comfortable as possible. I thumb through the pages, searching for the entry that I'd read yesterday.

I couldn't sleep again last night, thinking about Margaret's impending marriage to Edward. But just as I was finally settling, I heard her.

Margaret.

She was outside, calling my name. I don't remember much, but this morning, they found me outside by the cliffs. I'm afraid. Of what they might do if they think I'm mad. I'm afraid I might actually be going mad. But more than anything, I'm afraid of her. She's lurking in the waters. I know she is.

A mermaid that lures her victims by name. Could this actually be happening? I shuffle around the room, looking for my laptop. No, no, this is just the writer in me talking, getting the better of my imagination. Maybe inspiration is finally starting to hit. On the bright side, two 19th century lesbians entangled in a secret affair, one of whom is about to marry a dude, that could be my next bestseller if I pull it off right.

"Babe? Do you know the wifi passcode?" I call down the hall.

"FXG4572c1a3wx," Theo shouts back.

"Thanks!"

Still wrapped in my towel, wet hair sending sopping water down my back and sides of my neck, I log onto the Airbnb's wifi. It's desperately slow, taking forever to load the Google homepage. I move closer to the door, hoping maybe to get three bands instead of two on my wifi icon. *Mermaid. Legend. Rose Cove, Maine.* I type in my search words, hoping they produce something of substance.

I stretch out on the bed, scrolling. First thing I find is the local lore tab under the town's homepage. Nothing much to read except for local sightings of a beautiful mermaid sunning herself on the rocks below the cliffs date back to the before the town's founding in 1785. Nearby indigenous tribes warn of a trickster sea spirit that lures the lovelorn to their deaths by mimicking the voices of their beloved.

I feel a heat of anxiety creep up the sides of my neck into my face. Mimicking the voices of their beloved. She hardly heard Tess and I on the phone yesterday.

"Hey."

I scream, bucking at the sensation of something touching the top of my head. "OW!"

I turn, gasping an apology to Theo as he leans against the closet door, holding his nose with his right hand, and cupping under his chin with his other, catching the run-off blood spurting from his nose.

"Honey, what did you do?" I stand, the towel dropping away as I move to attend his injury. He pulls away, refusing my aid.

"I just came in to kiss my wife and she head butted me so hard." He turns back towards the door, headed for the bathroom. "I think you broke it."

I grab the towel from the bed. "Here."

"I don't want to have to pay for new towels." His injured pride replies.

"I'm sorry," I repeat, following him, watching helpless as he runs the tap and starts to clean himself off. "Anything I can do?"

"You were really into something," he says through a bloody grin. "Anything interesting?" I shake my head. "Just reading the local lore."

"Oh, about the mermaid?"

I nod.

"Think you found your inspiration?"

I nod again.

"Good, then my broken nose might be worth it in the end."

I chuckle, running a hand across his back. "Do you feel better?"

"Not really, but I'll be fine," he shrugs away from my touch once more. "Hey, maybe later we can do a walk together?"

Theo's face spreads out into a wide grin. "Thought you'd never ask. Want to get dressed and we'll go?"

"Oh, I was thinking later, later," I say, pointing back towards the room and my laptop. "Right now, I think I'm kind of onto something."

"Yeah, no problem." His smile doesn't quite reach the corners of his eyes.

It feels weird holding Theo's hand. We were never a PDA-type of couple, but we always held hands. Lately, there hasn't been much of it. His palm is warm against mine – familiar in the same way routines are familiar. We stroll along the cliff path, the grass bends low in the wind.

The sea below rolls along the rocks in long, choppy waves. It should be peaceful, but it's not. It has me slightly on edge.

Sensing my discomfort, Theo gives my hand a squeeze, asking, "You okay?" "Yeah," I say, too fast. Correcting myself, I reply in a softer, "Yeah, just, book stuff." "Book stuff," he repeats.

We walk a few more steps in silence, the cold wind picking at the edges of everything – my nose, my coat, my thoughts.

Theo slows down, turning to face me. "Can I ask you something?" My stomach tightens. "Of course."

"Are you happy?"

The question catches me off guard. "Why would you ask me that?" "I don't know, it just seems that with the book and everything, you seem a little unhappy."

"Of course, I'm unhappy. I'm under contractual obligation to deliver something marketable."

"But baby, everything is going to –"

My phone rings, the shrill tune cutting the air. I dig into my pocket, quickly rejecting the call when I see Tess's name. She must be on her morning run already.

"It's my agent," I say, shoving my phone back into my pocket, killing the sound.

"Aren't you going to answer it? You always answer it."

"She's just going to ask me about the book. I'll call her back later. Right now, I'm enjoying our walk."

I stand on my tip toes to place a kiss on his cheek like Judas Iscariot. I glance down at the space between us and reach out a hand. The wind rises again, dragging up salt from the sea. And for a moment, I think I hear my phone buzz again.

Chapter 4

I start my day with a large cup of coffee in the garden, wrapped in a thick, grey blanket. The soft fuzziness of the material provides a small bit of a relief against the pounding cold. Despite how beautifully the sun is shining, the cold winds feel like thousands of tiny needles against my exposed skin. I need the caffeine to kick in. The second night wasn't as eventful as my first night, but I still spent the majority of it awake, convincing myself the incoherent cries were just air moving through gaps in the walls.

"You're crazy to be out here," Theo appears, wrapped in his parka as he takes a seat beside me on the bench. The weathered wood groans under the addition of his 6'2 frame. "Then why are you sitting down?"

He smirks, dark waves barely moving in the wind given how much he gels his hair. "I didn't say I wasn't crazy too."

"Hmm." I offer him some of my coffee. He accepts a sip, grimacing at the French vanilla creamer I added.

We sit together in silence, watching the smattering of white and grey clouds glide across the sky. Just beyond the garden, are the cliffs, and below, the hollowed echoes of waves crashing on rocks nearly drown out the sounds of sea birds cackling in the sky. I look up, seeing a grouping of seagulls lazily glide along the gusts of wind.

"Have you ever heard from Tess?"

The question creates an instantaneous icicle along my spine. He's fishing for something. "Not for a long while. She found me on Instagram and congratulated me on the book last year," I reply, sipping the last of my coffee. The taste is no longer enjoyable.

"I see. I'm going to head in, take a shower. Care to join?"

I shake my head. "I'm actually going to drive down to the village, want to check out this little museum thing. Think it might spark something. Then I might find a café and do some writing. Hope you don't mind?"

He leans over, pressing a kiss to my cheek. "Have fun."

The town center of Rose Cove is one short block of weathered shops pressed shoulder to shoulder, their windows crowded with seashells, postcards, and other little knickknacks. The sidewalks are uneven, the buildings' paint jobs a little too chipped to still be considered charming. It reminds me of a movie set from the 70s that's been lost to time. After I park the car I get out my phone, following the directions one block over to the Founder's Home, where The Little Museum of Rose Cove is said to be. If anywhere is going to potentially give me answers, that would be the place. Disappointment collapses like a Jenga Tower in my chest when I see the closed sign hanging in the door. I get back on my phone, checking to see if it's closed permanently or just for the day. Not being able to find the information I need, I decide to make a morning of it.

I wander back around to the main stretch, peeking in the windows of each little shop I pass. Unfortunately, most seem to be closed for the off-season. At the very end of the main street there is a little antique shop that has a welcome sign in the window.

I swing open the little shop door, the bell overhead ringing with a delightful chime. No one is behind the counter, so I wander around, looking at the items on display. One item in particular catches my eye. The antique silver snuff box is delicately engraved with a mermaid. "She's a beauty, isn't she?"

A gasp escapes my lips, and beside me, the little old lady chuckles.

"Didn't mean to scare you, hun."

I giggle. "I've been a little on edge, I guess."

"Not from around here?" She asks, her voice soft and gentle.

I shake my head. "New York."

"That's a long drive to make for the off-season."

I glance down to the snuff box in the display case. "I needed the city break. What's the story behind that one?"

"The mermaid?" she chuckles again, pulling out a host of keys from her pocket that she rifles through before finding the one for the display case. Gingerly, she grabs the snuff box and presents it to me for further inspection.

"It's quite pretty," I admire.

"You must be familiar with the lore then," she says, closing the case. "Why else would anyone come to Rose Cove."

"Oh, I don't believe in all that. I just came for the inspiration. I'm a romance writer."

"Really?" she lights up. "Anything I might have read?"

"You've hardly heard of *What Stalks These Halls*."

Her eyes widen. "That one on the apps being called gothic Bridgerton?"

I raise a brow.

"My grand-niece has me on the TikToker for books."

"Booktok, yes," I can't help but giggle. "That's me."

"Oh, my. I didn't think I'd ever meet a celebrity."

"I'm hardly a celebrity. Just a writer."

"Well, I'd say you're getting a lot of inspiration from our local legend."

I shrug, still holding the snuff box. "That's the thing, I can't really find much information about it. I'm staying at this lighthouse Airbnb, and I –"

"You're staying at the lighthouse?"

I clock the switch of her tone, how it shifts from amicable to concerned. "Yes, my husband and I are staying the week."

"Are you two happy together?"

The question catches me off guard. "Why shouldn't we be?"

"Are you sleeping alright?" she continues her urgent line of questioning. "Why are you asking me such personal questions?"

Her demeanour softens momentarily, and she waves a hand. "Oh, no reason. Just sometimes folks who stay up there too long tend to get a little...restless."

I let out a small breath. "It's an old building. Noises, you know?"

"That's what they all say at first."

A flicker of unease courses through me. The old lady leans in closer, lowering her voice like she's afraid the walls might hear.

"My grandma used to tell us stories about the coast. Long before the lighthouse was built, the tribe who lived here had a name for what moves through the water."

"Mishabenook," she says, the word heavy and unfamiliar. "It means the one who borrows the voice."

A cold prickle spreads along my arms.

"Uh, thanks," I push the snuff box back into her hands. "I have to go."

"It's just a story, of course. Every town's got one."

"Yeah, I know but I have to run a few errands before heading back."

"Don't you want the snuff box?" she calls after me.

"Uh, I have to think about it. But thank you!" I grab the door to leave, the bell offering up a soft, hollow chime.

Chapter 5

After dinner, I sit down to write. I shoo Theo out of the living room, taking over. After re-arranging the living room in order to fit the vintage writing desk beneath the back window within view of the setting evening, I finally settle down with my laptop and a cup of decaf to get started. The writing begins, and within twenty minutes I find my flow, getting out a couple thousand words. Those words continue to grow and multiply, and before I know it, I'm staring at twenty-seven pages in the cold blue light of the laptop. Around me, darkness has fallen. Down the hall, the rumbling sounds of Theo's snoring remind me that I'm not alone in the cottage. I must've been at this for hours and not realized it. I stretch out my arms, the vertebras in my spine cracking one by one like popcorn. I yawn, glancing to the corner of the screen for a time. 1:32 am. Not bad. Feeling triumphant, I save the word doc under the title, Project Bestseller 2 – draft 1 and proceed to the kitchen to make myself a cup of peppermint tea before bed. Over the rising rumble of a boiling kettle, I hear it. Laughter. I abandon the tea on the counter, following the source of the laughter to the window.

It's just a draft coming in through the cracks, I repeat to myself. But I know that laugh. I heard it constant for four years. The symphony of pure joy that once would infect me to join along, now fills me with dread as I listen to every note. Tess.

It's not real. She's not real. This is all just lack of proper sleep and a writer's imagination. I decide the best course of action is to pull on my parka and my boots, and march out into the night to confront it. With my heart now pounding, I walk out into the cold February night. The sound of Tess's laughter seems to be coming at me from all angles on the wind. I walk out to the edge of the garden, looking out into the darkness. "This won't work on me!" I shout into the air.

For a moment, it seems to be over, nothing to be heard but the crashing of waves over the stillness of night. But then, it starts again. Not her laughter, but her voice, whispering my name. The raw pain and desire drawn out in every letter of, "Emily."

"It's not real, it's not real, you'll see it's not real," I say aloud, willing the sense of panic back down as I fumble with my phone, desperate to get a hold of the one person I know can talk me off this ledge.

With shaking hands I press the call button. Hopefully she'll be in a place where she can pick up.

"Emily, babe?"

I scream, dropping my phone at the touch of Theo's hand pressing against my back. "What are you doing out here at almost two in the morning?"

"I'm..." my shaking voice fails to provide an answer.

"And who were you shouting at?"

"I'm just..." again, the words fail to appear.

The silhouette of Theo's face turns, and his attention is pulled to the tiny source of light at my feet. He bends down before I can stop him, grabbing at my phone. It's still unlocked, the call still ringing, her name still dancing across the screen.

"So, what was that about you haven't spoken with Tess for a while?"

I'd always feared how a confrontation might play out if Theo were to ever know for sure. But the reality is way worse. Instead of the screaming and understandable fit of anger I was expecting, all I've received is calm. Plenty of tears and sense of betrayal, but calm. It's the kind of calm that doesn't feel like forgiveness, but rather detachment.

He sits across from me at the kitchen table, hands loosely clasped, eyes rimmed red. Behind him, the sun is breaking the horizon. He keeps his voice steady, like he won't allow himself to further crack.

He poses his final question. "Was it ever real?"

It lands heavy between us, adding to the exhaustion in the room. I open my mouth, but then quickly close it. Anything I say now will just feel wrong. Theo nods once, like my silence is the answer he was searching for.

"I think what hurts the most," he says quietly. "Isn't that you lied, but that you're still here...when I know you want to be somewhere else."

"Theo," my throat tightens.

"No." He shakes his head, pulling away from my advancing hand. "Don't. Please don't try to make it smaller than it is."

Theo is the first to stand. He heads for the door, grabbing his jacket off the hook and rummaging through the pockets. He pulls out the car keys.

"I'm going to stay somewhere else tonight, and probably the next couple nights if I'm honest. I'll come pick you up when it's time to head back to the city."

"Theo, please –"

He holds up his hand. "If you need the car for whatever reason just call me, we can figure something out."

"Okay."

At the door, he hesitates. Not looking at me, he says, "I hope someday you can be happy, Emily."

Then, he's gone.

Chapter 6

The silence he leaves behind lands harder than any display of anger would have. I stand there in the kitchen for a long time, staring at the table like it might spontaneously reproduce Theo. Outside, the midmorning light has gone grey. I realize that the wind has picked up. Not gradually, but all at once, like a gale is on the horizon. Metallic flashes across the sky, followed by the booming of thunder in the distance. The weather app says that we're in for two days of heavy rains. I consider calling Theo and begging for forgiveness, even if it's just enough to pick me up and get me back to New York. Or even just to move back in for the next few days and ride out the storm with me. I don't want to be here alone.

I listen to the heavy pelleting of raindrops on the windows. I decide to put pride aside and pick up the phone.

Theo doesn't answer, but he picks up on my second attempt. "Hey." "Hi, do you want to come back? I don't know if I can be at the lighthouse alone." I listen to his sigh of frustration before he responses. "Just ride it out for the next two days. I'll come pick you up Thursday instead after the storm has passed." "But, Theo, I'm...a little scared."

"Don't be. Just think of all the writing you'll get done."

He hangs up before I have a chance to argue back. He's probably right, I should weather this storm, as well as the one I've created.

The wind outside presses harder against the walls. The windows give a low, uneasy rattle. I move closer toward the window. In the distance, the ocean is no longer calm. It has turned, the waves are dark and churning, agitated in the way they crash upon the rocks. They're higher than I've seen them in the last few days, collapsing into themselves with frenzied violence. The horizon has blurred, sky and water bleeding into one another until no clear boundary is left – just a wall of charcoal grey.

And beneath it all, the uneasy humming of my name, threading through the storm. It calls to me in the voice I recognize all too well.

By Thursday morning, there is no sign of Theo. Granted, the storm has shown no signs of letting up. If anything, it has intensified, and there is a shelter in place warning. And with it, so has the torment. I've stopped answering Tess's calls, refusing to hear her voice. Instead, we communicate sporadically through text. Or the occasional voice note that I send. But I must be saying something wrong, because her last couple texts have been begging me to call her, to assure her that I'm okay, that I haven't lost the plot. But I can't give that thing any more ammo to work with.

It's no longer just my name. It's instructions. It's worse at night, and I need to stay awake and alert to move against its insidious magic.

Another gust slams into the house, harder this time, and the glass vibrates under it like it's straining to hold the world out.

"Emily," the name floats over the howling wind. My breath catches in unease. "NO," I look around for the ear buds I've been using to drown out Theo's snoring. I can't seem to find them. They'd be perfect for providing some relief. My eyes are heavy, stinging with tiredness, but I can't give in. If I do, then she'll really find me. July 2, 1901. The diary said so. "Emily..."

I step closer to the glass. The sea below is no longer just water. It moves with something alive, something that has decided it's not done with me.

"Emily, come to me, my love."

The voice rises and falls with the waves, as if the ocean itself is speaking. It calls again, softer and achingly close, like it's just on the other side of the glass.

"Come down to me, Emily."

My fingers press against the window before I realize I've moved closer to the center of the room. Another surge of wind hits the house. The lights flicker once, dimming the room into a pale, trembling half-dark.

Out in the stormy sea, something breaks the surface. A flash of silver. "Please, come with me."

"No, I can't!" I scream into the empty cottage.

It's been two days of no sleep, afraid to close my eyes for fear that I will hear her and be unable to resist.

"Emily, come with me. We can be together forever!"

I look down at my phone. To the last message from Tess.

Don't worry, sweetie. We'll be together again soon. Just hold on.

Just hold on. That's what I've been doing. Holding on for her. How can I trust a screen? I grab my phone, chucking it across the room where it hits the wall with a crack. "Emily, I need you to come to me."

"Tess!"

She's right outside. I know she is. She got that plane just to see me. I grab my coat and rush out into the storm, my body almost no match for the forceful winds. Rain is coming in from all angles, and despite the thick coat, I'm drenched within seconds.

"Tess?" I call out, following the sound of her voice. "Where are you?" "Here!"

I follow her towards the cliffs, my steps unsteady in the muddy grass.

"Come home with me."

My foot slips on wet rock but I don't stop, allowing myself to fall forward into the storm, into the dark and churning waters where secrets are kept.

Godrik

She went and got a slutty little nose ring over the summer break. Godrik Viathan cursed under his breath as the one person he would fall to his knees for, walked into his classroom. Lumah Halo was born of angelic descent but was also damned to contain the voice of a siren, which meant Godrik was forced to teach her the power of water magic. No matter how much he detested her.

And that slutty little nose ring.

Like the brazen female she was, she tossed her long, wavy locks over her shoulder, tucked in her golden-etched wings, and sat in the seat directly across from his desk. Godrik's stormy gray eyes narrowed, and his scale-covered fingertips gripped his intricately carved seat made of driftwood and precious coral. The action caused pieces of the red coral to fleck onto the floor, but he cared little about the mess he was making.

He couldn't take his eyes off her. All he could do was watch her, like the sullen fool that she'd turned him into.

Like a tribe of bratty, youthful aristocrats, three other twenty-something mystical students surrounded her — one spritely witch sat behind her, another female dressed in black sat on her left, and Godrik's disobedient bison-horned nephew sat at her right. Like Godrik, each of Lumah's lackey friends was born of demon descent. Each of them meant to be in this classroom learning the Shadowed side of Magic, the counterpoint of Luminous Magic, and the ultimate balance of everything.

Lumah, on the other hand, is an abomination, a flaw in the system, something that shouldn't exist at all, let alone be taught to hone her magic in his classroom.

Yet, here she was in the front row, and making his immortal existence miserable.

Rules were put in place for a reason, and since the moment Lumah was created, she broke every one of them.

Godrik enjoyed the flow of rules and the easy understanding that came with a structured system. Magic was fickle, and the world could easily be set into catastrophe should the magical force be off kilter by even a hair in either direction for too long. The equilibrium of light and dark kept things running correctly. Kept mortals from sheer panic and destruction of the perfectly imperfect purgatory they were given to live upon.

Of course, Godrik was a demon. His father is the serpent lord of Envy, the Leviathan, the fourth most powerful ruler of the kingdom of hell, and his mother is a sea nymph as wild as the untamed ocean itself. So, on occasion, Godrik liked to bend the strict structure for shits and giggles, but to twist the solidity of balance until it festered into something new was inconceivable to him.

Yet, Lilith and Michael did just that.

Together, they created a child unlike any other before, and called her one of them. The very idea of that sickened him. Additionally, neither the Holy Trinity above, nor the cursed nine below, did anything to punish them or the child. Godrik tried to take it upon himself last semester to attest that she wasn't worthy to learn here. Tried to show the system that she was a faulty violation, but she had proved him wrong with that polished voice and the manipulation it had over water magic.

And the clutch it had over his cursed soul.

Lumah was powerful, beautiful, courageous — and fucking witty to boot. He couldn't stand it. She was everything he avoided when he could. Godrik found pleasure in mediocrity, calculated ploys, consistent justice, and potentially reviving the relationship of light and dark when necessary.

Mundane. That's what he was. And that's what he liked. Everything else was a hiccup in his harmoniously bland routine.

A slow smile spread across Lumah's cherry-glossed lips, and she leaned over her driftwood desk. Making sure her plump porcelain breasts were on full display before him as her cleavage spilled over the top of her low-cut white t-shirt.

"Class started three minutes ago. Are you going to teach us something or sit there staring at me?"

Godrik's lips thinned to a single line of irritation, and horrid thoughts flashed within his lucid mind. *I want to drown you in the seven seas, rid myself of your haunting presence, and plaster your lifeless husk to my bedframe.* That's what his heart wanted to say to her. Instead, he took a calming intake of breath, unwrapped his sore fingers from his chair, and stood to his feet.

"Outside," he said, pointing toward the wall-to-ceiling glass windows, which faced the rocky cove and the churning ocean beyond. "The weather is perfect, the ocean is rolling with enthusiasm, and it's a fantastic day to learn about wave engineering."

Gasps of both excitement and shock rippled through the room, and his opinionated nephew questioned his decision with a fickle frown. "We are second year students. Many of us are still getting adjusted to our magic, isn't it dangerous for us to be so close to the riptides when a squall is approaching?"

"Yes. You are all young adults, free to make your own choices. Anyone uncomfortable with my decision is welcome to leave and learn nothing today." Godrik folded his arms and glanced around the room. "I'm not here to teach the weak; that's what Charity's class in the luminous wing is for. I am here to teach brave, assertive, water-wielding students how to hone their gifts and create small specs of havoc with them. What better time for that than in the midst of a storm?"

Many of the students hadn't yet learned anything beyond beakers and textbooks in their second year. His reasoning for going outside might cause some heavenly teachers to chatter over safety concerns, but Godrik couldn't stand to be trapped in this classroom with Lumah one second longer. He'd rather take his chances with crashing waves, raging winds, and blinding lightning, than suffocate from the turbulent feelings he couldn't control.

Lumah

"Good gracious, that man is stubbornly infuriating. This little fucking charade has already sent two to the infirmary, and half the class bolted before they even stepped foot on the sandy shoreline." Lumah seared as she clicked her boots impatiently against the side of a wet rock.

Next to her, Fawna Dagny, her freckle-faced best friend, shrugged and shook her short black hair like a wet dog. "Well, it is good practice. We'll never get a shot like this again until we are in our fourth year at least. As our teacher said, what better way to learn how to push ourselves than against a storm? Honestly, I think this is damn thrilling. If only all the teachers would —"

Lumah side-eyed her friend. "What? Sacrifice students?"

Fawna rolled her dark eyes. "They won't die, Lumah. We are born of supernatural lineage. That makes even the weakest of us tough to fucking kill." With a purse of her lips, Lumah watched a smug, sharp-toothed grin cross her friend's face as she continued. "And some of us are as immortal as the archdemons themselves."

"Well, that may be true, but he's surly enough to let us all suffer, and that can sometimes be worse than death." Lumah countered, twisting her soaked caramel hair into a swift fishtail braid.

By the time she finished her braid, the rain had begun to come down sideways, hitting her skin like the prickly spikes of a cactus plant. Before walking out to the cove, Lumah had thrown on a puffy turquoise jacket, but her hands, face, and legs were still left uncovered. And with every pounding of stinging rain against her flesh, Lumah grew more livid towards the teacher in question. If only the handsome asshole knew how to have a conversation and didn't hide away from feelings, no one would be suffering right now.

With a clenched fist around the collar of her jacket, she watched as a girl with red curls and gray leathery wings attempted to split the crashing water before it reached her. The girl flicked her fingers, manipulating the rainwater droplets so that they didn't impair her vision, then she pushed forward towards the blustering stormy waves, calling to her power with shaky, unsure movements.

Lumah sighed. The redhead was too nervous for such a risky task.

Rightfully so, too, if she couldn't bend her magic enough to manipulate the ocean, the powerful current would certainly drag her out to sea, filling her half-mortal lungs with more salt than one should swallow in a lifetime. It would be painful for the girl and pitiful to watch.

Lottie was the girl's name.

Lumah had only spoken a few words to her, but her heart sank in her chest when she noticed the size of the newly formed wave Lottie was going up against. There was no way this would end well for her classmate. Not only would the girl's nerves distract her magic but Lottie was the daughter of the laziest demon who ever existed, Belphegor, and a human mother. Her magic was a spark of what it should be for such an attempt.

"Reach outward. Feel the magic churning under your skin and own the waves!" Hollered Godrik over the howling wind. "Your strengths are in element manipulation and hydromancy, use them both now. The waves will listen to you if you believe in yourself."

The girl's eyes flickered in his direction as if to tell him she didn't believe in herself, but he ignored her fear and urged her forward with a snap of his webbed fingers.

Lumah flared her nose and turned away from the scene. Refusing to look at Godrik's sharp face any longer. And she sure as hell couldn't bear to watch Lottie get swept away in an embarrassing defeat. The girl wasn't strong enough. Her gifts were more useful on lakes or calm rivers, not against the temperamental ocean, and that scale-covered asshole knew it. Lumah cursed his name and closed her eyes. He was making a joke out of the class because he couldn't handle the feelings raging inside his body for her.

Fucking demons. They were fueled by heightened emotions, yet they handled them with all the grace of a caged bull.

Before she knew it, her body was shaking as deep-seated fury expanded from her core. Like uncharted waters, it swam through her churning gut, through her tensed limbs, and stung at her eyes. If he hated her enough to torture others like this, then she would greet his hate with surging contempt. She blinked away the threatening tears, letting their searing tribulation wash away with the chilly rain, and she lost herself to the low hum of her magic.

As her magic grew, she swallowed her harbored disdain for the man who was supposed to be teaching her how to control her powers. But right now she felt anything but in control. The seed of her swirling anxiety over everything settled its clenched anger within her fitful beating heart and searched for an outlet through the veins that held her power within their smallest capillaries.

"Here's your chance, Lottie, split the wave or take a nap at the bottom of the ocean!"

Godrik's voice slammed against Lumah's pointed ears harder than the cutting rain. With blue fire in her eyes, Lumah stretched her angelic wings and lifted her chin to the growing clouds above them. Under her breath, Lumah called out to her siren side, just as Lottie screamed. "I can't do it!"

And Godrik shouted harshly back at the waning student. "Yes, you damn well can, or you're not fit enough for my classroom!"

Lumah couldn't see the unbroken wave come down over Lottie, and sweep her away, but she could hear the girl's fearful squeal turn to a gurgled cry, and that was the last straw. Her siren magic burst to life, and she started to sing, low and mesmerizing. Like a hypnotic lullaby, her siren side left her vocal cords and sent a swarm of vibrations into the surrounding atmosphere. She sang to the storm cloud, calling for its intensity to stutter and stall. The way a hundred hornets would defend their home, her voice cut through the dense rain like visible, resonating sound energy, and the sweeping storm obeyed her command without retaliation. Then, with pulsing blue fingertips, she spun around and urged the thrashing saltwater current to break in two — just like Godrik had wanted the others to do.

Unlike the yielding clouds above her, the ocean tried to fight back. Unwilling to heed her magical call so easily.

Its turbulent projection aimed itself towards Lumah, looking to swallow her up as it did Lottie. But Lumah wouldn't bend.

Like the monstrous mouth of a water serpent, it lunged for her, but she steadied her feet and arched her wings horizontally, creating a fortress of feathers around her. Their water-repelling cage centered her song towards the threat directly ahead of her. Louder her voice sounded, and more forceful her magic beamed from her hands, until the air inside her lungs burned, and the magic in her veins felt like dull razor blades cutting at her flesh.

When she felt as if she would collapse on the sand below her feet, the ocean finally bowed to her, parting until Lottie was found, and the waves stilled to a low lulling roll.

Fawna and two others rushed to aid their fallen classmate. Once she was secured, Lumah turned to the remaining students and shouted. "This field experiment is over."

Beside her, so close she wondered when he'd gotten this near, a disapproving hiss sent chills down her spine. "You're not the one in charge."

Godrik's voice was gravely and threatening, but Lumah felt frustrated about the way her body wanted to bow to its captivating command.

Lowering her wings, and swallowing her feelings, she reluctantly turned to face the man who held so much power over her, yet refused to admit there was anything between their souls at all. When her eyes caught sight of him, his thick biceps crossed in tense irritation over his chest, her erratic breath startled.

Handsome wasn't a strong enough word to describe Godrik.

He was strikingly haunting, like the way fog captivates a person when it rolls over a crystal-clear lake on a moody fall morning. It was honestly unfair how addictive his features were to her. Every angle of him was perfection wrapped in scales, and it felt as if each piece of him was created just for her to enjoy. But before her staring turned to gaping, she straightened her shoulders and pushed aside the yearning that warmed every inch of her body and uttered with a sarcastic bite. "Well, the person in charge is a prick with the worst teaching skills imaginable."

His gray eyes narrowed, but she thought she caught the start of a grin before he spoke. "No one learns anything from being coddled."

For several breaths, the two of them stood at a standstill. She didn't dare flutter a wing, and he didn't so much as blink. This was the closest contact they had with one another since that moment in the parking lot last term. Months have passed since then, but she could still remember the way he tasted on her tongue, and feel the words he whispered upon her neck. They were sweet and passionate and nothing like how he spoke to her today.

Last year, he looked at her like she was something he craved to collect, to study, and to protect. But that was before she had whispered three stupid words to him. Now, he looked at her like he wanted to strangle the breath from her lungs and dig her grave so deep no one could ever uncover the treasure that cursed his damned soul. In their standstill, her betraying heart ached for him. For the torture that bled so clearly through his eyes, and the reasons he felt the need to shove those three words aside. A piece of her wanted to rid him of the pain he felt, take the words back, and pretend she'd never said them, but that part of her was foolish.

Because there was no denying what the two of them were, and as long as he refused to accept it, he deserved every ounce of agony that befell him.

With a rough exhale, Godrik broke their impasse. "Everyone, go pacify your feeble egos and leave this cove now. I'm sick of looking at you." He said the words to the class, but his stony gaze stayed locked on Lumah's luminous features.

"Feelings are mutual." Lumah flung her long braid as she turned around to rid herself of that beautiful, searing stare. She felt the tip of her hair slap against the side of Godrik's face.

That made her smile as she took a step forward.

But that smug smile turned to a surprised gasp in an instant. With the might of a clamped saltwater croc jaw, Godrik gripped the back of her neck, bracing her from walking away.

"Not you."

His grip was tight, and it scared her enough to make her flinch with shock. But it didn't hurt, and surely its hold wasn't enough to cause bruising upon her unyielding angelic skin. But those fettered, scale-covered fingertips along her delicate skin emitted a transfusion of desolate emotion through their hold.

Slowly, she turned on her heel. As she spun, his grip loosened as if shocked at the way he touched her, but it never left its placement upon her neck entirely. And when she faced him once again, his large palm rested against the nape of her throat. Lumah wanted to lean into it and absorb all the emotion that bled under Godrik's touch into her heart. She wanted to raise his palm and kiss his pain away with every peck of her love against his body, but she couldn't find the submissive energy to do so when he looked at her with such disgust.

So instead she pursed her lips and stood firm against his vexed attitude.

"You and I are going to have a little chat." He said through clenched teeth.

Behind her, Lumah heard Fawna chortle, "It's about fucking time."

Lumah

Everyone else was gone.

For an ungodly long period, the two of them — student and teacher, Angel and Demon — and the unspoken bond between them were alone with each other for the first time in months. Nothing but the calm sound of rhythmic ocean water receding from the wet sand beneath their feet and their synchronized, lilting breathing patterns echoed in the surrounding atmosphere.

And in the tenuous ambience, Lumah was losing her patience with this man. "So? Are we going to talk, or can I go to my room and change out of these damp clothes?"

Godrik rolled his neck and dropped his shoulders. "I think it's best if you transfer out of my class. Two other teachers teach water manipulation, and they'd suit your gifts better."

Lumah couldn't believe what she was hearing. She placed her hands on her hips and looked at him, dumbfounded. "Excuse me? You're joking, right? I'm not leaving this class. All my friends are in it..." she took a hesitant step closer to him. "...and you are the best water teacher in this academy. If you have me transferred, my father will not stand for anything less."

"Your father is not my concern. Even he can't force me to teach someone so untethered to their energy. You threaten the balance of everything without a single care in the world." He glowered.

"Me?" she gasped.

He nodded and pointed to the now calm ocean waves. Desperation and something like alarm swam through the creases of Godrik's eyes as he explained. "That stunt you just pulled has likely created a life of its own outside of our world and is now threatening the human world. Do you not see it, Lumah? You and I are a catalyst for an array of unfathomable consequences. Should you remain in this class, the human world will suffer greatly because of the war you and I wage without thought, and unlike us, they tend to die with ease."

Lumah stomped and flared her wings outward. The sun was attempting to penetrate through the clouds, and a loose ray caught the gold tips of her layered feathers. The ethereal tint shimmered like dancing fire along the frothy water beneath their feet, emitting her inside rage towards his words in an outward physicality. "I am not the one waging war, Godrik. I'm trying. Every day. To learn and live my fucking life like a normal person. For months, I've been trying to move on from the heartbreak that almost ate me alive because you rejected what we so plainly are. Because of you alone, my summer became a nightmare of stupid choices, and this morning I was looking forward to this class." She admitted.

Lumah paused for a moment to hold back any tears that threatened to break through her strong front. But when she realized there was none to hold back, and only pity stung in her eyes as she looked into Godrik's, she continued. "I was looking forward to something grounding and normal again. Instead of the chaotic disarray of dumb choices."

That earlier hint of a smirk slid across Godrik's face again, and he leaned in slightly, tipping his sharp chin in the direction of her nose. "Dumb choices like that gold fishing hook dangling from your nose?"

Lumah bit the inside of her lip and lightly touched the septum piercing in her nose. Then dropped her hand and shrugged. "Kesses was getting a tattoo and didn't want to be alone in the human world during the process, so I went with her and thought...yolo."

"Yolo? That's a mindless term for mortals who find it fun to flirt with stupidity." He cocked a dark brow. "Not the thought process of an angelic daughter of two immortals."

Lumah picked at her nails. "I've always been the best at making bad decisions with good intentions." She explained. Remembering how nervous Kesses was just to walk into the mortal shop and ask if they would do her blood-red crescent tattoo that day. She has a reason for her fright. Kesses's vampiric father fears the wrath of mortals and has demanded she never cross the veil into their world or be cut off from his wealth, but Kesses was never one who follows strict rules.

Neither was Lumah.

Lumah drew her attention back to the man who walked into all of her haunted dreams without consequence and threaded her fingers through the loop of his belt—tugging him against her. On instinct, Godrik placed his hands on her hips. "Godrik, being alone with you again might be the worst decision of them all. But it also feels like the safest."

She felt his palm flinch and his fingertips tighten upon the waist-band of her skirt. "That's where you're wrong, Lumah. In the arms of a demon, no one is safe. Especially not you. Like the angel you are, you're softer than you appear. You might wear a damn good lustful mask, painting your lips every shade of rouge and red, but there's nothing but innocent tenderness underneath that false tint." When he finished his sentence, he dryly swallowed.

Lumah watched as his throat bobbed at the lie that stuck in it. He wanted to make believe she was as innocent as a maiden on a wedding night, but he knew the sultry siren within Lumah's soul. And its feminine power made him as nervous as it did hungry.

With a pout, she whispered against his mouth. "Then take control, Godrik. Destroy me already. Fuck me, slap me, or kill me. The choice is yours."

"Fuck, you're mouthy." He rasped unevenly upon her lips, his pointed top teeth close enough she could almost feel them against her delicate skin. "It would be nice to rid my soul of you once and for all. Bury you so deep that no one would hear your screams or chain you to the bottom of the ocean, and leave you in darkness so black you'd forget that light exists. Creatures down there would worship me if I gave them a golden treat such as yourself." The tip of his nose rubbed against hers, and her siren hummed for more.

"You love to threaten me with words and intimidation, but you never follow through with them. Not once have you actually harmed me. Avoided me, yes. Hurt me emotionally, yes. Physically hurt me, no." Lumah grinned, pressing a knee between his partially splayed thighs. A baleful growl rumbled from Godrik's chest. A warning? Perhaps. But the danger only made her press him further. She raised her leg higher until the slightest sign of discomfort displayed behind his steel eyes. "In fact, again and again, you've allowed me to be the one who pokes at your comfort level and causes you bouts of harbored anguish. Why is that?"

A single finger of Godrik's found its way under Lumah's polka dot waistband, and goosebumps sprang from where his rough scales collided with her smooth skin. The untamed sensation that lived inside those goosebumps pooled around her pussy, and when he spoke against her mouth again, she had to stifle a rogue whimper from escaping her mouth.

"Anguish isn't the right term for the hollow resentment you continually drive into me." He seethed, pressing his forehead against hers as if the angled pressure would keep their lips from colliding.

Lumah couldn't control the little laugh that bubbled in her throat. "Why don't you stop the drama and kiss me already?"

He pulled his forehead from hers and muttered through a frown. "No. Your lips are poison and would be the end of my immortal solace as I know it."

"You know what we are. And beyond that, you want me. I bet beneath these belted pants, your cock is as hard as a coral, Godrik. So why not just give in?" Lumah questioned, generally curious, why he fought so hard against an incantation that could never be broken.

A piece of her knew the reason, but she still didn't understand. Couldn't understand, even when he spoke the truth to her out loud.

"I like the tranquility of loneliness."

She refused to listen to that answer. No one enjoyed being alone all the time. Not even a grumpy demon. "No, you don't."

Godrik backed further away. His eyes roved across her features in frantic pursuit, as if they were searching for where she found the audacity to tell him how he felt. "Yes, I do. Loneliness is consistent. It never fluctuates in the cascading void it splays across one's soul. It's quiet, numbing, and secure. I've known its bitter emptiness my entire life. And I quite like its barren comfort."

Lumah stubbornly shook her head and repeated with bolder confidence. "No, you don't."

Godrik huffed. Clearly frustrated with this roundabout conversation.

His frazzled breath hit Lumah's face like a cloud of aromatic arousal, immediately turning her legs into mush before him. Bracing herself, she released her knee held against his manhood, and Godrik took the chance to tear himself completely away from her. Running a hand through his dark, spiked hair.

"You are a holy terror who talks too much, has no understanding of boundaries, and loses herself in the type of behavior that leads to mutilating your soft body. You came into my life with jubilant passion and infuriating delusional ideals about love and matters of the heart. Never stopping to think that love is a broken concept. And a fucking curse upon one's soul. What gives you the right to tell me how I feel?"

"Because we belong together, and you know it. That's why you hate me so much. You try so hard to pretend you can't feel the connection that was written long before we ever met, but it steals the air from your lungs the moment I walk into the room. Your body shivers and heightens tenfold in heat at the slightest touch from me, and when you're away from me, my voice stays locked in your mind. And I know this because all of that is exactly what happens to me, too." Lumah blinked and stilled her drumming heart, then she mustered all her courage to say those three soul-sucking words once again to Godrik.

The words that turned him away from her months ago, and shattered her innocent outlook on life with every day he continued to stay away. "I'm your mate."

Godrik

Mate.

What a foolish concept. It wasn't a gift, like so many mortals fantasized it was. It was a damn curse. A hex placed on the demon gene centuries ago by a scorned witch. One that sealed their humanity inside their bodies and kept the dark from overtaking their souls.

For that, he was glad.

Sure.

He didn't want to be a mindless monster killing without care. He enjoyed stretching his mind with books, loved to indulge in a compassionate or complex debate, and enjoyed watching the seasons change year after year. Godrik would be the first to admit he liked to revel in the normal, mundane daily tasks which his humanity allowed.

But forcing his heart to love someone wasn't mundane. It was terrifying and torturous and all fucking consuming.

After wandering the supernatural veil alone for nearly a century, he thought he was safe from such a curse. Then she walked into his life.

"You don't know how I feel or what happens to me when you walk into a room. And I'll say one more time... you should transfer out of my class immediately and ultimately remove yourself from my life."

He didn't care to talk anymore. With the snap of his fingers, his magic transferred him away from that beach and into his cave beneath the academy.

Home. A place no one entered but him.

It was cozy, smelled of brine and summer moss, its walls were lined with a thousand years' worth of treasures — he uncovered and coveted alone — and best of all, everything was set up for one. One recliner sat beside a singular, stout bookshelf. One stiff pillow lay upon navy sheets, neatly tucked into the mattress of a waterbed big enough for his body alone to sleep comfortably. Even one banana sat on the counter, next to a single plate, and matching lone silverware, which were drying on a small rack.

Godrik walked to his small, triangular-shaped table and collapsed on the single seat made of smooth, blue sea glass. He massaged his throbbing temples. That word, mate, pulsed in his ears with every erratically angry pump of his heart. It's hexing four letters coming to him through her succulent mouth each time he heard it.

She was right. In the sense of fated mates and demon pairing, they belonged together. But it wasn't fair to either of them. They were opposite in every conceivable way. She was a beautiful, charismatic abomination, and he was a melancholic, intolerant demon meant to live forever in solitude.

Under his breath, he mumbled, "Love. What a fate of stupidity."

The following morning, Godrik entered the black stone halls of the shadowed side of the school six forty-five a.m., just as he did every day, and waiting for him outside his classroom was a familiar woman dressed in every shade of red imaginable.

"Lilith," he said, forcing a smile to drape over his lips. "What brings you out of the darkest corners of hell?"

She looked down her thin nose at him, unamused by his attempted joke. "Cute. You know I no longer reside in the caverns of that rocky, humid place. I live above ground now, and I am quite satisfied here."

"Ah, I forgot. You sold your lawless soul to the leader of angels," he teased. His tone was light, but there was a sharp edge hidden inside.

"Yes, and that angel wants to have a word with you about your teaching methods." She said, then without another word she clicked her tongue and clapped her hands. The two of them appeared in a puff of red smoke before an arched double door made of solid gold.

In the center of one door, black lettering read;

Principal Archangel Michael Halo.

Before Godrik had the chance to grumble, Michael swung the door open and gave him a smile that was all teeth. "Godrik! Good to see you. We have some things to discuss before classes start today. Come, take a seat."

Godrik followed Michael into the room, his hands behind his back and careful not to walk too close to the archangel in case he chose to abruptly stop. Godrik didn't care to swallow a mouthful of glistening golden feathers this morning. Lilith followed behind, her heels clicking against polished marble with every step she took.

When they reached a small step up, Michael took his place on one side of the glistening white desk. Flexing his wings around the high arch of his matching chair, while Godrik sat on the other side in a low-back off-white leather wrapped chair. Lilith stood on the right side of Michael, with one slender hand placed gently along the back of his seat.

"We will get right to it. Your stunt yesterday caused three highly prestigious students to pause in their skills until their injuries heal. Not to mention, thanks to you, our daughter pressed her magic too far and caused the start of the greatest hurricane the earth has ever known. We have wind weavers on it, trying to slow its track, but I fear it's too late to stop it entirely." Michael explained, his voice regal and level-headed.

Lilith, on the other hand, sounded livid. "I thought you were more practical than to do something so stupid, Godrik. Our daughter's magic is influential and faulty, a combination that requires delicate concentration and pristine teaching. I thought you understood control better than anyone and would serve her siren song well. Yet, here we are in a whirlwind of a mess, and you are at the center of its cause."

Godrik folded his pewter arms and ground his teeth. "Maybe her siren side should be left dormant. She has the ability to craft and tinker as well. Give her to the mermaids. Let her create reefs and care for creatures below the waves. She would be well taught with my sister in the underwater part of the building.

Lilith's red eyes flashed with sudden anger, but she kept her voice reasonable as she spoke. "Our daughter is well-rounded, it's true, but mermaids are born with fins and gills that make it ideal for them to learn under the water. Lumah may craft pearls with her hands, and breathe underwater, but her dense feather wings are not ideal for swimming. So, teaching her on land is more ideal."

Godrik shrugged. "Then send her to the clouds. She's shown a touch of weather magic in her bones. Let her try her hand with Wind Studies, or she could try out for the fast flyers." He looked at Michael. "Maybe she could be a champion in cascading around the skies like you."

Lilith answers again. "Lumah doesn't care for heights. Therefore, her wings are mostly for show, and her flying skills are muted by anxious feelings. And you can teach her weather patterns just as well as anyone else. Look at what the two of you performed yesterday. A problem, yes, but glorious none-the-less."

Michael's eyes studied Godrik for a moment, then he took a slow inward breath and released it with his own deep-rooted thoughts. "Your father has had well over a hundred children, and yet no one comes as close to you in water-born magic skills. And your particular advancement specializes in the musical harmony of the ocean. Changing tides, raging waves, and the enchanting sound of the siren. Our daughter's strongest asset is her voice." He says, his face full of joy. Then his brown eyes drop to his hands. "But its power will cause more damage than protection if not properly trained, and that's why we need you to guide her through any obstacles that may occur as her powers mature."

Lilith leaned over the table and reached out for Godrik's arm. "Teach her. One on one. Without heated anger, before more damaging weather patterns erupt and the humans we all have grown fond of disintegrate into nothing but memories."

Godrik tugged his arm away before one of her blood-red nails could touch him. "Why does it have to be me?"

Michael stood tall and broad, moving around to his side of the desk. "You know exactly why, but you choose ignorance over practicality, and that hurts us all."

"Not to mention your cruel avoidance pains our daughter." Lilith bit out.

Michael softly sighed. "The balance is fragile, and there are plenty above and below who want nothing but to see the earth implode on itself." Lilith and Michael exchange a quick glance. "But we want to protect the humans. They are flawed, but they are resilient. Eager to learn and their empathy is a characteristic we all could use a little more of."

Godrik ran a hand down his face, then leaned back in his chair. "Unfortunately, I've grown fond of the mushy mortals too. They give purpose to our society. But if I give in and let this pull to Lumah win, that will change everything we've structured our system around."

Lilith licks her orange-red lips and grins. Showing off the pair of sharp canines she possesses. "Exactly."

Michael flutters his wings and strides along the floor. "What you lack to see is that change is necessary. The human world is in flames. Darkness is consuming the human heart at a rapid pace, and without implementing change within our order, bringing a more balanced life within the specter world... our veil, then... we might as well call the four horsemen and begin the apocalypse now because this world is fucked."

Godrik couldn't help the sour look that crossed his face at the mention of the four horsemen, no one wanted to call on them. The four horsemen were a pack of bored, arrogant punks. Not demon, not angel, and definitely not human, they wandered the human world whispering in ears evil ideals and spreading plague but came back home to laze around and do nothing to balance their mutilated be-havior.

And balance was one of the few things Godrik enjoyed. "I'll do it. I'll start her training immediately."

"Fantastic." Michael clapped. "I always knew you were a smart man."

"Fate was right to bind you to our daughter." Lilith mused. Her red eyes glinted with something sinisterly familiar, but currently with his emotions building within him, Godrik couldn't quite place it. "The two of you are the equilibrium this world has been praying for."

Michael took Lilith's hand, and when the two of them looked at each other, Godrik understood that familiar glint in her eyes as hopeful ambition.

Godrik

Lumah walked into their agreed meeting place at exactly the said time Godrik told her to arrive. Not a second earlier or a second behind. He would have been impressed with her punctuality if it hadn't been for the distracting way she was dressed.

Forget that slutty little nose ring. Today her entire angelic form radiated with flesh-driven carnality.

One thick bare thigh at a time, she sauntered confidently through the arched stone doorway wearing a red leather miniskirt that rested low on her voluptuous hips. Godrik's eyes attached themselves to the short silver zipper centered in the middle of the tight red fabric, and his mind wandered to thoughts of what he might find should his fingers slide the chrome metal downward.

Panties? Or nothing but the folds of her heat?

Lumah waltzed closer. The click of her step against the natural stone floor brought his gaze to her above the knee black boots and the three-inch platform heels they stood on. A zipper lined the inside of each boot as well. He blinked and drew his fixated attention upward, assuming her shirt would also be covered in leather and zippers.

But it was actually worse. She wore a fucking thin white t-shirt, tied in an off-centered knot where her waist dipped inward, that read in gothic black font...God's girl.

And to top it all off, her caramel hair was wrapped in two messy buns, which sat high on her scalp. The way multiple braids wove from the buns downwards was identical to the hairstyle she wore the night in the parking lot last semester. When he had lost all control over his senses and crossed lines with a person — a damn angelic student — he never thought himself capable of.

"Fucking Christ, what are you wearing?" He couldn't stop himself from uttering. Placing one of his long arms outward to stop her from coming any closer to him.

She paused, her face bewildered for a second. With her pomegranate-hued eyes, she looked at him, and then down at her outfit, then seductively back to him. He watched in horror as she ran her tongue across her painted crimson lips and playfully turned to give him a full view of the outfit he turned his nose towards. "Clothes...and rather cute ones I might add. They flatter my hourglass frame, don't you think?"

Watching her turn made his mouth dry and his core stiffen. Godrik turned himself away. Distracting his thoughts by puttering around with potion bottles. "It's inappropriate attire to wear for the occasion. You're dressed as you should be in a lineup of human hookers, not the daughter of Archangel Michael learning magic from a son of Leviathan."

Lumah laughed. The sound of her voice pricked at his webbed ears and trickled down his spine like seductive needles attempting to penetrate his scale-covered skin and sew itself around his sappy, salt-drenched heart. As he fiddled like an idiot with liquid-filled bottles, she came up beside him and sat herself on the only clean section of the blue oyster shell counter.

"A hooker is exactly what I was going for, dear teacher." She mused, crossing her legs, and hitting his forearm with the tip of her boot.

A flash of anger rolled through Godrik's chest, and he stepped away from her. "Why the hell would you leave your dorm room thinking like that?"

"Because I knew it would get under your scales. If you were so bothered by my piercing, I couldn't help but wonder what else you'd find disgusting about me." She ran a finger along the zipper of her skirt. "Apparently, anything shiny and metal makes you squirm." She laughed in her throat. "Noted."

Godrik huffed out a heavy breath. "Enough of this foolishness. We are here to correct your wrongs, not count the things I hate about you. Yesterday, you pushed too hard and tossed the clouds above us into chaos around the mortal world. Today we will work on fixing that. Correcting the havoc you caused —"

She stopped him with a loud tisk. His jaw tightened as he waited for her to explain her irritating noise.

"That is the second time you have blamed me solely for the issue at hand. Yesterday, I let it slide. Today I'll have none of your tapered blame."

"Excuse me?" He practically seethed.

She straightened her posture and crinkled her nose. "The problem we caused. Remember, if it weren't for your arrogant resistance to what's formed between us and your unrelenting anger to despise all that I am, none of this would have happened. No one would be hurt, there'd be no unbalanced atmosphere, and no point in me being here now. But go on..." she said with a snarky flip of her wrist. "...explain to me how I'll be fixing your wrongs."

Fuck, she was snarky. Without thinking of later reproductions, he stepped towards her and smacked his hand over her mouth. At his gall, she chuckled beneath his grip. Hot air sprung from her nostrils, causing that slutty little nose ring to rest on his webbed forefinger. "No more talking, Lumah. Like a good god's girl, you're going to listen to me and do as I say. Got it?"

She nodded her head up and down in understanding, but he felt the slow lick of her tongue against his palm. A sign of her bratty disobedience towards him.

Keeping his hand over her mouth, he ordered. "Open your hand."

Lifting it off the desk, she did as he asked. With his unused hand, he pulled a clear bottle filled with a musky-blue syrup from the nearest shelf and flicked its corked top open with his thumb. "With this, you will create the illusion of soft summer clouds. The kind that sway with sunshine and help to dry out the abundance of rainfall. We will send them into the ethereal weather rotation and balance the chaos we've created."

He released her mouth and poured the thick liquid into her waiting palm. "Sing. Not with the tone of exasperation or indignation but from the pure happiness that illuminates inside your essence. That is where the balance will lie."

Lumah

Godrik placed the last puffy phantasm illusion into the threshold that led to the human veil, then he sealed the locking mechanism with his dark magic and a mutter of reserved vows. Lumah watched in curious wonderment, knowing the threshold of fabrication would never answer her, at least not yet. Not when she was still just a pup in a world full of ancient eternal creatures, but still she studied like she could uncover all the world's secrets by simply observing the unruly, yet magically talented male before her.

When Godrik finished, he turned around and courtly bent his head to her. "Beautiful, unblemished craftsmanship, Lumah."

She grinned at him proudly. "Look at all the good we can accomplish together."

He scratched his beardless chin. "Together we are a devastating earthquake that will transform the lands if we are not careful."

"I can be careful. Gentle. Doting. Even sweet. It's you who has trouble with all of those things." She said, fluttering her wings slightly behind her. "Sometimes you are such a grump, I ponder how you are trusted to teach in a school that defines composure and steadiness." With light feet and hopeful strides, Lumah moved towards her teacher. Her mate. The fucking asshole, she so longed to call hers. "Maybe you should learn that escaping into the fathom pit of loneliness is not a sustainable path to equilibrium. And our hearts are a perfect match of light and dark. Good and evil."

"The mating bond is not a balance. It is a vortex of descending water. Dragging two beings around and around boundlessly blindly until the fog of lust and love suffocates their individual souls and forces them into one dispirited state of mind." Godrik stretched his hand behind his head and absentmindedly picked at the scales on the back of his neck. "For a demon, love always starts as a curse and ends with woeful consequences."

Lumah's heart ached that he felt that way. Not for her own soul's sake, but for his. What had happened in his long life that made him so devoid of letting happiness inside? Many demons were surly, mischievous, and erratic, but he was a whole different beast. One with salty sorrow lapping at his core and she was going to be the one to turn that salt into sugar if it fucking wrecked her along the way.

Once she was close enough, she pressed two fingers against his lips. "I think you should be the one who shuts up this time and listens. I'm not talking about love, Godrik. In time, between us, that may form, but right now all I'm asking for is a kiss. A redo of what we began before the mating bond divided us."

He sighed and dropped his hand to his waist and for a long while he merely stared at her. She could see the wilted humanity forming in his eyes before he said the words out loud, and her heart pattered with enthusiasm and desire when his arms found their way around her body. Like a tsunami of flooded emotions, his lips parted, and he whispered a harsh "Fuck it."

Then he braced his warm mouth against hers and welcomed their bond with a tangle of teeth and tongues. As he severely lapped up the longing from her lips, she swallowed the hunger and the anguish that he fed to her. Heat flushed across Lumah's pale cheeks, and a stormy tingle swam within her core for more of him.

Her waist pressed into his center, and she let out a whimpered sigh when she felt his hard manhood against her swollen bud. But to her dismay, he slightly pulled away.

"Slow." He breathlessly said. "I don't want to rush this. Rush us. Together we will get to know each other's cravings better than the ocean knows its shoreline, but for now we will take our time."

Like a pouty princess, Lumah's swollen lips let out a subtle raspberry, but calming herself, she nodded. "Ok." Then in a flash she gave him a deliciously virtuous grin and contrasted it by grabbing a handful of his tight ass. "But promise me a kiss every hour until the end of time."

Godrik's features formed a genuine smile. Full of happiness and desire. Wide and joyous, he uttered. "Promise."

As those tender words hit Lumah's ears, three golden rings of luminous magic formed around the two of them. One at the base of their legs, a bigger one around their stomachs, and the last and smallest skimmed around their heads.

"The bond." Lumah breathed in astonished awe. "It's powered by luminous magic, not shadow."

Godrik appeared to be speechless as he watched the golden spheres of light accept their bodies as one and circled them three times around before forming into a singular large needle-like mass. In a magnificent, painless manner, the magic needle speared their chests and entered their hearts. Back and forth, the magic melded like a pendulum of fortuitous lightness and stitched their souls together.

Sealing their bonded fates for eternity. After a few minutes, the moment was over and the magic dissolved into nothing. Lumah's wings flung open in enthusiastic applause. "You claimed our bond was a curse, that just proved it is in fact not a curse but a blessing."

Godrik shrugged. "I suppose so." Then his eyes dropped and peered at something in the middle of her face. "So, now that I've given into your siren charm, will you be removing that thing from your nose?"

She stepped away and laughed vivaciously. "No way. As a demon, you're naturally addicted to torment. I'll keep it and wear it every day just to make sure I keep the balance between us even."

"Brat." He chuckled.

"Yours." She breathed.

"Mine." He groaned.

Ch. 1 - The Boat

The gods gave men free will, and with it, they start wars. They lie, cheat, and steal.

Subjugate others at every turn. So, in rebuke the goddess gave us wings, talons, and a song. It is in our very nature to sing and doom them.

We crave blood by design. Humans do by choice. I was never meant to fall in love with one of them, and I never will again. Because you see, it is not in our nature to love, but of course, as things go, even immortals may experience all things, given our many years. To this day I keep him close, so I can gaze upon him, to remind me of that love. To remember that moment, many years ago now, so that I may never go against my true nature again.

For man does what it always does, and then, in the end, so did I.

It was a joyous day. The sun was gliding across the cloudless sky. The rays of her golden

light warmed my deep tanned skin. The wind was fair, and with my wings outstretched it took little effort to coast the currents above the calm seas.

The human world was just beyond the veil. We had to wait for it to thin and a boat to pierce its fog. My sisters and I had been unfed for so long, our Islands disappearing into the mists of myth and legend, as it so often did. A ship hadn't been sent our way in many months.

We survived of course, on the many foods our islands grew and the fish from the oceans bountiful waters, but our desire for men's blood never ceased. We hungered for their lives and the thrill of ending them. Faces drowning with lust slacked mouths, pain and suffering, eyes ripped out upon our command, the feel of warm flesh beneath our talons, bones crunching at our whim.

We fed on the many blessings nature provided for us, but still, we would never be truly satiated. Always lingered the desire and the duty to enchant and sow chaos on the mortals, those men. Men who thought to rule all, conquer, and command.

They could never oppress us though. We are divine, we are their reckoning. We craved their deaths above all else, and with the cloudless skies and thinning of the mist's veil, all of us were a chatter for the coming feasts the goddess would send, and today there would finally be one. I had spotted a ship.

It was not too far away, and when I began to sing, I could see from above, how my song fell upon the sailor's ears. It was gentle like a whisper, to steer the vessel towards our awaiting claws. Soon, it would be close enough, all my sisters would see the ship and lend their voices to pull it in.

As I glided the warm updrafts above the ship, I took the moment to observe the men on the deck. It had been so long since I laid eyes on a human. Despite my hunger, I couldn't help but be curious of the stupid creatures. I knew little about them other than stories I'd been told of their wretched ways, our role in the world, and how susceptible to our songs they are.

Their forms were of an intriguing physique though, and many worked the decks with skilled hands. I wondered what they were transporting? By the looks of them they were not soldiers, nor were they simple fishermen. Most likely slave traders or pirates. The goddess tended to send us ships of mortals who earned their demise by our hands.

Always so busy and seemingly focused men were, but one sound from us and all sense left them. Already the man at the helm was steering the ship off course, and the other crew were halting their jobs to stand in place, listening to the lulling melody of my voice.

My keen eye spotted a figure shaking his other crewman and arguing with them, pointing in the direction of where they had been heading until I whispered them off course. My interest was piqued. Perhaps this man had been below deck. I sang louder. It raised a fervor on board, men abandoning their post to gaze out across the sparkling seas.

Our Island was almost in sight now. My sister's calls floated in on the wind. Soon, the human ears would hear the sweet haunting melody of all our voices, and the ship would be doomed.

All except for the one. He was busy gathering things and throwing them hurriedly into a long boat. I observed as he lowered it and began rowing away.

I could not abandon my duties quite yet. I had to ensure the ship would hear my sister's awaiting calls, but it was no matter. The man would not go far.

My long wavy chestnut hair flew about my shoulders, coming to rest draping down my back as I pumped my wings to hover. There was no doubt now the crewman had caught the tempting songs of my waiting sisters. Their sails and minds full of what knowledge and pleasure awaited. I could smell their desire from my height.

So overpowering, the urge to fly fast rejoin my brood and take part in the coming slaughter. My taloned feet flexed under my body, but the single manned boat paddling away. Curiosity overcame and I left the ship on its final voyage where the rocks would run it aground, and eager hungry sirens awaited.

I circled back in a wide arch changing course in the sky to fly towards the boat, tailing it closely after descending. Savoring the moment.

The man I observed worked the oars expertly and with vigor. He was built well with muscular arms and broad shoulders. Hair the darkest of black, and tied back with a leather strap. It was longer, falling to his shoulders, sweat beaded at his nape and ran down soaking into a linen shirt. I'd never been this close to a man who wasn't driven mad, and found the moment mildly interesting. Like a cat who watches a mouse before it pounces. I smiled to myself then opened my mouth, a simple hum would do, from this distance, to drive him senseless, do whatever I bid.

The sound washed over the space, my eyes flashed with the expectant adoration before the kill, but nothing happened. Just the slapping of oars against water. I sang louder. The

The man did not turn, did not falter, did not acknowledge, or notice my presence. Now I was really curious.

I came to land behind him in the boat, my strong feathered legs balancing, my large talons clicking against the wooden bottom. It sent the small wooden vessel to jostle. In an instant the man was on his feet and spun around eyes wide with shock. I smiled wickedly, standing tall, knowing my tresses lay across my shoulders, bare breasts exposed. I kept my wings splayed out and above me, bent my arms poised in front of me and waggled my fingers in a sort of greeting. "jump overboard and swallow the sea human until your stomach explodes."

I waited for the blissful ignorance to take hold before he did as I commanded. Instead, I watched something new spread across his face, one I couldn't help but notice was as finely built as his body. The look of shock faded as determination set across his heavy brow. His eyes darkened. It caught me off guard, and when he swung the heavy oar at me, it struck my wrist.

The pain was sharp, unexpected. I hissed and lunged forward, snatching it from his grip before he made to hit me again. My strength startled him, but only for a moment. He quickly armed himself with the other oar. Then it was the two of us, both equipped with oars, in a teetering long boat, surveying the other with uncertainty. Never in my life had I ever been met with anything other than blind willful ignorance, and through my confusion and the throbbing in my wrist, I found the situation quite comical. A laugh erupted from my mouth.

The man was poised to strike, but my laugh caused enough bewilderment to break his determined brow. He surveyed me, dropping his oar momentarily before raising it again.

"Stay back, vile creature." He gruffed.

Vile creature. To be called such by a human was humorous, and another bubble of laughter found its way from my lips. I cared not for humans, but I had grown accustomed to lustful adoration. Being called vile was as amusing as it was frustrating. I eyed this man with curious disdain.

"Vile, is it? How is it you are immune to my song, human?" I drawled, lowering the oar.

I could easily kill him but needed to know what set this man apart from all the others. His brows furrowed, deep blue eyes focused on my lips as I spoke. My hands dropped the oar. I ran them down my hips, smoothing some of the tawny ruffled feathers, and tucked in my wings to take a seat.

He nervously looked around, lowering his oar slightly, the muscles in his arms momentarily relaxing.

"I know what you are."

I tossed my head, sending my hair bouncing around me, bracing my hands on the side of the boat. I twisted my chest, the movement caused my breasts to sway softly.

"And what is that exactly?" I questioned.

Again, his eyes were focused on my mouth. "A siren. We've all heard the tales."

He turned to look in the direction of the ship. I had a theory. I took the moment, letting out a loud shriek, shattering the silence. No reaction, no indication whatsoever he had been startled.

Then he continued. "The crew, they weren't acting right, said it was the most beautiful thing they'd ever heard." He looked back menacingly at me.

"But you can't hear, can you?" I asked.

He stiffened, lowering his eyes, then shook his head.

"No, I cannot." His shoulders slumped, indicating this was a source of embarrassment.

"But you know what I say by reading my lips."

His shoulders straightened, his head raised, "yes, that is correct."

I figured as such by the way he was so intense with my mouth. His oar rested at his side now. The boat drifted wherever the current took it.

"Please sit." I motioned to the other seat.

As much as I was raised to hate men, I'd never actually talked to one before. One word from my mouth and they were cutting out their tongues, splitting open their bellies wading into the waters. Their blood calling in the sharks. This was unique.

The man considered my request and looked around, contemplating his next move: the vast open seas around us, the oar in his hand, then back at me. He slowly sat down, resting the oar across his lap.

We appraised each other then in a sustained silence, and for the first time, I found myself wondering what a human was thinking. I absent-mindedly rubbed at my wrist.

"Does it hurt much?" He offered.

"Does what hurt?" I replied.

"Your wrist." He motioned towards my arms.

I looked down, removing my hand. "No, not particularly, not anymore, more of a shock really. I can't recall the last time I've been hit, if ever." I replied, eyeing him carefully.

He brushed his hand over his forehead and down his black, sweat-slickened hair. "I suppose I'm sorry about that then, though you do plan to kill me, and my men." He gazed out back towards the horizon where the ship had disappeared.

"Oh, your men are most certainly dead." I casually relaxed back onto my arms. "And I haven't decided what I'm going to do with you, yet."

Our eyes met once my lips were done moving. Again, I wondered what he was thinking. He said nothing. The silence grew, broken only by the sounds of screams floating in on the winds. He could not hear this, but I could smell the iron tang of blood in the air. It sent a shiver down my body, ruffling my wings and causing my talons to flex, scraping against the wooden bottom of the long boat. His nose wrinkled, could he smell death as well as I?

His eyes sharpened. "I never believed in the stories of creatures like you," he said.

"A creature, is that what you think of me?" I smiled coyly.

"Well, what are you then?"

"I'm a siren, and a woman."

He seemed to consider this.

"I've never seen a woman like you before, I mean you are beautiful, the most beautiful creature I've probably ever seen, but the women I'm used to don't have wings or feathered legs, or talons." He gestured towards my feet.

"Well I've heard stories about your kind, and the women you're used to are treated poorly, second class, bartered, sold, beaten, and abused, but we are their retribution." I retorted, spreading my legs and moving my hands upwards. "And, I can assure you, I'm a woman in every way that counts." I watched the flush of red spread over his face. His eyes stared at my hands, then quickly averted his gaze to the endless expanse of water before coming to rest back at my face. I giggled to see the man so flustered. I crossed my legs leaning forward.

"So, then human, what do they call you?"

He gave me a questioning look, cocking his eyebrows before shrugging his shoulders, resting his elbows on his knees with resigned compliance. "They call me Loukas, my name is Loukas, and what is your name, if I'm allowed to ask?" He said with a flash of a smile.

"My name is Maisandra, but my sisters call me Maia." I replied. "I must admit I'm curious about you, Loukas, tell me about yourself, what were you doing on that ship, and what is your life like on your mortal lands?"

I could see something brewing in those dark blue eyes, mulling over a response. "I was part of the crew on that ship. Master Navigator and cartographer." His speech was clipped at first, but as he continued to tell me of his life, he became more animated.

When I posed a question, he answered, and in turn would offer one back to me. I went from never having spoken to a man before, to having a conversation with one.

To hear him tell me of his life and ambitions opened something in me, I couldn't deny. Curiosity, interest, and I hated to admit it, appreciation.

I suppose knowing his name made him real. Hearing him say my name made it harder to see him as some mindless soul caught in a song.

We floated in a liminal space, he and I, while we spoke. The mists were closing again, gathering around us, shrouding out the endless blue ocean. The sun was beginning to dip down towards the horizon, painting the sky in hues of vivid orange and pinks.

While he talked, I appraised the strength of his hands, the roughness and calluses across his fingers. Scars from a life lived peppered his arms. The way he pushed down his hair and wiped at the sweat gathering at the nape of his neck. My nose inhaled his scent. Without our song coaxing out lust or fear it smelled sharp and spicy like Oak. My eyes closed and I felt myself walking in that scent, a forest of him.

Time slowed, his voice drowned out by the rustling of the leaves from that unfamiliar place. It lasted for a moment. When my eyes opened it was to the usual sound of waves. His voice back to the forefront. He had begun to tell me of his life as a child living on the streets after his parents died.

"I took up residence outside a local pub, The Imperial, sold olives to drunk patrons I'd stolen from the groves, I still live in that neighborhood, and I still frequent that pub, but now from the inside." He laughed, more to himself, reminiscing of the memory. Strands of his blackened hair escaping their strap silhouetted against a deepening sky.

I raised my hand to silence him. "The hour grows late, and I'd like to hear more of your story, but we should head for land."

The bright marmalade sky was quickly darkening and dusk was upon us, clouds had gathered, and soon darkness would swallow. Without the moon's light, it would be hard for me to find my way out of the mists and towards shore.

He looked off in no particular direction "Where my men went to die?" It was posed as a question.

"I think not, that is our main island, the one we all share, but we each have our own roost. I will take you to mine." We looked at each other for a moment. A short quick nod of his head told me he understood. I raised myself, grabbing a length of rope from the bottom of the boat. "Here, tie this off."

His skilled calloused fingers quickly knotted off the loose end, and then I was up. Springing from the seat with a powerful thrust, spreading my wings, I towed the boat as the dying rays of the sun goddess bled into the air, losing its daily battle against the moon. We reached my Island before the red disc slipped below the horizon. The last of its light shimmering on the waters' surface.

Ch. 2 - The Rookery

Most of my Island was surrounded by coral and rocks that jutted out sharply from the sea, but a small area had a deposit of sand that opened to a beach. I guided the boat there. Coming to land on the soft, sandy embankment. My talons sunk into the loose, warm ground. Loukas jumped from the boat, battling the surf as he hauled it onto shore. His body strained with effort, muscles tight and rigid. When he had finished, he made his way up the beach and raised his head to look at me. Exhaustion clearly written across his face.

"Come, let me get you something to eat." I said.

The clouds were cleared out here, and the moon's crescent was prominent in her position in the sky. Its glow allowed him to dimly survey his surroundings. A silhouette of trees and white sands. He followed close behind as I made my way into the forest, down a small path that cut inland towards my domicile. No human had ever set foot on this land.

The birds and snakes watched from the darkness. Bats flitted out from the canopy searching for insects that trilled in a chorus heralding the evening. Loukas peered out, sensing their eyes, on alert, looking up at the stars and the sky. "Where are we?" He asked, "I do not recall this land on any of the maps."

"We are on my Island, one of the many my sisters and I inhabit, hidden, shrouded in the mists. Don't worry, no harm will come to you here."

Soon, the small winding path opened up to reveal a cleared space. I walked to a wicker basket that held rocks, and struck a firestone, lighting a nearby torch. My home bloomed into light. Its walls were made with coral mined from the sea and timbers from ships. It was open to the air, and spacious, but I hesitated walking inside, nervously playing with the feathers of my folded wings tucked into my sides. A human in my home?

Loukas made no motion to come towards the house and instead took in the scene. Coins glittered and dotted the grounds and sands. Gems and jewelry heaped decoratively all about the area.

His eyes widened. "I've never seen so much gold."

It took a moment for me to process. "Yes, it's a weakness of ours, I suppose. We do love shiny things, and you humans covet it above all things as well, do you not?" I paused, looking

back at him. His mouth was agape, and I could tell he was in a state of shock. Standing over the wealth of centuries. I continued, "Of course, we have no need for it, makes for beautiful decoration though, how it captures and reflects the light, and your ships have brought us much of it over the years."

I started a fire in the firepit, then left him and walked inside my home. Consciously aware he did not follow. When I emerged, he was sitting around its warmth. I handed him a plate of salted fish alongside a pile of heaped fruits, which he gratefully devoured.

We spoke with the crackling flames between us. As the stars broadened the night sky. I regarded the encroaching closeness of our bodies, and deepened questions we posed the other. We became absorbed in the truth, history, and secrets we divulged, an intimacy of history and shared knowledge. Conversing effortlessly as the embers flamed between us, until sleep eventually overtook.

Ch. 3 - Awakening

The warm scented winds of tropical flowers enveloped us when we awoke the next morning to golden sunlight. I showed him the beauty of the land. How the islands here provided all my kind ever needed.

Its trees heavy laden with fruits, the grounds ripe with root vegetables, and the crystal waters swimming with fish one just needed to pluck from the seas.

A balance and a gift we honored. Secrets of nature's inner workings I divulged.

Loukas spoke of farming and hunger, famine on his lands, and the poor. He readily ate all the fruits and berries on our leisurely walks. I had no concept of starvation, but reasoned that our constant desire for mortal men's death was akin to the hunger he spoke of. I felt pity for humans knowing they could die from hunger. It seemed we both were learning many things, and while his knowledge of my island was growing, it was not without its dangers. He reached out to pluck a round berry of the deepest blue from a thorny bush. I grabbed his hand.

"Those dark berries, we call them Thana, they feed only the birds, and will cause death for you and I alike if too many are consumed, do not eat them." He looked at them thoughtfully before dropping them to the sand.

"So you aren't invincible after all" he said with a teasing smile.

"Immortal for us doesn't mean incapable of death." I countered. We walked out towards the water's edge to the tide pools. "See here the black spiny urchin. Its poison would prove fatal for you, so watch your step in the shallow pools. As for me, it would be a mere annoyance."

Loukas was enthralled, nodding and taking in all my land's wonder by day, and I was fascinated with his stories of the mortal world by night. The glow from the fire, always between us. Curiosity of the other grew over the course of each day's passing, and deepened with the moon's nightly observance. The glow from the firelight casting a net around the other, that found us both caught, and so on the third night together, the flames of passion ignited.

More than my wings opened for him. His touch was eager on my feathered thigh. His lips grazed mine, teeth nipping lightly against my throat. An undulating dance of skin against skin. A pleasure I'd never known. With heavy breathing and a pounding rhythm, we moved as one. He filled a part of me that had ached for him. My wings fluttered as I rode atop him, his rough hands gathered me, pulling and thrusting, grinding with a ferocity that coaxed moans from my mouth. Sounds I'd never heard myself make.

A tightness began building, a warmth from my core, a quickening of breath. Increasing with every motion. Releasing a shuddering crescendo that felt much like a wave crashing against my body. I screamed from its impact to a rumble of satisfaction springing from Loukas. A look of satisfaction mirrored between our two faces. A collapse of exhilarated exhaustion that left us a tangle of flesh and feather woven tightly in each other's arms under the twinkling stars.

The next morning, I rose early and watched him sleep. His sun kissed shoulders rising and falling at a steady pace. A throbbing soreness in my midsection. The previous night playing back in my mind. It was not unheard of for a siren to lay with a man, but it was done with sadistic haste and brutal control, always ending in a swift death. Yet here one was softly breathing on my sands. It should not be this way, he was mortal and a man. It pained me to imagine him gone, but our curiosity had been fulfilled, and I knew it was time. I watched him as he gradually woke up. He rolled lazily with a grin, I couldn't help but smile, he was so handsome, but I shook my head.

"Loukas, it's time for you to go. I will tow you back out to sea, you only need to head a few days Westward until you reach your mortal lands."

He rose slowly, wiping the sleep out of his eye. "Say that again, I wasn't focusing on your mouth." He said, staring at my body with a look of lust I knew all too well.

"I think it's probably best if you return to your home."

He walked up, circled and grabbed me about the waist from behind. "So, you aren't going to kill me then, and I think I know why?" He said, nuzzling his bearded face against my cheek. Again, a grin spread across my mouth. He spun me around to face him, then held me in place. "Because you care for me, maybe even love me." His intense gaze stole my breath as much as the words themselves. I opened my mouth, my thoughts tumbling to fall on something to say. "Because I love you too." He finished breathlessly, pulling me in and brushing my lips with his. "And I'm not leaving."

Ch. 4 - Tangled Stars

And so, he stayed and so went our days together in bliss. Learning and playing against each other's deepest desires and exploring our bodies' most tender places. Mornings were filled with plucking fruits and planting seeds. I'd set out to fish from the air, and he from his boat. He was interested in the sky, using parchment to track the stars. He walked the island to map its shape. I could have flown him, but he said, "If humans were meant to fly, we'd have wings, and I think the height would scare me, plus that would be too easy."

He enjoyed his mathematics and his compass. Plotting the stars and the land with formulas and care of the cartographer that he was. When he wasn't charting the skies, he was making cordage and ropes. Splitting fibrous grasses and weaving nets. I helped him with this endeavor, it kept our hands otherwise busy while we spoke in the dusk, but no matter the day's affair, every evening we ended up in each other's arms tangled under stars.

It seemed nothing could part us, and had I been paying attention, I may have noticed the dark shapes against the sky. The shadows playing on the sands. My sisters circled and were coming to call, but I was otherwise ensnared with Loukas's head between my legs. My wings as open as my thighs. Eyes closed to what danger flew above.

The pounding of their feet upon the sand was heard by me and felt by Loukas.

So preoccupied in our feasts of the flesh, it was that finality which alerted us to their presence.

Isadora and Nysa walked slowly, hissing with spite.

"Maia, we'd wondered where you'd been. Nobody had seen you since the ocean brought us the ship. We were worried about you, that you may have been hurt, but I see now you are lost, sister. Truly lost to lay with a man." Isadora said, looking with disdain at Loukas.

"Gore your eyes out human, and eat them." She smiled.

Loukas, for once, seemed nervous, sitting up and broadening his shoulders. He inched closer to me, and was wise not to say or do anything.

Isadora stalked around us. "So, he does not follow my commands."

I stood, slowly turning to face her. "No. He can not hear our song, and yes, I've gotten to know him, we are as one he and I."

Isadora threw her head back and laughed. "He is no different just because he cannot hear your voice. Do not be swayed from your calling. Step-wide so I may finish him." She spread her wings and flexed her fingers into clawed arches, then lunged. Her eyes set on Loukas's throat.

Loukas scrambled back on his heels sending sand flying up as Isadora's powerful legs hurtled her forward.

I sidestepped, grabbing her arm and pulling her off her feet, then slammed her down. Her shoulders and wings dug into the sands from the impact. My hand lashed out, striking her face. "I said to leave him alone. He is mine."

Isadora's eyes cut to mine, anger flashing across their surface. She regained her footing, wiping a trickle of blood that beaded up and wept like a tear down her cheek. Walking towards

Nysa, hands out displaying the red smear.

"She strikes her own sister." The words came out in a hiss of disbelief. Nysa grabbed Isadora's outstretched hands.

"Is this truly what you will do, to save this man, lash out against your own?"

Her words struck me in their seriousness. I looked at Loukas who stood behind me, then at Nysa and Isadora.

"I love him, I will let no harm come to him." I said, crouching slightly in a defensive position spreading out my wings. Instead of anger, I braced myself for it. I watched as their wings dropped. Disappointment fell across their faces. They looked at one another, then Nysa stepped forward and held my gaze with a sadness I had never seen.

"You strike a sister and choose a mortal over your own kin. We demand a feather ripped from your wing, and with it yourself from us."

Her words hung heavily in the air. Behind me, Loukas shuffled his feet. I could smell his fear. So too could my sisters, their talons cutting into the sands.

His fear, instead of inciting the bloodlust I knew flowed through my sisters' veins, wound itself into the pit of my stomach, drawing out a sense of protection, instinctual and fierce.

"He is mine." My voice was as forceful as my hand, which grasped and pulled one of my feathers. Pain shot through my left wing.

Nysa stepped forward, her eyes downcast, mournful. "He, nor you, will ever see us again. Your song is lost to us, Maia."

I struggled to keep the tears that gathered from leaking down my cheek. Isadorsa rubbed at hers, smearing more of the blood that I had drawn. We exchanged one final look of a thousand words, and then they rose from the ground, and were gone. Fading into the distant sky as the mists rolled in. Loukas came up behind me, stroking my wing, wrapping me in a hug.

Ch. 5 - A Feast

After that day, I could not help my sadness. I mourned the life I had given up with my sisters, even though I cherished the one I chose with Loukas.

He must have felt my pain. He gave me space and busied himself around the island.

He went over his maps, drawing and plotting the seas, making cordage and ropes in a feverish pitch, as if to show me his usefulness. He spoke of fishing deeper waters, and occupied himself with reinforcing the boat. He salted fish, made baskets, and dried fruits all with distance and a watchful eye.

He gauged my sadness with gentle apprehension and carefully planned self-appointed tasks. I appreciated how quickly he had adjusted to life on the island, proving himself competent and functional. I could understand his belief that I required both space and time to process what had happened, but the thing I wanted most was his affection and attention.

I would go off on daily flights, contemplating the situation. I secretly kept my eye out for a glimpse of my sisters, or the island. It was all but lost to me now in an endless fog. I grieved both them and the distance it caused with Loukas.

I decided to speak to him of my loneliness and my need for reconnection. So, I was delighted at what I saw on my arrival home from one such flight at dusk.

The clearing was decorated with candles and a table set up with a banquet upon it. Loukas was waiting, tentatively shuffling from foot to foot.

"What is all this?" I asked, touching down onto to the sands.

"I wanted to surprise you, do something special." He took my hands. "Here, sit."

My cheeks warmed from the smile replacing the sadness I had worn just moments before. My eyes danced around the scene.

Flowers and vines. Candles and the moonlight. My home had never looked so lovely.

Loukas walked off into the darkness beyond the candles glow, quickly returning with a silver platter piled with food.

"I was hoping you'd return soon. I didn't want dinner to be cold, hurry up and eat while I get our drinks," he said excitedly, placing the dish down before me. He ran off, returning with two goblets. "I've been planning this for a while, a long while, it needed to be perfect."

I took the goblet he handed me, quenching my thirst. It tasted like our wine, but different, a deeper note of something I couldn't place.

He eyed me hopefully. "Do you like it?"

"Yes, oh Loukas, this is so thoughtful of you."

He drew me close, planting a kiss on my cheek. "Just wait until you've tasted the fish. Close your eyes, let me feed you."

I giggled and rolled my eyes, but agreed. It was sensual, him feeding me. Flavors mingled and rolled around as I chewed. He knew I hadn't been eating and was ravenous.

"And what do you think?"

I opened my eyes. "It's delicious." I replied. Loukas sat opposite of me, his blue eyes piercing in the candlelight.

"It makes me happy to see you eat. Cheers," he said, holding up the goblet.

Our glasses clinked together and I drank deeply, the mulling herbs, tickling my throat. He looked so handsome sitting there with a look of satisfaction on his face. I wanted to show my appreciation by dancing my fingers around the plates before eating more of the stuffed fish and olives.

"Here, try a bite of this." He said, placing a piece of bread between his thumbs dipped in a spread before bringing it to my lips.

"It's quite spicy." I laughed, drawing my goblet towards me. It was empty.

"Take mine." He leaned forward, my fingers grasping around the stem. I swallowed more of the sweet liquid, the tickle in my throat growing. His eyes bore into me as he sat, his elbows on his knees, carefully gauging my movements.

I coughed to clear my throat, drowning more of the liquid.

"Why aren't you eating?" I managed, hoarse.

He rolled around one of the grapes. "I ate while you were away. This is all for you."

The burn was almost unbearable now. "Oh, Loukas, it's so spicy. What did you use to season it?"

He smiled, but not in the way I was used to. His lips slowly curled into a sneer. "Oh, a little of this, and a little of that."

I didn't like the look on his face, and the burning had started to spread throughout my body. I wanted to cough, to move, but found I could barely draw breath. My limbs felt heavy, the hand holding the goblet dropping to the sands below. My body lurched sideways, falling to the ground. My wings were heavy upon the sands.

From my vantage point, I saw the last of the liquid from the goblet, pouring through the white sand grains, and there at the bottom seeds. Seeds I recognized as those from the berries of Thana. I was paralyzed, couldn't move, or talk. My mind was reeling.

Loukas came into view, staring down at me, a knife in his hand. I was screaming in my head for him to help me. To my horror, he raised his arm bringing it down and hacked at my wings with a ferocity I could never imagine. The pain was indescribable. My feathers, cut and flayed, blew about in the wind.

"Stupid bitch, if you're still alive, I hope you can feel this. You and all your sisters are going to be fucking dead. Monstrous creatures, all of you." He stopped to look me in the eyes, "and if you're not dead yet, you will be."

His wicked smile grew as the blade drew near. Its pull felt icy across my throat. My neck sliced open. I lay there unable to move, struggling to breath, hot blood pouring down my throat. I tried to raise my arms to clutch at my throat or reach for his hand. Unable to do either, only able to listen to the sound of my breath gurgling. He stood kicking sand in my face, and stalked out of view.

I kept thinking this wasn't really happening and at any moment he would come back to save me, but was forced to watch as Loukas drug out treasure – my treasure – my coins and gems down the sandy trail. In the nets and baskets he'd made, the ones I'd helped him make.

Could just make out by the candlelight him loading the boat. He made the same trip a few times, and each time he passed, I willed him to look at me. To help me, to love me. I watched as he raised the sail. Leaving me for dead. The boat grew smaller, vanishing into the darkness of the night and the mists as he sailed westward away from me.

If he had looked at me, but one more time, he would have seen the tears running down my face, pooling with the blood, soaking into the sand.

Ch. 6 - Rebirth

The slit on my throat ran from ear to ear. The length of it had leaked slowly, with the Thana berries all but stopping my heart. A broken heart, but one that still pumped. I lay there paralyzed for so long, I could feel my skin binding itself together. Pins and needles rushed through my veins. The pain of betrayal, stabbing, and knitting my fractured heart and sliced throat back together.

From the sands, I'd watch as the sun rose, and the moon set, for the sun to rise again. I wanted to die from the heartache, but over the days, my breath became normal again. My fingers curled, a toe wiggled. Immortality gradually regenerated what grievous injury almost ended. I must have eaten many thana berries, for the paralytic was slow to leave my system.

When I finally managed to move my head, the pain was unbearable. Seeing my desecrated wings tossed far flung from me, their feathers shorn and bloody, I felt a desolate sadness. My hands probed my neck. The wound there, healed, my voice, but a whisper.

I stood, and walked shakily to a mirror. Its polished bronze surface reflected in the sunlight, I cursed what I saw.

A thick ropey scar upon my neck, stumps where my wings used to be, dried blood cascaded down my body with grains of sand stuck to it. My hair looked wild, my eyes had turned black. My scream came out in a stream of clicks and hisses.

Appalled, I turned away from what I saw. I rushed to the waters edge, but my movements were impaired and laborious. I fell to my knees and crawled the remaining way into the gentle lapping waves.

I cried then for my sister's, I cried for my wings, and for my song. Lost, they were all lost to me. As I rocked myself in the surf weeping the sadness away, a fire began to burn in me. The deep pain ached into a fury. A seething boil that radiated off of me.

The sea began to bubble. Washing the blood and sand away. I witnessed the tawny feathers of my legs and from my wingless stumps molt into the turbulent surf.

I wanted to pray to the sun goddess, and stared up at the sky, but for her to see me in the light of her rays felt like a humiliation. To see myself was too much. To let a man do this to me. To have dishonored my sisters, to have fallen so far from grace.

Ashamed I ran from the day and hid myself. I never wanted to catch my reflection again. I waited for the dark of the evening to emerge. I walked the sands and stared out where Loukas's ship sails had disappeared in the cover of night.

His name, a curse, I uttered with a whisper that grew stronger by the day. A whisper that through time became a voice that could speak again, but my song was forever lost to me. Nothing more than painful clicks and a whistled hiss. Perhaps some cuts are too deep, some pain irreparable I thought.

The moon became my companion, its gentle glow and darkness a comfort. I watched the flitting of the bats against the silver skies longing to join them in the skies, and confided to the moon my failings and humiliation. I kept waiting for my wings and feathers to grow back, but they never did.

Instead, a metamorphosis I was not expecting. Soft downy fur sprouted from my legs black and thick. Bony protrusions emerged and elongated from my stumps. Thin inky black skin, soft and supple, grew like webbing and wrapped around them. The flesh was warm, veiny, and wide. Slowly forming an expanse of wing that grew nightly.

One evening, when I found I could flap them they lifted me off the ground under the pale crescent. I joined the bats that I now closely resembled.

The moon goddess had heard my prayers and given me flight. I was now a daughter of the night. I found my screams and whistles could guide me. I could see farther and better than I ever had in the day. My talons were sharper, my body was once again healed.

There was only one thing left to do to make myself feel complete, and as I sailed into the mists under the soft glow of the moon, I hungered only for one thing. Loukas.

Ch. 7 - New Lands

My whistled screech cut deep into the swirling fog, as my new wings proved to be quite efficient at rapid changes mid-flight. With this new maneuverability I was able to whirl and spin in the air in ways I'd never previously, and with each pump of their soft skin, I was propelled further than any siren had ventured into the outer seas.

Windswept currents that smelled of salt and seaweed met my nose, but in there carried across the waves, was the fetid scent of humans. Even as I grew tired, it was the pungent smell of man that kept me going.

The fog was endless, but when it finally broke, my eyes beheld what my whistles and clicks had been forming in my mind.

In the distance was a great landmass, and scattered across the glittered sea, were boats. I had made it to the mortal lands.

It could have taken months or years to track down Loukas, but his retelling of his life was accurate to the very last detail. At least in that I came to find he had not lied.

Sun-dried brick houses sprawled across the earth. I circled high, smelling the winds, searching for the spicy oak scent of Loukas amidst the onslaught of odors. The city was large and overwhelming in its stink, and so I found a densely packed grove of trees just outside the sprawl to land in.

A dirt path cut through the trunks of olive trees, and to my delight, a horse pulling a man on a cart. Instinctively, I tried to sing, but the shrill whistle and clicks only proved to startle the beast. The horse whinnied and stopped short, blowing out his nostrils and pawing at the earth. The driver seemed not to have noticed anything, and snapped the reins to plod the horse further. So I stood out on the path.

When the man saw me, he recoiled in shock, and slapped at the horse's back with frightened fervor.

I only needed to raise my hand to nullify the animal. Snatching the reins with the other hand, I demanded, "tell me human, do you know of a Loukas?"

The change was unexpected and immediate. He grew the faraway look with a slack jawline, his hands going limp at his sides.

So, my song was taken from me, but my voice still had power.

"I know many Loukas'." The man said hypnotically, a sleepy smile crossing his face.

"Do you know of a Tavern called, The Imperial?" I asked, hopefully.

A raise of the man's eyebrows "I know of that place, yes" he said, dreamily.

"You will take me to it." I said, as I nimbly jumped into the back of the cart wrapping myself in a piece of cloth to conceal my wings.

"Of course, my lady."

A slap of the reins and the cart lurched forward. I regarded the countryside as it turned to cramped city streets with all their civilization had to offer. I saw the hungry eyes of the poor, down beaten backs of the slaves, beggars, and barefooted children. I thought of Loukas as a child on these streets and wondered what my riches had done for him here. Perhaps he had done some good for what I imagined was his community, but once at the tavern I needed only speak to a few people.

Spellbound by my voice many knew of him and were forthcoming with the information I sought. He'd come back boasting of his riches, and had moved to a villa high on the hill above the city.

I took to the sky, and as I drew closer, my nostrils picked up the spicy oak scent of him. The villa was large with a courtyard. Slaves busying themselves about, and then I saw him, laying in the sun being tended to.

I landed quietly and worked my way through the home, bewitching the slaves I encountered. Getting testimonies from them as to their treatment. By all accounts he had acquired a taste for brutality along with the finer things in life. Young girls, gaunt and beaten by his hand. Forced to do things that at one point had sent my wings to flutter. I shuddered in disgust.

In their dreamlike trance they told me he bragged of seducing a siren, discovering her secrets, killing the creature, and stealing her gold. His plans to go back and finish the job. That he spoke of great treasure he'd promised the crew he was forming, and the glory they would win, knowledge they would learn, by killing and torturing the creatures.

I took my time weaving around the home, finding a room with maps to my Islands spread across a desk. I burned them in golden bowls. I had seen enough.

Walking back from the depths of the house towards the courtyard standing in the dimness of dusk. He still sat drinking and ordered the slaves about. Slapping one when she dropped a platter of food. Screaming at her to get him more wine. I stopped her as she passed "bring me that cup of wine first." The poor girl came back with a scarlet bruise already forming on her cheek, holding the cup before me. "Now take it to him." I whispered.

Then I waited. Watching him in all his gluttony down the liquid. Only then did I emerge from the shadows "Hello again Loukas." I said in a purr.

He listed sideways on the chair, the berries paralytic taking its effect. not enough to kill him, just enough to leave him as he left me.

Helpless, scared, and vulnerable.

I spoke slowly to make sure he saw every move of my lips. I knelt down beside him. "I see you have made use of my treasures."

His chest movements barely perceptible, but his heart was still pumping so loudly I could hear it, waves of fear pulsing from his pores. It smelled sweet and delicious.

"I gave you the choice, you could have left, I would have probably given you the gold, had you but asked, I loved you." I said, walking my fingers up his broad chest.

"I really loved you, but you betrayed me, and I really should thank you." I splayed out my wings and lifted the elongated arched claws of my fingers in front of him. "As I lay there dying, it evoked something in me, something the goddess saw, and she blessed me with new gifts." I said, grabbing his chin, roughly turning his head back towards me as it started to loll. The poison coursing through his body. "I wanted to share them with you, and I want you to be there when I share the news with my sisters. I think it's only right."

A sound like a moan escaped his mouth. I lay a finger across his lips.

"There is nothing left to be said between us." I stood, flexing my fingers, and raised my wings against the darkening sky. Lifting up, gripping him in my taloned feet, claws sinking into the soft flesh of his chest.

I took off into the dusk. The expanse of the ocean before us.

Ch. 8 - Eastward

The waves were tumultuous below us, churning with frothy delight as I made my way back toward our lands and away from the stench of the city. The mists waited. I used my whistles and screeching to navigate through the blinding whiteness and swirling fog. Until a sound I'd missed met my ears. The lulling song of the sirens. My sisters waited.

The berries' poison was wearing off from Loukas. He began to jostle underneath me, fingers prying at my talons, whimpers and groans.

The closer we got to the islands, the louder and more desperate his moans became. I cared not for anything he must have been feeling, all I registered was the sound of the songs, the waves, and the wind through my hair. It was the goddess calling me home. My sisters, having heard my whistles, were standing on the sandy shores looking up at the skies. Many of them lent their voices to my appearance in the sky.

I circled above, calling out to them. "Forgive me, my sisters, for my weakness. Of my curiosity for that which the goddess created us to slaughter. I was played a fool, and deceived by the very man I betrayed you for, but as I lay forsaken, the goddess granted me new life, and with it, I bring my gift to share with you, my penance and my revenge."

Loukas was squirming and bellowing. I glided down closer to the island. In the crowd I could see Nysa and Isadora. We locked eyes with one another, and I bowed my head. They looked stone-faced before smiles curled up at the corners of their lips, nodding in quick succession with approval.

I could feel Loukas' hands frantically grabbing at my legs below me. My hand reached down letting my fingers twist and wrap themselves within the black mass of his hair, before I released him from my talons. Lifting him up to be eye level with me. I could feel the cold dark rage radiating out from my gaze. It settled him.

The whites of his eyes, large with fear. "This is all for you Loukas." I smiled wickedly

watching his eyes focus on my lips. Then I called down to my sisters, "And for you, my sisters!"

His mouth moved to say something, but I slashed with my free hand cleanly and deeply into his neck. The razor sharp claws severing his body from his head. Blood shot up in a great spurt from his muscular shoulders, his arms and legs twitched as the body hurtled down through the air away from us.

I held his head so for those last moments of consciousness he could truly appreciate it. His eyes continued to blink in surprise, his mouth opened and shut gasping for air.

I saw it all unfold like a bloom, time slowed down. The feathered wings of all my sisters taking flight gathering and ripping at the falling body. A flurry of teeth and talons. Flesh torn from bone. Intestines strung out and slashed. We watched together as his body was eviscerated into nothing. I turned his head to face me. I looked deep into his piercing blue eyes for the last time as they were beginning to glaze over in death. I saw him focus on my lips. "I've been planning this for sometime, and if you're not dead yet, you will be." I said, smiling.

A flash of recognition crossed his features. I brought his face to mine and sunk my teeth into his lips, tearing them from his jaw. He tasted good, better than I had remembered a man could taste.

Ch. 9 - Remembrance

"I tell you this story my little young Siren, so that you may learn from my mistakes, and know of your father," I said to my daughter, born many moons after that fateful day. "This skull here is the only thing that remains of him, I keep it close, always, to remind me of man's capabilities for deception."

I handed my daughter the skull. Her hands tensed, sharp claws scratching the surface. Her black eyes staring into the empty sockets that once held the piercing blue ones of Loukas. Her nose scrunched, smelling his deceit still leeching out from the bone.

"In the past, we had to wait for the goddess to send us ships, but she has blessed you and I with the ability to see through the mists, and aid our sisters." I said, coming to brush my hand against her cheek, and down the soft warm skin of her wings. "We can now hunt into the outer seas, and though my song was cut from me." My fingers left the ink black of her wings to graze against the scar on my neck before lifting her chin to look into the fathomless beauty of my daughter's eyes. "Yours, my dear, is intact, and you were born to sing. You have been blessed with all the goddesses' gifts, both old and new. So come now, let us seek a ship, for we all hunger."

Chapter 1

The salty breeze caressed my cheek and whispered of my impending doom.

It was as though every stone crevice had taunted me for years, refusing to allow me to forget for one second what awaited me. Not that I could, anyway. The reminder was in every breath, every lesson, every sunrise. And now, I had run out of those.

"Maris?"

I blinked the thoughts away as I looked from the open window and met sparkling brown eyes in the mirror. My only friend stared at me expectantly as she ran a brush over my scalp. Her blonde hair fell in wavy tendrils, pinned on one side by a shell barrette that framed her heart-shaped face perfectly. Her cheeks and lips were naturally tinted pink, giving her an effortless beauty that I could never attain. The light teal dress offset her sun-kissed skin, and she looked every bit an ocean goddess.

"What?"

Talia gave me a chiding smile. "I knew you weren't listening to me."

"I'm sorry. I was just…"

"It's okay." Her hands dropped to my shoulders, giving them a squeeze. "It's a big day." She picked up the pearl headband, sliding it onto the crown of my head, twirling some wavy strands around it to hold it in place.

I clasped my hands in my lap and blinked away the wetness from my lashes. They would not get the satisfaction of any tears. My breath caught as fear tightened around my ribs, while dread coiled low in my stomach. Why me?

The white pearls were a stark contrast to my dark blue, almost black hair, but complemented the porcelain color of my skin. I didn't fully recognize the face staring back at me. My bluish-jade eyes were rimmed in navy, shimmering teal painted my eyelids with dark blue in the creases, and a nude pink coated my lips. The freckles dotting my nose faintly showed through the powder dusted across my skin. My face masked the turmoil inside.

"Talia," I said as I turned, grabbing her hand. "I—"

"Maris," she interrupted. The sharp look on her face melted into the serene look she normally wore. "Tonight is such an honor. Remember that."

"I know, it's just—" The words stalled. For a heartbeat, I considered saying it: *I don't want this.*

"Tssh, there are so many who would love to be in your place. There is nothing higher to aspire to. I only wish I…well, Thalen chose you. You are THE chosen. The favored." She gave a tight smile and tilted my chin up to look at her. "This is what Thalen demands of us, and you are the lucky one. You get to serve him in his kingdom for all eternity."

I silenced the words that wanted to break through. That I didn't think it was an honor, nor did I feel lucky. But such words uttered aloud would be blasphemous.

Talia smiled and closed her eyes for a few seconds. "There, let's get you dressed." She pulled me from the chair, and I numbly followed her, dropping my robe as she placed the white underdress over my head, then the white ceremony dress, trimmed with silver brocade in swirls reminiscent of ocean waves. She tugged the ties on my back taut and secured them into a bow.

"Beautiful," Talia reassured and gave me a quick hug.

The knock at the door caused me to jump as I pressed my index finger back into an uncomfortable position to keep from wringing my hands.

Talia opened the door and lowered her head as Priestess Undine swept in. Her shrewd eyes scrutinized me from head to toe before clasping her hands. She had graying short hair that framed brown eyes, and lines creased her square face, telling of her age.

"Well done," she praised. "It's almost time." She placed a hand on my cheek and smiled. "There's no reason to be nervous. You are ensuring the safety and prosperity of the kingdom. This is a joyous evening. You have been a wonderful gift, excelling in your lessons and devotion to our sacred Order, and following our expectations. Thalen will be pleased."

I chased the warmth of her hand as she dropped it, longing for some sort of affection. Not that she ever had. Priestess Undine had a singular focus of serving the ocean god. Her role in the Thanyktas Order was teaching those, like Talia, who wanted to join the Order, and helping the High Priests as an intermediary to the people of Thanykotos. She was also the keeper of the Chosen One. Her light teal ceremonial robe, decorated with silver trim and belt, and bejeweled ocean wave pin spoke of her status.

"Come," Undine stated, heading for the door.

I willed my feet to move as dread swept through me, pausing in the doorframe to take one last look at my room. My throat closed as sadness threatened to choke me, but I swallowed hard as I followed Undine and Talia through the halls.

Five years ago, my life ended when I was chosen as the next sacrifice. A ceremony known as the Quinquennial Rite was conducted to gather all the girls between the ages of fifteen and eighteen. High Priest Erwyn selected a name in a random draw to be the next sacrifice to the ocean god. They viewed being chosen as the highest honor. The girl went to live with the Thanyktas Order, where she learned all about the customs and how to live a life dedicated to Thalen, and bestowed upon Priestess Undine.

I had done everything I had been asked. I excelled in my studies, using them as a distraction from the inevitable, and presented myself as the perfect, pious sacrifice, all the while longing for some change in my fate.

All in preparation for this night.

Waiting for someone to see me, to notice me, to take pity on me.

To free me.

They performed the Thalasic Tidal Rite every five years to continue garnering the favor of the ocean god Thalen. It ensured there were calm seas, and the kingdom thrived because of his benevolence. It was based on an ancient pact between Thalen and the kingdom. Annual rituals, called the Thanyraic ceremonies, were performed to appease the god between Rites where the High Priest spoke incantations of gratitude while standing in the surf, and the priests tossed in a seashell that washed up with the tide as a sign of rebirth and renewal.

After tonight, another sacrifice would be chosen, and I would be forgotten.

My heart pounded in my chest as I left the safety of the stone building and took in the revelry. The kingdom celebrated the Rite with music, dancing, and food—a joyous occasion for everyone but me.

After all, I'd be dead.

The air smelled of salt and brine mixed with roasted meats. The ocean was calm with steady waves lapping at the beach's edge. The kingdom of Thanykotos was built along the coastline of the Thalasias Sea in a crescent shape. One side had a rugged, jagged cliffside, while the other had a security fortress that jutted out into the sea and trading ports, while the beach rested in the middle. The weathered stone buildings of the priesthood were constructed between the beach and the cliffside. Those in service to Thalen resided there, as well as those chosen as his sacrifice.

I had called it home for the past five years. Once chosen, I was not allowed to live with my family or communicate with them. I saw them only at the ceremonies from a distance. The Order afforded me the courtesy of saying our goodbyes yesterday, in a meeting that lasted only half an hour. The kingdom compensated the families of the Chosen Ones well for the loss of their child, but everyone understood the importance of the Rite, even my parents. They had hugged me and said their praises, and I had hugged my younger sisters. I might as well have already been dead to them.

My only friend walked ahead of me, and my mind raced with our memories. I grabbed Talia's elbow. "Will you miss me?"

Talia blinked. "Of course." She hurried her steps to catch up with Undine.

"Behold! Our Chosen One!" High Priest Erwyn held out his arms in my direction.

I faltered, slowing my pace and wanting nothing more than to not take another step forward. There was an arched doorway leading away from the beach, and I wondered if I could make it and disappear. My eyes met Priestess Undine's sharp gaze, and I lowered my head to the priest in a show of respect. The moment vanished.

"Come," Erwyn said, taking my hand. He led me to the dais that overlooked the ocean and the ceremony.

I averted my gaze so I wouldn't have to connect with those staring at me and sat down on the old wooden chair. Sucking in a deep breath, I worked to calm my nerves, but nothing seemed to help. Is this how the others had felt?

Why was I paying with my life for an ancient pact? What did Thalen want with me, anyway? I was a nobody. Only in this chair because of my name on a piece of paper.

Clapping startled me, and I had missed whatever Erwyn had said. My lips quirked into an awkward small smile as the audience reacted. My fingernails dug into my palms leaving crescent moon shapes in my skin while the breeze lifted strands of my hair, reminding me what was to come.

"Chosen One," someone called. Then another. Soon, the word spread through the crowd until it became a chant.

The ocean looked even darker than normal, like it knew my life was seconds away from becoming its next claimed soul.

Growing up, I had loved being so close to it, but now, I hated it. Hated what it stood for. Hated its power, its demands.

My stomach churned, and I worried I might be sick. That would be a terrible look for the Chosen One. From what I remembered, none of the ones before me had been scared or nervous. They were like Talia. Always peaceful. Always serene. The perfect acolyte.

Then there was me.

I wanted to question everything. But I was also envious. Why couldn't I just be more like them? This would all be easier to accept.

Watching the crowd dance and laugh, enjoying the night, stabbed me in the chest. How could it be so easy for them to dismiss that I was sitting here in my final moments waiting to die?

"Would you like to dance?"

I jerked, coming face to face with the most handsome man I had ever seen who felt...wrongly familiar. He was tall and broad, with short-cropped black hair and deep ocean blue eyes framed by thick lashes set in an angular face with a sharp nose and jaw. His full pink lips tilted up on one side. Like it was a smile I should recognize. A dark eyebrow lifted as I realized I was staring.

"Oh, I can't. I..." I tugged at the fabric of my dress. "I'm sorry. I'm not allowed."

His brows dipped. "Not allowed?"

"Right. I'm the guest of honor...or whatever." I shrugged. "Thank you for the offer."

"What about a walk? Food?"

I shook my head.

"You seem nervous."

Ugh, I thought I was hiding it better, and here this stranger noticed. Why was he here and bothering to speak to me? No one else was. He looked almost familiar, but I couldn't place where I knew him from.

"Is this an honor for you?"

I bit my lip. No way I could answer that honestly. I wanted to scream no. Instead, I said, "Of course."

A muscle in his jaw ticked as he studied me.

"The Thalasic Tidal Rite is our most sacred ceremony, as we honor our gratitude and devotion to the all-powerful Thalen," High Priest Erwyn said, his voice carrying on the wind for all to hear.

"I—" I turned to find myself alone. Where did the man go? I surveyed the crowd, and there was no sign of him.

"This Rite, we have Maris to thank. Our Chosen One. Our gift to Thalen. Her sacrifice ensures our safety, prosperity, and favor. Thalen will continue to grant us calm seas, advantageous trades, and the well-being of everyone in this kingdom."

He motioned to me, and I stood. My time was running out. Was there a way to avoid this? What would happen to everyone if I did? No, remember the people, remember the people. It's not just about me.

Remember your lessons, I scolded myself.

But I wanted more. Did anyone even know me? I didn't want to be known as simply a Chosen One. Forgotten in five years, as if my life meant nothing. My eyes found Talia's, and she gave me a slow blink and tiny smile. Erwyn was speaking, but I couldn't hear for the ringing in my ears.

I could do this. I would do this.

I'd do it for my family to ensure their well-being. But deep down, I wanted to curse the ocean god. How did we know Thalen even wanted this? Because the priests said so?

Get it together.

Taking a deep breath, I focused on the ocean. I was going to face this, cloaked in bravery, and pushed away the uncertainty.

"We have a long history of devotion to the ocean god. We must continue, so he remains pleased with us." His eyes swept over the crowd. "Sacrifice is required of us all, and we give it willingly. As you serve us, we serve Thalen. I am honored to stand between you and him as High Priest. There is no greater calling than to serve him. And our Chosen One bears the greatest honor of all." He paused, bowing his head. "For that, we are eternally grateful."

The crowd bowed in my direction, and that was my cue. I walked down the two steps of the dais and fell in line behind Erwyn, flanked on every side by the priests. I lifted my head with a false air of confidence as we left the beach and stepped onto the stone walk that wove alongside the priests' building and cliffside toward the ledge erected just for these ceremonies. The crowd filled out along the beach's shoreline below us.

Run. Run, run, run.

The thoughts rushed unbidden through my mind as my body shook. I didn't want to do this. Why wasn't there a way out? I had a family, dreams, a life. They took everything from me.

As I passed Erwyn, the wind whipped through my hair and dress as the stone ledge ran out from under my feet. The waves crashed against the rocks below, mocking me. Their rocking acted like a monster ready to gobble me up.

It was such a long way down. And dark. It was so dark.

The priests hummed deep in their throats as Erwyn began his incantations, taking his place directly behind me. He spoke in a language only the priests knew, and according to them, Thalen. The deep, ominous sound made my skin prickle.

Save me, save me! No! I don't want to do this! I screamed in my mind.

"Thalen, the powerful, accept our gift for the Thalasic Tidal Rite in exchange for your protection and blessings. We honor you. Let this be a sign of our unyielding devotion."

Terror gripped every muscle as I froze in place, staring at the water. What would happen if I turned and ran? Would they kill me here? Did I have a chance of getting away?

"It is time," Erwyn muttered.

"No," I whispered.

A hand met my back and pushed. Hard.

The wind hurtled around me, fluttering my dress around my calves, and doing nothing to stop my fall.

Time slowed as I twisted to look over my shoulder to watch the priests staring at me with stoic expressions. This was just another ritual to them. There was no empathy as they so willingly took a life. One that didn't belong to them, but their entitlement said otherwise. All this for a god who hadn't been seen or heard from in decades.

I fought the scream that desperately wanted to bubble out, but I would not go out that way. They would not know my fear. My body turned as the dark water waited to eat me whole. My arms flailed around me in a sorry attempt to slow my drop.

Cold stabbed every part of me as my brain registered my crash. The roar of the wind dropped to a deeper pitch as the water closed around me. A wave swallowed me down, down, down into the watery abyss. The current tossed me around like a rag doll despite my trying to kick to the surface. I didn't even know which way was up.

My lungs screamed, burning, convulsing as they demanded air I couldn't take. Anger surged through me that this had been my life of a meager twenty years. There was so much more I wanted to become. Not this. Never this.

I kept kicking and searching for the surface. If I got a breath, I could swim elsewhere. Stow away on a ship. Anything but this.

My body screamed at me, and my struggles faded. My legs failed to power through the current as I sank. Everything slowed as sleep lulled me. A hand wrapped around my ankle and yanked. I opened my mouth and screamed into the watery void, bubbles carrying my cry as the darkness overtook me.

Chapter 2

A dampness tickled my cheek, then pulled at my body. The darkness lingered in my mind and then... there was the wetness again. My body rocked back before gently pushing forward.

My eyes blinked open as something scraped my cheek, and I squinted against the light. My fingers dug into the grainy earth. I pushed myself up, recognizing the beach underneath. A wave sloshed around me before retreating again. The ocean calmly lapped the shoreline while the birds screeched overhead.

My teeth chattered from the chill of my wet dress and the wind. I racked my brain for what happened. Why had I fallen asleep on the beach? I lifted my hand to tuck my hair back when something hit my cheek.

An amulet.

My brows furrowed as I stared at the small silver rectangle, with four sides, and a piece of blue jade encased inside. At the top was a wave where it attached to the chain. A white pearl connected it to the open part of the chain, and it glinted in the sunlight. It was one of the most beautiful pieces I had ever seen.

But where had it come from?

Scanning the land before me, my eyes landed on the dais chair. My heart plummeted as the memories slammed into me, followed by a disbelieving relief. I wasn't dead.

I wasn't dead. Panic seized me. What did it mean? Falling into the water was the last thing I remembered.

Twisting, I stared out onto the ocean, but nothing seemed amiss. How had this happened?

A scream jolted me out of my thoughts.

I scrambled to my feet as a woman screamed and cried while pointing at me. Within minutes, there was a small crowd, including priests.

"Thalen rejected her!" someone yelled.

"Thalen rejected our sacrifice! We're all doomed!"

I shoved the amulet into my pocket.

Erwyn appeared, fury written on his face. His brow narrowed into a crease as he glared at me. "What is the meaning of this?"

My mouth opened, but no sound came out. I didn't know how to explain something I didn't understand myself. My heart hammered against my ribs as a sharp ringing filled my ears. I needed to run, to get away from here, but my body refused to move.

"Thalen rejected her!" a woman cried.

I studied the fear written on their faces as my stomach flipped.

"What do we do?" a priest asked under his breath.

"This has never happened before," Erwyn seethed. "What did you do, girl?"

"No-nothing," I hesitated. "I just woke up here and—"

"Thalen has never rejected a sacrifice in our history."

Had Thalen rejected me? That thought settled around me, and I started to tremble. This was bad.

"Thalen must be displeased with us," another priest whispered.

"Nonsense," Erwyn said. "It's not us. It's *her.*"

They stared at me, and I wanted the sand to split open and drag me under.

"What did you do?" Erwyn hissed. "Tell me!"

"I...I didn't do anything," I insisted. "You were there. I fell into the water and woke up here."

"Get Undine. Were your preparations completed?"

"Yes!"

"Your allegiance to Thalen?"

"Yes!"

Erwyn took a step toward me and grabbed the back of my neck, his face mere inches from my own. "You understand, this does not happen. What is wrong with you that we missed? What did you do!"

"I didn't do anything!"

"Liar!"

"Cursed!"

"She's cursed!"

"Cursed! Cursed! Cursed!"

I closed my eyes to their chants, doing my best to block them out and go somewhere else in my mind. I flinched as his grip sent a sharp pain down my back before he shoved me forward, causing me to stumble and land on my knees in the sand.

"What..."

Erwyn cleared his throat. "Priestess Undine, we seem to have an issue with your Chosen One."

Priestess Undine looked at me horrified.

"How is this possible?" she asked.

A gasp sounded, and my eyes landed on Talia stepping out from behind Undine. Her hand covered her mouth as she stared at me with wide eyes.

"Talia—"

"Silence!" Erwyn snapped.

"Cursed!"

"You will find out what happened," Erwyn threatened. "This is unacceptable."

"Thalen rejected her!" a shout came from the crowd.

Undine's eyes widened as her jaw clenched. "Get up, girl."

I pushed to my feet as she grabbed my arm, her nails digging into my flesh. I wanted to cry out, but I swallowed it instead. She half-dragged, half-pushed me toward the priestess's building, my feet scrambling to keep me upright. Water droplets ran down my skin, a constant reminder of the event. A warmth radiated from my pocket. Why had my fate changed?

Undine threw open my bedroom door and shoved me inside, slamming the door behind us. I tripped on my wet dress and fell onto the stone floor, cracking my elbow and hissing at the sting of pain.

"What is the meaning of this?" Undine spat. "This can't be happening. You cannot escape your fate, Maris! You were selected as the Chosen One, as were all the others before you were."

I rubbed my sore arm. "I don't know."

"You completed all of your studies and duties."

"Yes."

Undine paced. "Thalen has never rejected a sacrifice."

I winced at that truth. Why me? I felt like I had spent most of my life asking that question. But why would Thalen reject me? He had thrown me back onto the shore like trash. As if I meant nothing. Something in my chest splintered at the thought.

"Why did he reject you!"

I met her brown eyes. "I don't know! It's not like I saw him."

"Then how did you get back here? I saw you jump into the water myself."

Jump? That was a farce.

"I just woke up here."

"You have no memories?"

"No."

She wrung her hands as she stopped pacing. "Maybe you are cursed."

I shot her a look. "I'm not cursed. You've been here. I've done everything that was asked."

"Indeed. Perhaps he rejected your heart."

My hand brushed the amulet in my pocket. I didn't know how I had ended up with it, but it was going to remain my secret for now. I didn't need more scrutiny than I had, but I needed to find out what it meant and how I had gotten it.

"This is most unfortunate," Undine chastised. "You will have to stay here until we decide what must happen next." Her tone made it clear that *next* might mean my death. She glared at me. "Thalen must be quite displeased with you. Your soul may be forfeit to him now."

"Maybe it's not just me?" I muttered.

She stepped towards me, and my cheek exploded with pain. "Never say such a blasphemous thing again," she hissed. "You're at fault here. I suggest you plead with every part of your being for Thalen to show you forgiveness for your insolence."

I jumped at the slamming of the door and then sank onto the couch, massaging my cheek. Tears pricked my eyes, and I furiously brushed them away as they fell. This was so unfair. All I wanted was to have a normal life, but that was never going to be granted to me. Dying wasn't the worst of it. This may be worse. They may decide to kill me anyway. Not only was the Order disappointed in me, but the entire kingdom was terrified of me.

I retrieved the amulet from my pocket and studied it. The blue jade stone was the same shade as the ocean and my eyes, and the silver twinkled as the light hit it. I closed my hand around it and pressed it against my chest. Shutting my eyes, I wracked my brain for any shards of memory. I was on the platform, Erwyn pushed me, and I fell. The water sucked me down and... And what? I'd tried to swim, but it was so disorienting... It was a black hole. What happened between being in the water and waking up on the beach?

Taking a deep breath and sniffing, I headed for my bathing chamber. My mind was made up. I was taking control of my life.

Chapter 3

The stone echoed the voices down the hall, and my slippered feet padded with gentle thuds as I made my way to the library. Shadows housed me while I did my best to remain unnoticed, hurrying on my way with my head down. The need for answers drew me out of my room, where I was sure they wanted me to remain. But I needed to know if there was a record of a refused sacrifice before or...if I was just that lucky.

I spotted Talia outside the library building, and relief washed over me at seeing my friend. "Talia!"

Her eyes widened as her steps faltered.

Was that horror on her face?

"Hi...Maris." She glanced around, clasping her hands. "What are you doing...out?"

My skin prickled as unease settled in. "What do you mean?"

"I just don't think you should be wandering around, considering. What are you doing?"

"Going to the library."

Some of the tension loosened from her shoulders. "Ah, that probably is best. Study and improve your devotion to Thalen."

My brows scrunched. "No, I—"

"Well, I better go. Good luck."

I watched her hurry away. Like she wanted to get away from me before anyone saw. Like I was...cursed. The word repeated in my mind.

Why had Thalen done this to me?

Sighing, I pushed open the library doors, the comforting smell reminding me they were still my friends. Light streamed through the stained-glass windows, illuminating the rows of books. There was an ornate dome in the center of the ceiling, with the other levels circling the dome to prevent a blocked view. There were ocean motifs painted in the dome, including one of Thalen rising out of a wave with a gold trident. I made my way towards the archive section, where the historical accounts of the kingdom were housed. A slight pang of overwhelm hit me as I looked at the multiple shelves. Where to even start?

I knew there had been no rejected sacrifices in the recent past, so I chose one from back in the previous hundred years.

My finger ran down the list of names. Girls like me, whom I had never heard of. They gave everything, and now they were only names left in a book. No one even spoke about them anymore. I never wanted the same fate.

I flipped through the book, scanning the entries. There was nothing personal about the individual girls. It was all rhetoric about their service to Thalen.

"What are you searching for?"

I startled at the voice and stared into familiar blue eyes. It was the man from the Rite. His handsome features left me lost for words. He sat in the chair across the table and scooted my book closer to him as he peered at the page.

What on earth was he doing?

He glanced back at me and raised his left eyebrow. "Is it a secret?"

I snapped back into myself and gave a one-shoulder shrug. "Maybe? I don't know."

"Hmm."

That velvety sound caused a shiver to rake down my spine. Never in my life had I seen anyone as beautiful as him, and I wasn't accustomed to the flare of attraction, to...familiarity? It was like my brain no longer worked properly. How do I form a coherent sentence again?

His lips twitched as humor lit his features, and his posture relaxed into the chair. He was enjoying my discomfort. Weren't all men the same in that regard? Except...this felt different. Not as condescending. More...playful.

"I'm just surprised you're...talking to me, is all," I blurted out.

His fingers drummed against the table. "Why's that?"

"Considering...everything..."

He shifted in his seat, folding a set of large, muscular arms on the table. His black cotton shirt stretched against the expanse of his sculpted chest. He smelled like the sea, a mix of salt and driftwood that invited me in, teased my senses. Those deep blue eyes focused on me, leaving me feeling utterly exposed.

My mouth went dry, my thoughts scattering under the weight of his gaze.

"Am I not supposed to?"

"What?" I blinked.

"Talk to you."

"Oh, uh, no, you can. I just didn't expect many would want to."

"And why's that?"

"Because I'm still here." I cleared my throat and shifted in my seat.

He tilted his head. "It's what you wanted?"

I looked back at the book, unsure of how to answer that. It would be heresy to admit that out loud. That I didn't want to be the sacrifice for the Rite. That I was relieved to be back. That I didn't die. I wanted a different life, although I wasn't sure what that looked like. This was all I had ever known. I didn't know if I'd ever be free of it.

"Hard to say…"

His jaw clenched, and his eyes sharpened.

What was it about him that had me wanting to spill my darkest secrets? No, I had to be smart. I couldn't afford to say anything that would cause me more trouble than I was already in. My eyes traced his features. I'd love to run my fingers through his tousled black hair, up his sculpted chest and grip his broad shoulders, pressing into every hard plane. How would his full lips feel pressed against mine? My only experience was a few stolen kisses on the beach with a boy when I was fourteen. Those were chaste. Nothing like how I imagined his would feel. Full of heat and demand as he took what he wanted, as he gave me what I needed.

The loud thud of a fallen book snapped me out of my revelry. A flush crept up my neck as embarrassment set in at my thoughts. My eyes flicked back to his. Was that heat reflected back?

His hands clenched into fists as he pushed away from the table and stood. He walked away and disappeared into an aisle of books.

The breath I had been holding left in a whoosh. What was wrong with me? I had never had thoughts like that about anyone before.

Focus.

I pulled the book closer to me and worked through the names once again. Nothing of these girls being rejected was mentioned. Everything about the Rite happened as normal. It was hard to believe I was the only one. Had none of these other girls feared dying? What was wrong with me?

A black book slammed down in front of me, causing me to jump. My eyes shot up to find intense blue ones fixed on me.

"This is the one you want," he stated low in my ear.

A chill caused me to shiver as I studied the book.

His hand gripped my chin, pulling my attention to him. "You will study this one?"

The earnest look on his face had me deciding my fate. "Yes," I whispered.

"Promise?"

"Yes."

"Good girl." He leaned in as my breath caught in my throat. His fingers caressed my jaw, his thumb brushing ever so lightly across my bottom lip. My heart pounded at his touch and the possibilities. His eyes dropped as his brows furrowed into a faint line. His fingers trailed down my throat and picked up the amulet I wore around my neck, examining it. "Where did you get this?"

"I...I don't know," I confessed.

"Explain."

"I woke up with it."

"A gift from the sea." It was more of a statement. He turned it one last time before pressing it against my chest, the warmth of his fingers heating my skin in every place they touched. He traced the outline of the amulet in a slow, tortuous arc. He straightened and slipped past me.

With the spell broken, I blinked rapidly. "Wait! I don't think I got your name..."

He ignored me and continued on his way until he disappeared from sight. A wave of disappointment hit me as I wracked my brain for a name. If he had given it to me at the Rite, there was no way I'd remember now. My skin tickled from the memory of his touch, hoping that wasn't my last run-in with him. I moved the book to read the spine.

The Record of the Thalasias Accord.

My forehead scrunched. I had never heard of this accord. We were taught about the Thalasic Tidal Pact. I looked in the direction where he had disappeared, but only an empty aisle remained. How had he known what I was searching for?

Ensuring I was alone, I slid the book into my dress, wrapping an arm across my middle to hold it in place. With one last look around, I fled from the library back to my room.

Chapter 4

The next few days passed in a blur as I poured over the book, soaking up the history of Thanykotos. This book contained records the Order didn't teach. I had no way of knowing if it was taught to the priests, but I suspected not. How did he know about this book? Where had it been hidden?

After my visit to the library, I was banished to my room for the foreseeable future. No doubt, thanks to Talia. She was supposed to be my friend, so it was hard to understand why she'd do this. Surely she didn't think I was cursed like the others. She knew me. I chose not to dwell on it since I had something more important to discover.

This record of the Thalasic Tidal Rite was hard to reconcile with what I had been taught my whole life. After the third time, I stopped counting how many times I reread it, making sure I hadn't read it wrong. According to this, the Thalasias Accord was the pact agreed upon between Thalen and the then rulers of Thanykotos. It called for an annual celebration to express the kingdom's gratitude to Thalen for his aid in calm waters and prosperity. This allowed the trade ports to remain full and desirable. This did not sound like everything I had been taught. The pit in my stomach grew each time I read it.

The Thanyktas Order was established to pass on the histories and teachings to future generations and to perform certain rites to thank the ocean god. Five hundred years ago, a High Priest named Firth claimed to have received a message from Thalen calling for a sacrifice during the Thalasic Tidal Rite to ensure the kingdom's devotion to him. By sacrificing a young woman of the kingdom every five years, their sacrifice proved to Thalen they were wholly devoted to the god and dependent on his favor. There was no record of anyone questioning this. That year, they sacrificed the first girl to the ocean god.

I wanted to throw up.

Firth enforced this ideology, and the Order continued the practice for each Rite thereafter. A few later priests added their touches to the Rite, thus making it what it was today. Thalen, who once interacted with the people, fell dormant but continued favoring the kingdom, which prospered into great wealth.

How had they let one priest change it from its original intent? And why had the sacrifices been women only? Why couldn't it have been anyone? Probably the same reason women can't join the High Priest order. I rolled my eyes, and the truth made my blood boil.

These were the kinds of questions that had kept me up late into the night. The other one that plagued me was: why had Thalen gone along with this?

Another short entry caught my eye that described several years of hardship and turmoil, with ships and ports being claimed by the sea. The kingdom became poor and hungry, and the people demanded that something be done. An ocean goddess was blamed for distracting Thalen, and Firth, along with the Order, kidnapped and banished her, cursing her to be forgotten. They claimed it was for the kingdom's salvation. Now I wondered if that's how they so easily ushered in the Rite. I couldn't help but feel empathy for her.

My fingers closed around the amulet as my heart dropped for all of those girls. It never sat right with me they made it out to be some heroic act. Not only was it perfectly calculated, but it was not even needed.

The history had been twisted by the very ones who were meant to preserve it.

The amulet warmed against my touch, and for a second, I wondered if it was infused with magic. But that was silly. I needed to let go of my fantastical ideas. This world wasn't magical.

Now, the thought of what to do next weighed heavy. I was an outcast. Cursed and banished. I didn't know how I was going to get out of this debacle, and I wasn't convinced they wouldn't kill me. If I started speaking the truth from the book, they would just add heresy to my growing list of offenses. I massaged my temples, working to release the building tension headache.

The crack of thunder boomed, shaking the glass in my windows, followed by flashes of light. The cacophony played outside, each taking turns to perform.

My brows furrowed as I placed the book on the couch and stood. The sky was dark with ominous clouds, and the black sea was rolling with white foam as large waves gathered and crashed against the rocks below. I cranked the latch, opening the window. The wind whipped in with a howl, blowing strands of my hair into my face. The weather was like nothing I had seen before as unease settled deep within.

The wind fought me as I pulled the window closed, doing its best to force it back open. Air circled the amulet where it hung suspended.

I froze.

The circle of air turned the same blue jade color before escaping out of the window and back towards the ocean with an answering clap of thunder. The amulet bounced once as it landed back on my chest. My hand clasped around it as I stared at the sea. Lightning streaked across the sky, and thunder boomed, startling me back to reality. Grabbing the latch, I pulled the window shut until...

I paused, squinting my eyes down at the beach. A group gathered, their teal robes fluttering furiously in the wind. There in the middle was someone dressed in a white dress with golden hair streaming in the whipping wind.

Talia.

"No!" I shouted. "No, stop!"

Everyone ignored me as my voice was lost to the wind.

I slammed the window shut and shoved my feet into my slippers, throwing open my door and barreling down the hall. My amulet bounced against my chest as I ran. I heard a few chastising remarks from those I passed, but I didn't care.

They were recreating the Rite! And they were sacrificing Talia! They couldn't do this. Not anymore. They didn't *need* to do this.

I burst through the door, the wind almost knocking me off my feet. I grabbed my dress to keep it from wrapping around my legs as I scanned the beach. The group was no longer there as my heart pounded in my ears. My eyes widened as I took in the sea while holding onto the balustrade, and fear gripped my muscles. The ocean churned and roared as the black sky covered us in menacing rolls. A flash of white caught my attention as the group made their way up the rocky cliffside.

"No! Wait!" I ran down the last few steps, my feet landing in the sand.

"Not so fast there." Priestess Undine grabbed my bicep and jerked me back.

"Let me go!"

"The cursed one can't be here. You're not supposed to leave your room until we decide what to do with you."

I tried to wrestle free from her grip. "Can't you see? Thalen doesn't want this!"

"How would you know what Thalen wants?" she hissed. Her other hand closed over my jaw in a vice grip. "They should've already killed you for your heresy. Thalen rejected *you,* Maris. We cannot let that go unpunished."

"No—" I choked as her hand squeezed my windpipe with a strength I hadn't expected. My hand slapped hers trying to loosen her grasp so I could take a breath. Nothing was working. I refused to go out like this. I had to help Talia. Convince them that no sacrifice was needed. I had to make them listen.

My fingers brushed the amulet. *Help.*

It warmed against my chest.

Then the priestess' grip on me was gone. She screamed as she went flying through the air, arms flailing and reaching for me as she was dragged out and thrust into the sea. My breath came in sharp pants. I couldn't believe my eyes. There were no signs of Priestess Undine.

I hiked up my dress in one hand and took off running for the ledge on the cliff. My feet slapped against the stone as I climbed, the waves crashing below. I made the mistake of looking down, and I faltered. The stone was wet from the storm's anger, so if I slipped...

Looking up, I couldn't think about that.

I continued on as the priests lined the same spot they had days ago. I knew they were humming or chanting, but the wind kept me from hearing it. Talia stepped in front of High Priest Erwyn. She looked like a ghost in her white sacrificial dress, her hands clasped at her chest in prayer. Such a compliant acolyte.

She'd always had something I hadn't. The way I had wanted to be like her over the years. Now I saw there was an undercurrent of something between us. Had she resented me for being selected as the Chosen One?

I would have gladly traded places.

It didn't matter now. I would not allow another sacrifice.

"Stop!" I screamed as I reached the landing and faced them.

Surprise flickered on the priests' faces.

"Maris," Erwyn scolded. "You are not invited. Leave. Before you mess up another Rite!"

"No!" I moved closer. My body shook with nerves at the memory of being in this place. Of falling. "Can't you see? You're not supposed to do this!"

"It has to be done," he stated. "We must honor the Rite."

"No—"

"Maris! Shut up!" Talia cried, fury written all over her face. "You had your chance!"

"Talia, this isn't the way! It's not—"

"Just because you weren't good enough doesn't mean I'm not. It should have always been me! Don't ruin this for me!"

My chest cracked at her words. Not good enough rang in my ears. I'd never claimed to be good enough. I had never wanted to be the Chosen One of the Rite.

"Talia, I'm trying to help—"

"Go away!" she screamed. Her hands clenched into fists at her sides, and her cheeks reddened.

"Yes, take heed, Maris," Erwyn said. "Talia is the worthy one."

She shot a smug smile in my direction.

"Can't you see this isn't what Thalen wants? Look!" I gestured around me.

"How would you know what he wants?" Erwyn spat. "He rejected you. You are cursed."

"He is not happy with you all. It's not me. I know the truth! There was never supposed to be a sacrifice!"

"You think I would take your word over hundreds of years of the Order's teachings?" He barked a laugh.

"It's true! It has to stop!"

Erwyn rolled his eyes and turned, motioning for Talia to do the same. She faced the sea once again and closed her eyes with a serene expression, her mouth moving in silent incantations.

"Wait!"

A priest grabbed my arms, pinning them behind my back as Erwyn continued with his chant and the priests hummed.

"Let me go!" I fought to wrench my arms free. "Thalen doesn't want a sacrifice! Stop!" The storm picked up, with dread filling my stomach. This was a terrible place to be if the rain started. The clouds swirled in a circular pattern overhead.

"Don't do it! Talia—no!" I screamed as Talia stepped off the ledge. Her white dress billowed in the wind, causing her to look otherworldly. Her hair fanned out around her as she lifted her arms, dropping into the waves and disappearing into the black abyss.

I tore my eyes away and glared at Erwyn. "How could you?"

He pursed his lips. "It had to be done."

A scream pierced the storm. Talia was ejected from the water amidst the spray, limbs flailing in every direction. Her eyes connected with mine as terror laced her features, and her arms reached out for me.

But I was too far away.

She let out a bloodcurdling scream as she fell and crashed onto the jagged rocks on the cliffside below. Her white dress turned crimson as she stared with unseeing eyes.

I choked back a sob and drew in a ragged breath, my hand shaking as it covered my mouth. My mind whirled at what had just happened, and I tore my eyes away from the sight of my friend. Why hadn't she listened to me? My stomach rolled, and I thought I might be sick.

Erwyn looked in shock as he turned towards us, swallowing hard.

"This is your fault," I hissed.

His head dropped before he glanced at the other priests. They stood in stunned silence as they looked to him for guidance.

"We...we're going to have to find a new Chosen..."

"No! I warned you. I—"

He stepped closer to me. "You cannot breathe a word of this. Do you understand?" He shuddered at the clap of thunder as the storm intensified.

I pulled one arm free and pressed my hand against the amulet, finding comfort in the gesture. "Can't you see how angry Thalen is? He doesn't want this."

"He is asleep," Erwyn spat. "Don't tell me about my god."

The ocean roared as the water rose into the air. The wind whipped and howled faster as the dark clouds rotated around the rising water. A gold trident pierced the center of the clouds, and lightning streaked across the sky, the electricity crackling. The water receded, revealing the form of a body. Black hair, glowing blue eyes, muscular torso draped in a black sleeveless tunic cut in a V in the front, and gold bands on each bicep.

I gasped, covering my mouth with my hand. It was the same man as before in the library.

Thalen?

He pointed his trident towards the shore, and the storm unleashed, wreaking havoc on the land. I watched in awe as stone crumbled, the shore flooded, and screams filled the night. My hair blew into my face as I turned to watch the ocean god. His wrath was evident as he commanded the destruction of what lay before him. He was going to leave the kingdom in ruins.

"No," I whispered. "Stop." I took a breath then yelled, "Thalen, STOP!"

Those glowing eyes lurched toward me as he took me in.

It was unnerving to have the ocean god's attention suddenly focused solely on me. A ripple of nerves ricocheted down my spine, and I touched the amulet for strength. "Take me! Don't destroy the kingdom."

There was a pause in the storm as it revolved around the god. He moved across the water until he was standing on a pillar of water before me. His brows dipped in rage as he looked at the priests, who stared in disbelief before falling to their knees.

"Unhand her," he commanded, his voice booming with authority.

The priest dropped my arm and took a step back.

"Repeat yourself."

"I..." My voice trailed off as I took him in. The man from the library was here, just diminished. His god version was on display for all to see. I knew I should quiver in fear at his power and strength, but I was drawn to it. There was a small part inside that felt emboldened by him. Those full lips I still fantasized about, like I could almost remember what they tasted like. Despite never having them against my own. There was an inexplicable pull to him, like I was caught in an undertow.

The amulet hummed against my skin, and my fingers wrapped around it. A soft glow shone from the jade. The wind whipped around me, fluttering my hair and dress. I realized the god was still waiting for my response.

"Take me instead," I said. "Don't destroy everything."

The hollows of his cheeks sharpened as he clenched his jaw. "It's deserved."

"Maybe so. But take me and continue the Accord."

One eyebrow flinched. "You found it?"

"I did."

"Tell me."

"There was never meant to be a sacrifice. That was put into place by a priest named Firth. You just wanted a celebration for your favor." I bit my lower lip. "But...why did you let it continue?"

"It was something humans came up with. I had lost...I figured they'd stop one day when nothing changed for them. I was mistaken to have put any trust in humanity. All they did was twist words and beliefs for their own selfish gain."

"You didn't want the sacrifices?"

"No." Thalen folded his arms across his chest.

"Why did you send me back?"

"Because you didn't want it," he stated. "Your mind screamed it. I didn't want it in the first place. I couldn't take you. So I gave you back." His eyes rested on the amulet. "The sea gifted you something of mine."

"Oh..." The amulet warmed against my skin. "I didn't take it."

"I know. I've been waiting..." he hesitated. "They deserve my wrath and vengeance." With a wave of his trident, the storm raged in full force once again, the rain pelting the earth, but not me.

Not me.

I mentally ran through the index of topics in that book. I had focused on the Rite and pact, but there had been mention of a myth about the ocean god. There had been an ocean goddess once who was taken.

Think, Maris, I scolded.

The goddess was taken and set to return...but why?

"Thalen," I pleaded. "Take me. Accept me. Let me be the last."

He looked at me. "You will not return a second time."

I nodded.

"You will give yourself for *them*?" he said the last word in disgust.

"No," I said. "I am giving myself to you. I am the Chosen One. I want to be *your* Chosen One, not theirs."

Heat flared in his blue eyes. "You must give yourself willingly."

I lifted my chin as I stared at him. This was the right choice. I felt it deep in my bones. I couldn't explain why, but I was meant to be with him. The sea called to me, and I was going to answer. This was my path. My fate.

I extended my hand out towards him. The amulet hummed. The teal wind reached out, caressing my cheeks and hair before swirling down my body. It circled the amulet before extending out towards Thalen. To his chest.

To his *amulet*.

How had I not noticed?

Thalen moved closer to me. The wrath etched on his face fell to hope as he reached out his hand. "Are you sure?"

"Yes," I stated, full of conviction.

"You choose me?"

"Yes." The wind whipped around me as if in excitement.

The ethereal glow in his eyes faded to reveal the familiar ocean blue. "Come to me," he breathed.

I took the remaining steps to the edge of the cliff. There was nothing but crashing waves below. But I was not afraid. Not like last time.

I returned my focus to Thalen and his outstretched hand. The teal air still connected our amulets in an arch.

"Come to me, Maris."

With a smile, I stepped off the cliff.

But I didn't fall.

My feet landed on misted water. I took another step, then another, never taking my eyes off of him. My hand slid into his, and he grasped it, yanking me to him. My body pressed against his hard one, and his other hand held the back of my head in place against his chest.

The moment we connected, all the memories rushed back to me. The stolen moments from before. A kiss in the shadows. Laughter in each other's arms. My being taken from him. Cursed to return at an unknown time. The caveat that I had to choose him to be reunited despite the odds against us. If not, we would be forced to be separated for eternity. Tears pricked my eyes.

"I've waited so long," he murmured.

I breathed in his scent of salt and driftwood. Oh, how I had missed this!

"How did you know?"

"I'd always know the other piece of my soul," he said, his lips pressing to the top of my head.

I leaned back to look at him. He was as beautiful as I remembered.

Thalen moved his hand, and a wave wiped the cliff's ledge, washing all the priests onto the jagged rocks below. Their cries were sweet music. The waves and clouds retreated, revealing a full moon in a sky of stars. The ocean no longer whispered of my doom, but of something I had been waiting lifetimes to remember.

"Take me home," I whispered.

"As you wish," Thalen said with a smile.

With a swirl of his trident, the sea mist enveloped us, and we plunged into the ocean, down deep where we belonged.

Together.

Chapter 1

I fucking hate mermaids.

They're clingy and desperate for attention. Usually, I stay well clear of them when I need a bed companion, but the women in Wallsmith are no cleaner than deck rags, so I had to make do with the options in front of me.

This one had been following my ship for weeks, singing to me from the sea. My brain can resist the call of a siren, but my body knows what it needs.

My mistake was inviting her onboard.

Her long red hair cascaded down her back as she rode me, her tanned, newly formed legs bent at either side of my thighs. I gripped her hips and pushed her up and down, needing to feel the entirety of her body connecting to mine. Her tits bounced gloriously, and I held them in my palms. A perfect fit.

She was beautiful but not worth the hassle afterward as she lay at my side, stroking her long fingers up and down my arm.

"Time to go," I said, pushing her off and rising from the bed. I pulled my trousers on, then laced up my boots.

"Black," she whined, not moving. "Come back to bed."

"We're leaving port. You need to go."

"Let me stay."

I walked around the bed and left the door open as I pissed into the latrine, hoping the unseemly sound would disgust her. When I plodded back in, she was still in the same position, white sheet just below her exposed breasts.

"Out."

I couldn't leave this room until she left or else I'd never have heard the end of it. Godwin had been egging me for months about this fucking mermaid and he'd never let me live it down if he saw her traipsing out of my quarters.

A knock on the door saved the mermaid from getting ripped from the sheets by her hair.

"Captain, we're ready to go," a deckhand grunted into the wood, then his heavy boots stomped into the chip depths. The crew knew not to come into my quarters. Ever.

I turned to force the mermaid out, but when I looked back, she was gone, the circular porthole flapping after her sudden descent.

Good.

Throwing on the rest of my garments, I trudged out onto the deck to check the status of our departure from port.

"Everyone's on, Captain. We're ready to go," my First Mate, Goodwin, told me. I grabbed the spyglass and looked out to sea. The sky was dim with sunrise brewing on the horizon. We were ready to set sail.

The sea looked willing to greet us, and I grunted approval to Goodwin, who then yelled down to the crew to start preparations.

As I gazed onto the deck, at the many men moving the ropes and pulling the anchors up, one person caught my eye. A young boy, too clean to be on my crew. He was pulling the mast rope and looking back and forth as he went. His suspiciousness was like a beacon to his misdeeds. A stow-away.

He must've snuck on. And I was going to find out why.

But not until we're far enough away from port that when I threw him over the edge, he wouldn't be able to swim to safety. No one steals onto my ship and lives to tell the tale.

Turning the ship's wheel at the helm, I put us on course for Isle Loyish and the abandoned ship I heard was there. A ship full of gold.

I heard a tale of it in our last stop at port, and I was immediately itching to get my hands on the loot before anyone else. The minute we finished our rum, we set sail.

Maybe this boy heard us making plans for Loyish and that was why he jumped on my ship. He'll soon jump off when I get through with him.

With enough open sea between us and the nearest land mass, I instructed Goodwin to escort the new crew member into my quarters. He was waiting there, pacing the floor, when I entered the room.

He looked at me as the door closed. The striking blue eyes immediately told me I'd made a mistake.

That was no boy.

"Captain, I—" she grunted, a poor attempt at masking her voice. Before she could say another word, I sauntered over and pulled her hat off, revealing a tumbling mass of brunette hair. She gasped, stepping out my reach but the damage was already done.

With the hat out of her face and her hair down in waves, I saw the full effect of her beauty. And she was breathtaking.

Piercing blue eyes, the color of the sea. The color of my soul. Full lips set in a pout that made me want to bite. I shouldn't have been reacting that way. I'd just fucked that mermaid, that drive was out of my system for now.

But this...

This was different.

"What are you doing on my ship?" My voice was husky, like a predator stalking prey.

She looked back and forth between my eyes for a few silent moments, looking as if she was unsure if she should tell me the truth or a lie. I'm able to know the difference either way but I was interested to see what she pulled out. I cocked my head to the side, waiting.

"I'm here for someone," she said, quiet but firm.

I hoped whoever the fuck she was here for was prepared to die by my sword.

"Who?"

She didn't speak. Instead, she looked out the small porthole to the open sea. I stepped in front, blocking her path and setting us impossibly close. She didn't step away, only looked up to meet my eyes. Once again, I was haunted by the blueness of hers. I could get lost in them and I almost couldn't control my need to do so.

"Who are you here for?" I asked again, my voice softening.

She sighed. "My father."

I drew back. "There are more than fifty men on this boat. Any idea which one he is?"

She looked up at me like I'd underestimated her, like I was the idiot. I loved the way she wanted to defy me.

"Goodwin," she said.

He'd never mentioned a daughter. Let alone one that was a grown woman.

"Does he know that?" I smirked, and she rolled her eyes. The need to punish her grew as my body reacted to her closeness.

"He knows I exist. But he hasn't seen me in over ten years."

Her pulse was racing. I could practically hear her blood pumping through her veins. She was affected by me as well. And this wasn't fear. This was something else entirely.

I no longer wanted to talk to this woman about her father.

"What is your name?"

She had the right instinct to look nervous now as she mutters, "Calena."

Her eyes jumped to my lips as I moistened them.

"Calena," I repeated, the word tasting like heaven on my tongue.

"Calena," I said again, taking a step closer.

She took a step back, but I didn't let her get far, pulling her in with an arm around her waist. She gasped again but didn't pull out of my embrace. Delicate hands rested against my chest as if ready to push me away at a moment's notice.

"What am I going to do with you, Calena?" My nose found her neck, and I took a big whiff of her scent.

Fuck, she smelled good enough to eat.

I licked her in the same spot, just to confirm my suspicions. Her breath caught again, but she didn't push me away. Instead, she leaned closer.

"Black," she breathed out. My name on her lips was my undoing.

My lips crashed onto hers, and she opened for me immediately. The palms that were resting against me gripped tighter as she kept hold on me. I devoured her, shoving my tongue in as if it were the abandoned ship I was on the way to pillage. This was my gold rush.

I lifted her up, and her legs tightened around my hips. One hand under her butt, the other gripping the back of her head so she couldn't break away from me even if she tried. But I had a feeling she wasn't going to. She wanted this just as much as I did, and she showed me by grinding against me, the friction almost too much to bear.

"Isaiah," she moaned as I moved down her throat toward her collarbone.

I froze.

No one has called me that since my mother died twenty years ago.

I should punish her for the use of my name but hearing it pass her lips made me grow even harder than I already was. Fuck, I didn't know what to do with this girl, but whatever I decided after, I was not letting her go now. Ever.

She's mine.

Throwing her down onto the bed, she used the freedom to scoot all the back to the headboard, her leg thrust out to keep me back.

"Wait," she said breathlessly, and I do, because I'm not a fucking heathen. But it took everything I had in me to be patient with my little stowaway.

I stood at the edge of the bed and cocked my head at her.

"Wait?"

She nodded frantically, catching her breath. Her pupils were dilated to the size of saucers. I knew she wanted this as much as I did. Why was she denying us this pleasure?

I kneeled on the bed, moving inch by inch closer to her. I didn't touch her, but I came as close as I could. The leg she had put out to push me away held steady, her foot hitting my chest as I crawled closer.

"Calena." Her name was a warning. Before she could pull it away, I gripped her foot, moving it up my body until her ankle was against my lips, and I kissed it lightly. She jolted her leg out of my grip, but

I didn't waver. Instead, I placed another kiss on the other side of her ankle. Then I drifted up her leg. Slowly. Placing kisses on her calf. The side of her knee. Her outer thigh. Her inner thigh.

Calena sighed, her body becoming putty in my hands. I inched closer still, my knees settling inside of her legs, opening her as wide as she can go.

"Black, this isn't—we shouldn't—," Calena sputtered, but I ran my finger up and down her core and she almost cried out in ecstasy. She was so wet and ready. It's intoxicating.

Oh, she will be the end of me.

I didn't give her another chance to protest as I dove in, my tongue lapping up the wetness she was so ready to take from me. The wetness that was mine to claim. Everything about her was mine. I took as many licks of her as I liked, tasting her sweetness. Savoring the ultimate flavor of her.

Calena writhed beneath me, and I firmly gripped her hips to hold her down, not nearly done with my meal. My tongue flicked, twisted, and turned, and I knew she was about to give into the pleasure I was giving her, whether she wanted to or not.

"Black," she cried, gripping my hair in her tight fists. I savored the burn of it against my scalp. It had been a very long time since I've done this to a woman and I vowed I never would to anyone else again. I was ruined.

"Fuck!" She screamed as I gently nibbled on her core and used my tongue to soften the sting. One of her hands held tight to my head while the other gripped the sheets as I knew she was about to explode. Her pants ceased. Not a single word or sound was uttered for a few seconds, but I didn't stop and as her fingers tightened on my scalp, I knew she's right there. One last kiss.

Calena wailed, releasing herself fully, without a care as to who can hear her. I typically wouldn't care either but I didn't need this going around to the crew that there's a woman on board, so I released my grip on her hip and covered her mouth with my big hand as I lapped up her sweetness.

I was about to move up her body to continue, but she bit my hand and I reared back.

"Silencing me?" She questioned and at first I thought she meant to push me away, but I saw the flirty glint in her eyes. She was challenging me. She was showing me she was not one to be messed with.

Well, neither am I, my little stowaway.

"You don't want to hear my cries? Cries that you've pulled from me?"

Fuck. She was good. Pulling the waistcoat down from my shoulders, I loosened my trousers and released myself from my pants. Calena's eyes widened slightly at the sight of me, but she didn't give anything else away.

"I want to hear every sound you make. I just don't want the rest of my crew to have the same pleasure." I pulled her down by her knees until our cores were flush together, and Calena squealed at the sudden movement. I wanted to bottle that sound. Take it to bed every night.

When I entered her, it was a peace I've never felt in my entire life. Like I was meant to be here, in this woman. For eternity. I knew she felt it too but she looked at me like I had just given her meaning. I knew she had given it to me too.

"Fuck me," she said, and I didn't know if was a command or an exclamation but I took it as both as I plowed into her, harder and faster with each thrust.

I fit into my little stowaway like a glove and now there was nowhere in this world that she could run that I would not hunt her down. She was my sanctuary, my blessing. My goddess. And I worshipped her as such.

Ripping open the front of her shirt, the buttons flew across the room as her perfect breasts were exposed. I gave attention to both, licking one while playing with the other. Calena moaned under my touch and pushed her chest closer to my mouth in encouragement.

"You are mine," I said gruffly as I moved from one breast to the other. Calena nodded her head over and over, but I wasn't sure she actually heard me. Gripping her neck, I pulled her eyes to mine. "Mine."

Calena muttered, "Yours", and I kissed her in a way that had her lips sore for days. I continued to pound into her over and over until she was a puddle beneath me. Calena gripped my arms and gave out that same cry she did before when my mouth was between her legs, and I kissed her to silence her again. She let me, but I felt the smile on her lips.

With two more hard pumps, I released into her, then collapsed at her side, not wanting to crush her under my weight.

Not only did I just fuck my first mate's daughter, but I claimed her as my own. And now, there's no way I could let her leave this ship.

Chapter 2

"You're sick." Calena looked at me with disgust, the sheet covering her chest in a way that made mine ache. Not only because it was covering her beauty, but it was the same sheet that I fucked that goddamn mermaid on, and she held it the same way just hours ago. Calena deserved more than a secondhand sex rag.

She looked at me like she hated me and she probably did, especially considering I just told her she was stuck in this room for the time being.

"I'm not some prisoner you can chain to your bed and fuck whenever you want."

"Of course, you're not."

"Then let me go." She rose from the bed onto her knees, and the sheet fell, revealing her perfect body to me. I held back a groan and pulled on my pants to hide my growing hardness.

"You're not going anywhere. I need to figure out what to do with you. In the meantime, you are to stay here and not cause any trouble on my ship."

"I came here to find my father. You will not keep me from accomplishing that task."

"And what do you think is going to happen after that? Hm? Happy reunion with daddy aboard my ship?"

That silenced her. She came on my ship with a reckless idea and absolutely no plans afterward. *Stupid beautiful girl.*

I moved to run my palm down her hair, but she dodged my embrace. With a sigh, I threw on my shirt and waistcoat. "I don't want to chain you in here, Calena. But I will if I must."

She sat back on the bed. Her look of defiance was the last thing I saw before I left the room, locking the door behind me.

Entering the deck, I immediately spotted my first mate.

"We need to talk."

He nodded and went to enter my quarters.

"Not in there." I inclined my head toward the helm. Goodwin gave me a questioning look before walking back up the stairs toward the ship's wheel.

"Tell me about your past."

"My past?"

He looked at me like I'd lost my mind and maybe I had, but I felt the need to protect this girl above even my own crew.

"You were married?"

"Aye," Goodwin narrowed his eyes. "I was."

"What happened to her?"

"Who knows. She turned out to be a good for nothing whore."

"Did you have any children?"

Goodwin's head twisted in my direction. "Why are you asking me this?"

Good question. I didn't want to give anything away about my little stowaway, but I needed to know if he knew she existed.

"Just need to know if there's any loose ends out there for this gold retrieval. Don't want anyone waiting around trying to get something from you."

He looked at me through a furrowed brow. "My whore wife died years ago. There were rumors of a daughter, but I don't know her."

And there it was. The answer. Calena was telling the truth. Goodwin was her father, and she's come to what? Reconnect with him? Get something from him? Goodwin has nothing to offer as far as I'm aware.

Unless she heard about the gold and she's coming for her fair share.

Fuck. Of course, she was. She heard we were going in search of the abandoned ship and knew she could get what was owed to her from her father.

Grunting, I turned on my heels and headed back toward my quarters. Goodwin called after me, but I ignored him. Unlocking my door, I rushed inside before he could follow and locked it behind me.

"What do you want with Goodwin?"

Surprisingly, Calena was still laid in the bed, naked, the sheets pooling round her beautiful form. "What do you mean?"

"I mean," I said, moving closer. I didn't dare join her on the bed, for risk of her taking advantage of my need for her in such close quarters. "What business do you have with him?"

She looked at me, and I could tell she was once again contemplating telling me the truth or a lie. I wasn't sure which she decided when she finally said, "I've come to tell him something."

"And what is that?"

"That's between him and me. And if you let me go, I'll be able to go about my business and get out of your hair." She grabbed her shirt from the floor and threw it on her shoulders before I could protest.

"Let's get one thing straight." I reached out and gripped her neck after the shirt settled down over her chest. It was big enough to be a dress and I wondered briefly where she even got it from. "You aren't going anywhere."

Her ocean eyes searched mine, and I knew she wanted to defy me yet again. Instead, however, she did something else. She nodded.

"I'm not going anywhere. But let me talk to my father. Please."

Her plea was the only reason I released her throat. Calena sat back on her heels and looked at me like I'd just given her the best gift of all. I hadn't even agreed, but she started to kneel her way toward me at the edge of the bed and I found the oxygen leaving my brain and heading south quickly.

"Please, Black." She inched closer, her face inches away from the part of my body that was aching for her touch.

"Say my name."

Her mouth opened in a small gasp but then she smiled. "Isaiah."

I gripped her neck again, pulling her face up to meet mine. Our lips crashed together and I lost myself in her touch the same way I did just hours before. Calena was my goddess, and I would worship at her altar every single night for the rest of my life. She knew the power she had over me, and she didn't exploit it. Instead, she guided me along her body, showing me the parts of her that wanted the most attention, and I happily obliged. I kissed her lips, and she kissed mine, and I realized what desire truly was.

Calena pulled back before I was ready to release her, but she didn't give into my moans of protest. "Let me talk to my father."

I needed to think logically about this. Goodwin was the only man on this ship that had the directional sense to get us where we were going. It was also one of the reasons I'd kept him around so long. I couldn't have him distracted by this...situation.

At the same time, I didn't know how long I could keep Calena locked up. She was fiery as hell—something I admired about her—and I knew I wouldn't be able to keep her at bay for long. If I could just keep her away long enough for Goodwin to get us to this isle, it would be much better for everyone.

But Calena wasn't going to be happy about this.

She looked up at me with eyes that said she'd give me anything I wanted if I gave her what she came here for. And fuck, it was hard to do this but...

"No."

She reared back like I'd struck her.

"No?"

"Not yet," I said to appease her. "I need to get us to our location first and then I'll let you speak with him."

"You don't get to decide—"

I gripped her neck, pulling her face to reach mine. "That's a dangerous sentence to finish, love."

Calena shut her mouth, but her lips formed a delicious pout. I couldn't help but attempt to draw a kiss from her. She didn't relent, but that was okay, I still savored the taste of her.

Releasing her throat, Calena fell backward onto the bed.

"You're not locking me in here again."

"It's that or I actually do chain you to the bed. Your choice."

If looks could kill, I'd be dead a hundred times over by now. She sat on the bed and crossed her arms but didn't fight me further. I knew her freedom was important to her, so if she couldn't venture out of the room, I knew she'd rather be able to roam free inside of it.

"I'll be back," I said as I left, not giving her another chance to try and change my mind.

Goodwin was standing on the other side of the door when I opened it, and I pushed him backward and shut it quickly before he could peek inside.

"Are we there yet?" I asked, walking past him to the galley.

"Almost," he replied, trailing behind me. "The winds are blowing east, so we were taken slightly off course. We're back on track though."

"Where did you learn this directional sense, Goodwin? You're able to guide us in ways even my compass can't."

Goodwin shrugged. "Just something my father taught me, I guess. And his father before him."

I grunted. I didn't feel like taking any kind of lesson from Goodwin, so I guess I had to keep him around to point me in the right direction. Even though he was absolutely useless at everything else in this world, not worst of which is being a father.

Looking out into the sea, I spotted that flash of light that occured just as the sun slides down past the horizon, signaling nighttime. Goodwin had said it wouldn't be more than two days' travel to Isle Loyish so by nightfall tomorrow, we would be at our destination.

Enough time for me to reign my little stowaway in.

The crew ate their meals below deck, and a few men brought me my usual dinner. They didn't look twice when I requested another serving, knowing better than to question their captain.

I brought the plate to my quarters to give to Calena. I expected her to be pouting on the bed still or even asleep given the lateness of the hour but instead, I found her snooping through the maps on my desk. She whipped around when she heard me enter, but she was not quick enough to hide what she was doing.

"Looking for something?" I asked, placing the plate on a free corner of the desk. She stepped away from the desk sheepishly.

Calena looked at the food, then at me, clearly nervous about something. Then it dawned on me. "You think I'd poison you?"

"I don't know what you'd do," she whispered. I pinched her chin between my fingers and drew her gaze to mine.

"Hurting you is the last thing on this earth that I'd ever want to do. You belong to me now. And I take care of what belongs to me." I moved her gaze to the plate. "Eat."

I released her and stepped back, watching as she sat down at the desk and descended on the plate as if she hadn't seen food in weeks. And who knows if she had. I didn't know anything about her before she came on this ship.

"Where did you grow up?"

"Centip Valley," she said automatically, in between massive bites of the chicken leg.

"And what did you do there? Before you came on this journey to find your father."

Calena swallowed and then took a large gulp of the wine I brought with her plate.

"I worked on my uncle's farm. Tending sheep and pigs."

"Did you like it?"

Calena scoffed. "What do you think?"

I couldn't help but laugh. I would hate doing a job like that. My life had always been about the sea. If I'm landlocked for too long, I go absolutely crazy. When I looked up at Calena, she was looking out the window at the crashing waves. If I didn't know any better I'd think she felt the same way.

I allowed her to eat the rest of her food in silence, not requesting any more information from her, even though I was dying to know everything there is to know about her. One day I would learn every nook and cranny of my little stowaway but for now, I let her relax.

She looked absolutely exhausted, and I knew now that she had a full stomach, she would sleep soundly soon.

However...

There was one thing I needed to know first.

"Calena?"

"Hm?" She responded absentmindedly, picking at the last few crumbs on the plate.

"How did you know my first name?"

Calena put her fork down. With a gentle voice, she explained. "My mother used to tell tales of a great pirate. Isaiah Black. Strongest, bravest, fiercest man who's ever sailed the seven seas. When I saw you on the helm after I snuck on the ship, I knew immediately that man must've been you."

Blinking for a few moments, I take in her words. I knew my name was out there—my legacy left behind at each port of call—but I never imagined this woman would end up being the one I would let use it.

Calena looked back down at her plate, a blush forming on her cheeks.

"Come," I said, and she glanced toward me. Pulling off my pants and shirt, leaving only my undergarments, her eyes widened in shock, then lust, then...apprehension. "Calena," I gestured for her to come to me again and she did, hesitantly. When she's standing directly in front of me, I chastely kissed her lips.

"Time to rest," I said, pulling back the covers on the bed and climbing in, gesturing for her to join me. She was hesitant at first, but it didn't take long for her base instincts to kick in and she climbed in after me, resting her cheek on my bare chest.

"Rest well, my Calena."

She hummed a reply, but I didn't hear it before her breathing turned into quiet snores. Calena had fallen asleep atop me in a matter of seconds, and I knew, just based on that, that this would be the soundest sleep I've ever had.

Chapter 3

The space next to me was cold when I awoke, and I immediately bolted from the bed. Calena was nowhere in sight, and the door to my quarters was wide open.

Fuck.

Throwing my clothes on, I grabbed for my pistol before realizing it wasn't where I left it last night.

Double fuck.

"I said shut up!" Calena yelled from the deck. Once I stepped out, I gaped at the scene before me. Calena was standing in the center of a circle of men, barely dressed in more than she slept in, but the most troublesome part was that she had my gun trained on my first mate, and he stood before her with his hands up. If I had known this was what she wanted out of a reunion with her father, I would have gone ahead with that threat to chain her to the bed.

"Cal—"

She doesn't look my way.

"Don't come closer, Black."

I took a step forward. "Don't make commands on my ship." I moved another step, but she cocked the gun. I halt all movement.

Calena still didn't look my way, keeping her attention entirely focused on her father. "Goodwin," she said, her voice full of venom.

Goodwin looked over her shoulder to me in desperation and asked, "Captain, who is this?"

Many of the crew had stopped their jobs to pay attention to the spectacle. I wanted to holler at them to resume their work on my ship, but I couldn't take my eyes off Calena.

"I don't look familiar to you? Because I'm the spitting image of her, so they say."

Goodwin's eyebrows narrowed in confusion before widening in shock. He knew exactly who this was. Then he looked at me again.

"Don't look at him. He can't help you now."

Without another word, Calena shot Goodwin in the left shoulder.

Every crew member drew back in shock, myself included. Was she aiming to kill and just had very bad aim or was she toying with him?

"Does it hurt, Dad? Does the bullet feel like the same pain you made my mother endure?" She shot him again, this time in the right shoulder, and I knew her aim was true. She hit him exactly where she wanted.

"All she ever did was love you and what did she get for it? A battered face and a couple of broken ribs. A daughter she died for while trying to keep her alive. A good-for-nothing husband who treated us both like dirt beneath his feet." She walked forward, making every step intentional. "Do you have anything to say for yourself?" She asked him, but he was too preoccupied by the pain in his shoulders to even register that she was inches away from his face. He cried out when she pressed her thumb into the wound in his left shoulder.

"You are a coward. And the world will be better without you."

Calena raised the gun and placed it directly between his eyes. She took in a deep breath, cocked the gun a third time. Goodwin sobbed in front of her.

Typically, I wouldn't give a damn about one of my men dying, especially if they deserve it but he was the only man that can guide us to Isle Loyish.

I needed him alive.

"Calena, wait."

"No." She didn't look at me. She defied me by pushing the gun closer into his forehead.

"I will let you have your revenge as soon as this man gets me to the place I need to go."

"As it were," Calena whispered, "he's not the only one with directional sense." Then she pulled the trigger. "I learned it from my father."

Goodwin's lifeless body hit the deck like a sack of potatoes. Calena's knees buckled, and I stepped forward to catch her before she ended up on the floor next to him.

"Haus, Franc, take care of this body." I gestured toward Goodwin, and the two men hopped to the task immediately. Calena reached out and grabbed the compass that was hung around his neck, pulling it off swiftly, and they grabbed him by the arms and feet and hauled him overboard as if he was nothing more than debris.

"Clean the deck," I commanded.

"Aye, captain."

The rest of the crew set to work, leaving us alone.

Grabbing Calena's shoulders, I pulled her slightly haunted gaze to mine. "Do you really have the same sense that he does?"

"Yes," she said, breathing heavily. "I only worked on the farm in the beginning of my life. After my mom died, I spent the rest of my time traveling on ship after ship to locate him. Learned a lot about directions doing that. Also learned I love the sea maybe as much as you do."

She smiled at me, and her sudden happiness was breathtaking. She did what she came here to do, and I found my happiness in her as well. I placed a brief kiss on her forehead before standing her back up. She looked down at the compass, opening it to help her guide us to our destination.

Shrugging out of my jacket, I placed it over Calena's shoulders as we made our way to the helm. Calena confidently gave me my heading, and we set sail. Just a few more hours until we arrived at Isle Loyish to find the abandoned ship of gold.

As the ship coasted along, I knew it was time to take care of my little stowaway. She did defy me in front of my whole crew. That cannot go unpunished.

I turned to look at her, my voice hard. "My quarters, now."

She nodded, not even pretending to be shocked by my sudden shift in mood. She was smart enough to know what was coming.

When we entered the room, Calena walked right to the bed.

"I'm not sorry," she said immediately. "I would do it again." She stopped her movements and slouched down onto the bed. I took a few steps until I was standing over her.

She looked up at me. "Say something."

"What would you like me to say?"

She opened her mouth and then closed it. When she opened it again, I hooked my thumb inside and she closed it, sucking my thumb deeper into her mouth. My eyes threatened to roll back into my scalp from the feel of her tongue circling my thumb. The way I wished it was another part of me.

"You defied me in front of my crew."

Her lips peeked open, and I removed my thumb but kept the hand around her neck, gripping ever so slightly.

"That's what you're upset about? Not the fact that I killed your first mate?" She looked up at me with the look of deviance that I've come to adore.

"I will not be defied in front of my crew. And you will be punished for it."

Gripping her neck, I pulled her up so she was standing. Her frightened eyes pierced mine, and I relished in her fear. Before she realized what I had in store, I moved, pulling her stolen pants down to her ankles. She gasped as I sat on the bed and laid her across my lap.

She drew in a sharp breath when my palm stung her delicate skin.

"This is my punishment?" She asked. I smacked her again—hard—and she moaned beneath my touch.

"Yes," I said, before smacking her again. Then again. "When you misbehave, you're punished." I smacked her one last time before I pulled her up by her long, luscious hair. She twisted around and sat on my lap, hissing at the contact of her freshly punished ass onto my legs.

I kissed her fiercely, gripping the back of her neck to keep her against me.

"But also, yes. You did kill my first mate. And now I need a new one," I said as I pulled back so she could see the depths of my feelings on the topic. I didn't give a shit about losing Goodwin. He wasn't a great first mate and clearly an even shittier person. But I needed a first mate.

"What are you going to do about that?" she asked in her deviant way. Like she enjoyed being punished and wanted more. I'll give her more. I moved to twist her back to my lap but a knock on the door drew my attention away and I immediately grabbed my gun to kill whoever interrupted us.

"Captain," the tentative voice called. "We've made it to Isle Loyish."

Those are probably the only words that could've got me to stop what I was doing. Calena looked at me, and my grip on her waist tightened briefly.

"Our ship of gold." I kissed her, and we left together, walking onto the deck as not only captain and first mate but lovers with no intention of ever letting the other go.

Chapter 1

My mother had requested the skeleton hang in the central glass case display. Blue light shimmered along its cream-colored bones, its skull and torso that of a human, save for its sharp teeth and long claws, while the lower-half portrayed the anatomy of a fish tail. After hours of searching through her sketches, I finally picked the one that she'd marked as the most accurate to what she'd witnessed.

It was far more haunting suspended in a glass case, than drawn on paper.

"We can't move forward with the exhibit, Ms. Windsor," Ms. Day, the museum attendant, said.

"Why's that?" I asked, circling the skeletal creature, checking for any mistakes I might've missed. "Are there issues with the materials?"

"No, that's not the problem."

"The plaques have misspellings?"

"The plaques are perfectly well, Ms. Windsor."

I tapped the glass case. "Then what's the issue?"

"There have been complaints, Ms. Windsor."

I raised a brow. "Complaints? By God Himself, what could the people possibly be complaining about? Too much museum and not enough time? It's a good problem to have, you know."

"No, they're saying"—she took a deep breath—"that none of this is real."

Curling my fingers along the glass, I scoffed. "Of course, it's real."

Ms. Day wrapped her hands behind her back. "The museum's credibility is being compromised and it's not just because of the mermaid's manufactured skeleton. It's everything in this exhibit—the prophetic warnings of soul deals with the sea, the concept that a soul can be restored—"

"Soul deals are not to be treaded on lightly," I replied.

Her lips thinned as she straightened her back. "*This* issue isn't to be tread on lightly."

Sweat built along my neck and slid down my high-collared dress. I stepped away from the glass. A large tome sat on an intricately wood-carved dais. I brushed my fingers over its open page, the drawing depicting a piece of rare algae my mother had discovered years ago.

Ms. Day continued, "If we could just move these pieces to the myth and legends department—"

"If it's the museum's credibility that's at stake, then putting historical evidence in a myths and legends department is counterintuitive. Have you ever thought of different exhibits that are getting complaints? The bird and foliage exhibit was rather dirty and smelly last I stepped in there."

"*Ms. Windsor.*"

I paused, rubbing the gold locket hanging around my neck in between my fingers. "I won't have my mother's work be reduced to fiction."

Ms. Day didn't waver as she said, "It's better than not being remembered at all."

As I opened the locket, my mother's bright smile contrasted with my close-mouthed scowl. She'd had a head full of wonder and a heart full of adventure, determined to share the magic she'd found with the world. Yet all I seemed to do with my life nowadays was hide behind books, attend high-teas I didn't care for, and argue with museum attendants.

An emptiness in my chest ached. I ignored it. Nothing mattered more than making sure my mother's exhibit got the proper attention it deserved, and if knowledge wasn't going to get her the credit she earned, then I'd have to go a different route.

"Ms. Day, did you know that the sea can harbor souls?"

"I beg your pardon?"

I smiled. "The sea can hold your very essence–the thing inside of you that craves purpose beyond everyday needs. For example, your current desire to please your boss to the point of causing my mother to roll in her grave."

Ms. Day scoffed. "You've misunderstood me completel–"

"However," I interrupted, "there's a way to regain one's soul from the sea. An algae in a cave just north of here. What if I retrieved some as evidence for the exhibit?"

Ms. Day's face paled. "And how would you prove its effectiveness?"

In all truth, I didn't know. My mother had died in the expedition to retrieve the algae, so she never knew how it worked; only that she'd found an ancient text pointing to its use. There was also no clear answer as to *how* the sea gained souls in the first place. Either way, I needed Ms. Day to believe I was more than just a walking encyclopedia with old money. I needed her to believe my mother's exhibit was worth the time and effort, so much so I would figure out the mysteries myself.

A horrifying thought, and yet, a part of me wanted to; a part of me that I'd been shoving aside ever since my mother had passed.

"Ms. Day, label the exhibit as 'under construction.' I'll be back in a month and everyone will know my mother's claim to the sea is as legitimate as the Wright brother's recent claim to the air."

"Ms. Windsor, I'm not sure this will go over well—"

"Or should I retract all my donations from this place?"

Pursing her lips, she cleared her throat. "I'll pass the message along."

"Very good," I replied, "I hope that when I return, the bird and foliage exhibit will be cleaned up a bit too, hm?"

It wasn't ladylike at all to be seen running through the streets of New York City in a freshly washed organdy cotton dress and newly-bought buttoned boots. Nor was it ladylike to shove my way into the local bait shop with sweat dripping down my powdered nose. But when my mother's last wish was in the throes of being dismantled due to some plebeian "complaints" about her work's legitimacy, sacrifices had to be made—far bigger sacrifices than just my clothes and makeup.

Lord have mercy.

This was the last place I should be, but it was the only place I could think of that could get me what I needed. At home, all I had were books and theories. Here, there were adventures and risk-taking; fishing wires looped on the walls and hooks peppered across the ceiling.

I took in a deep gulp of air and ignored the shakiness in my fingers.

"*William*," I shouted over the cacophony of fishermen crowding the cluttered counter.

The familiar mop of red hair peeked over the pack of men like a drop of blood in a sardine can. Heart beating fast in my chest, I laced my hands together and squeezed as tight as I could.

"I'm a little *preoccupied* right now," William shouted back, his voice carrying a touch of annoyance, "if you've got a boat that needs a wax, come back next week."

He hadn't recognized me.

I should go somewhere else.

No, I couldn't risk it. My mother's exhibit was on the line, and my offer wouldn't take more than a minute or two of his time. I'd pay him or whoever he suggested a sizable sum. Everything would be fine.

So why was I sweating so profusely through my clothes?

"It's urgent!" I replied.

"Aye, wait your turn, woman!" a stout man with a measly comb-over and dirtied jumper hissed.

I pulled out a ten-dollar gold coin. "Help me get to the front and this is yours."

The man's brows raised along with a curling grin. "Of course, madam. Right this way."

He snatched the coin from my gloved hand and shoved his way to the front. I followed, offering an array of quiet apologies while the stout man cursed like someone who'd returned from war. Once we made it to the counter, I caught a breath in my throat.

William's sweat glistened along his lightly freckled skin, his white sleeves rolled up to his elbows. The tip of his tongue peeked out of his mouth. He was scouring through a metal box filled with spoon-shaped lure hooks. His familiar, unfettered concentration reminded me of the times he would help my father fix his broken lure contraptions or tend to my mother's crabbing cages.

He was the only reason I'd bought my own fishing rod all those years ago—a broken one, of course. And no matter how many times he fixed it, it always seemed to "break." To my delight, William's visits had turned from monthly to weekly, stretching over an entire year until one day, he left his toolbox behind and brought a different box; one that fit in his palm and was meant for me.

Twisting my fingers together, I pushed the memories aside.

"I heard there were mermaid sightings a few days ago," one of the men next to me whispered to William. "Rumor has it I could make a fortune if I catch one."

William cackled. "Don't let those silly myths get to you now, or you'll forget to catch real fish for your shop."

William tossed a handful of the spoon lures to the man, who caught them mid-air. After the customer slid a few copper coins across the cream-colored linoleum, William finally looked up. He slammed the metal box so loud, everyone in the shop jumped.

"*Calliope?*"

My confidence waned. "Hello."

Mouth gaping, he gathered himself, pushing his hands on the countertop. "What are you doing here?"

"It's nice to see you too, William," I said with a smile.

"Nice to see me?" He pushed a hand through his red matted hair. "Did your father send you for something?"

Gulping, I rested my gloved hands on the counter. "I need a sailor to take me up the Hudson to Gorgona Cave."

His stare felt like it lasted an entire minute, questions seeming to flit through the green and brown specks in his eyes as his frown deepened.

I observed the spoon-shaped lures instead, uncertainty gnawing at my insides with each breath.

"Store's closed!" William yelled. "We'll be open again tomorrow!"

An uproar shook the shop. William didn't let down, continuing to shout at everyone to leave.

"You good-for-nothing woman," the stout man cursed at me. "Should've known better than to trust a bit of gold given by a siren."

William grabbed the man by the collar. Gasping, I stepped back, holding onto my gold locket.

"Now, Rudy, is that how we treat a proper lady?" William questioned.

The stout man—Rudy—vigorously shook his head. Looking away, I did what I could to push away the heat blazing across my cheeks.

"Glad we can agree on that," William grinned. "So, why don't you offer Calliope Windsor your sincerest apologies, and maybe I won't add an additional charge to your next purchase?"

The stout man wobbled on his feet, offering me an overly extravagant apology, and then left the shop in a mad dash.

"You didn't need to scare the man," I said.

"You don't know Rudy like I do."

"Well, I at least didn't mean for you to close the shop so early in the day."

"It's fine."

Judging by the tension in his shoulders, it wasn't fine.

Without looking at me, William was unable to hide the anger in his tone as he asked, "Why do you need to go to Gorgona Cave, Calliope?"

Patting down my dress and re-positioning my hat again, I straightened my back and approached the counter. "I need a rare piece of algae for my mother's exhibit."

"Just get some from the harbor and call it a day."

"William, please, you know it's more than that."

"*You* believe it's more than that."

"I'm not asking for your belief, I'm asking for your help," I retorted. "It shouldn't take more than a couple of weeks at most, and I'm willing to pay—"

"A high price," he finished, facing me. "You always are."

I bit my lip. The fire that had been building in my gut since Ms. Day said she'd move my mother's exhibit to myths and legends was gone, replaced with a fresh wave of guilt I'd been avoiding the past year.

"You don't need to be the one to take me," I replied. "I'm just asking if you know anyone who could."

His eyes softened. "Why can't you just let this go?"

My chest hurt, his question the same he'd asked the day I'd left.

"Let's not behave like children today, William," I replied with a forced laugh.

He rested an elbow on the counter. "You're right. Let's talk like real adults who don't barge into each other's establishments and interrupt a decent day of wages."

My eyes fluttered closed in frustration. "I didn't ask you to close your shop."

"Just answer my question."

"I need to do it for her," I reached across the counter and, despite my better judgment, pressed my hand onto his arm. "For my mother. Please."

Heaving a deep sigh, William slid his arm out from underneath my hand. The counter's chill seeped through my gloves. He turned around, rubbing his hand along the back of his neck.

"It's been a while since I've seen you," he remarked, each word said carefully.

I paused, lacing my fingers together. "I know."

He looked at me over his shoulder, brows furrowed—worried.

Collecting myself, I said, "The museum's threatening to move my mother's exhibit to the myths and legends section unless I can deliver the algae she found. And while I know you have your thoughts and opinions on her work, I believe all her years of tireless research deserves to be legitimized." I let out a sigh, my shoulders relaxing. "It was one of her final wishes, Will."

Hands on his hips, he took a deep and long pause.

I shouldn't have come.

Regret and worry flooded my senses. How could I be so foolish to think I could somehow sail across the sea to save my mother's exhibit? And to ask the man I'd left on his knee without a single explanation?

"This was a mistake," I stuttered. "I'm so sorry, I'll go—"

"Be at the docks by dawn. Any later and I'm calling it off."

I widened my eyes. "You don't have to take me."

"The second-best sailor here is Rudy, and there's no way in hell I'm letting him take you out there," he paused. "Do you still have the sailing gear I gave you?"

Stilling my hand on the locket, I replied, "I do."

A small silence spanned between us, his muscles tensing underneath his shirt.

"Good," he said. "Bring all of it and I'll supply some extras."

Straightening my back, I cleared my throat. "Right, of course. And I'll pay you enough wages to cover three months of work at your store to make this worth your while."

William's eyes widened.

"Do we have a deal?" I asked, steadying my hand between us.

Looking between my face and my arm, William said, "I don't need your help with my store, Calliope."

"I'm not offering help. We're conducting a business transaction. Now, what do you say?"

Hesitation lined his brows until, slowly, he extended his callused hand and shook. "A business transaction," he breathed, his hand holding on for a moment longer than I anticipated.

"Great," I replied, swiftly turning and opening the shop's entrance before a well of emotions broke through the dam I'd built. "I'll see you at dawn."

Before William could say another word, I ran through the streets a second time that day, finally arriving in the sanctuary that was my mother's home library. I was set to sail tomorrow, but now the real issue surfaced: how in the hell was I going to prove it could restore souls?

Chapter 2

Deep purples and blues stretched across the morning sky, the colors glittering along calm waters. The dock creaked underneath my tennis Oxford's, the shoes embarrassingly underused this past year, given I was the daughter of a researcher and adventurer. But with my mother's museum exhibition at stake, it was time I did something more than study historical texts about the ocean or attend parlor parties with people who I didn't care to know.

I needed to retrieve the rare algae she'd discovered years ago. She'd sworn on her life the sea could harbor someone's soul–their love, passion, and purpose–much like a pirate hoards their treasure. Then, the person would be like an empty vessel, hungry to fill themselves again. According to her research, this algae was the only way to retrieve one's soul again.

All I had to do was sail to Gorgona Cave, bring a sample back to the museum, and prove its effectiveness. Then, my mother's research would finally be confirmed as *real*, not myth or legend, and all the "complaints" about the exhibit's credibility would be laid to rest. She would be cemented in the museum as a true researcher; a piece of her that could live on, and I could visit as often as I wished.

The only thing was figuring out under what circumstance a soul ended up in the sea, and how this algae could restore it. Not to mention, I had a month with only a handful of documents written by my mother. I'd already read through them a hundred times.

God help me.

"You actually came," a deep voice shouted.

William jumped out of his boat and onto the dock. He wore the same outfit he did every day since becoming a sailor and bait shop owner three years ago—a white shirt, khaki trousers, and brown leather suspenders. His shoulders had become noticeably broader in the past year while his red hair had grown to meet his shoulders. He was every bit as handsome as I'd recalled, which was rather unfortunate seeing how I was planning to ignore him as best I could on this trip.

"Of course, I did," I replied, rocking on my heels.

William scoffed, "Right, why would I think you wouldn't? After all, we're doing this for your mother."

The sting sliced where he'd meant it to hit—my heart.

"Are we ready to depart or are we still waiting on supplies?" I replied, desperate to change the subject.

"Ready when you are," he said, offering his hand to help me aboard.

"I can do it myself, thank you."

"Fine by me."

He jumped back into the boat, the ship teetering on the water beneath his weight.

I braced my hands on the boat in preparation to climb onto its deck, but something familiar caught my eye. Breath hitching in my chest, I kneeled down, running my fingers along the boat's name. Its deep blue calligraphy swirled like ocean waves, guarded on either side by depictions of red-tailed mermaids.

Calliope.

My heart sank into my stomach.

Even after leaving him in a whirl of tears and shouts, William had kept the ship's name—*my* name. Water licked up through the crack between the dock and the boat. Gripping my gold locket, I rubbed it between my fingers and stood. I stared at the man whom I'd believed had hated me with every bone in his body.

"Are you coming?" William asked, a tinge of annoyance in his tone.

I had to do this for my mother—face the man I left, despite my regrets, and sail on cold and treacherous waters.

Before I could think better of it, I flung myself over the railing and landed on the wood deck. The water's motion surprised me, my feet slipping on the wood. Falling towards the newly scrubbed floor, I ended up stumbling into William's arms instead.

He gripped my hips, his fingers sinking into the sensitive part of my skin. Tobacco and leather lingered in his hair and on his clothes, memories resurfacing of dinners in his home where we drank wine until we fell asleep in front of the fire, and mornings where I refused to get out of bed just so I could smell and kiss him until he left for work.

Longing laced through my chest. My cracked heart threatened to open itself, as if it believed he could touch it and make all the pain disappear.

"So sorry," I said breathlessly, my face flush to his broad chest as I gained my footing.

"It's alright," he whispered, his shaky breaths brushing my ear, sending a shiver along my arms.

He slid his hands up my waist, under my cotton shirt, finally settling on either side of my body. My skin was soft and sensitive where his touch met mine—a touch that felt like home.

Get a hold of yourself, Calliope.

I scrambled away from him, patting down my cotton pants and adjusting my small hat. Will brushed his arms and turned his attention to a canvas sail.

"Well, uh, go ahead and get settled," William said with a small cough. "The downstairs bedroom is where you'll be sleeping and there's a fully stocked galley kitchen. I'd imagine you'll want to stay down there for most of our travel."

"Right, yes, thank you," I replied, clearing my throat before heading downstairs as fast as my feet could carry me.

William released the boat from the dock while I stood in front of the bedroom mirror and promptly pointed at myself as a disappointed mother would to their child.

"Calliope Windsor, get a grip. Remember why you left this man. He's better off without you—that's what you decided. For the love of God in Heaven, remember why you're here: to get the algae for Mother's exhibit. That's all. Not to swoon over him, even if he has become a handsome, grumpy, strong, kind, sailor of a man . . ."

It wasn't a very convincing talk considering how disheveled my brown hair had become and the way my dark eyes were lined with tears. I looked lonely, maybe even scared. Perhaps I'd been feeling this way for longer than I preferred to admit.

"For fuck's sake," I shook my head. "If my mother could survive hurricanes and shark attacks for her research, I can survive a few weeks of sailing with Will to get her algae."

Then the decision was clear: if I *was* to survive these days of sailing, then I'd quarantine myself below deck.

The first three days I spent studying my mother's research on algae while William remained topside. By the time night fell on the third night, I'd learned nothing new. The algae remained as much a mystery as the sea's ability to harbor souls, everything described with hunger and emptiness. While I criticized William's lack of belief in my mother's research, I was beginning to understand where the frustration came from, especially with an idea as abstract as a soul. If there were schools of philosophy stumped on the concept, how could the sea understand them let alone hold them in its depths? Was it like keeping crabs in cages? Fish in nets?

I opened the locket and stared at my mother's smiling face. "I believe you, you know this, but *how* is any of this possible?"

Her words from years ago echoed in my mind at the question:

The sea isn't entitled to give us answers, Calli. Its ways are mysterious and ever-changing, deeper than any text could explain. That's what makes it so fathomless.

It was a lot more exciting when I wasn't relying on its mysteries to save her exhibit. Shutting my mother's research journal with a thud, I threw it on my bed and walked upstairs. My mind was getting too clogged with unnecessary questions. Some fresh air would help.

Salt-soaked winds flooded my nostrils, the breeze catching my long hair and sending it up into the sky. I smiled until the ocean waves caught my attention. Instinctively, I caught myself on the stair rail and stilled. I loved the ocean, in theory, like when it was depicted in books and explained through scientific means. But in its fullest reality, it terrified me.

"The water won't bite," William commented, lying on the deck and eating what looked to be an apple.

"How close are we to Gorgona Cave?" I asked.

"A little over a week," he replied.

A wave slapped the side of the hull, its cold spray catching my arms.

"Fantastic," I managed to say through a trembling throat.

A small grin played on William's lips as he stretched out his arm. "Come on, if you're going to vomit, it's going to be over the railing, not on my newly polished deck."

"I'm fine," I assured.

"Very convincing. You should consider going into show business."

"Maybe I will."

Standing with his arm still outstretched, he leaned closer. "Calliope, you look like you're about to shit yourself like that one time when we went to the Inter-State Fair in Jersey."

I scowled. "That was because the hot dogs you swore were 'the best in town' were diabolically unsanitary."

"You still shit yourself."

"I was *sick.*"

"Still. Shit. Yourself."

I glared at him. A playful smile tugged at his mouth, the sight so charming and ridiculous it was impossible to hold my composure. We broke into laughter. William's voice was deep and full, a sound I'd always tried to elicit from him any moment I could. Hearing it now made the ache in my chest grow wider.

I'm here for my mother, not William.

I stopped laughing.

Playing with my locket, I took a step backwards. "Maybe I should just go back downstairs—"

William swooped my arm into his and strutted us out into the middle of the deck. Stars burned in the night sky, reflecting on the water like a piece of glass. The effect caused my stomach to churn. I grabbed onto William's arm. Surprise lit my chest as he draped his hand over mine.

"I've got you, Calli," William whispered.

Something in my chest fluttered at the way he said my name. His eyes were locked on mine, and he was so close I could feel the heat from his body radiating onto my skin.

Taking my hand in his and placing his other on my hip, he hummed one of his favorite music pieces. Before I could think twice, he was leading us in a simple one-two step dance.

I should've stopped us, but I couldn't muster the discipline. This past year I'd sequestered myself away in studies and benefactor business. This moment right here was what William had always brought to my life—whimsy and color.

"So," he continued, "you still think I'm handsome and strong?"

My stomach dropped.

"William—"

"And I'm kind, which is very nice, but grumpy?" He squeezed my hip, "I think I'm pretty chipper for a man who works at a bait shop in New York City."

Scrunching my eyes shut, I let out a deep breath. "Why were you eavesdropping on me the other day?"

"I was going to show you the restroom, but instead I heard you talking about me, and before I could step away in time, I heard you explain to yourself how you decided I was better off without you."

Gulping, I averted my gaze. "I'm not wrong."

He stepped closer, the space between us a single hair-width apart. "You can't speak for me like that. It's not fair."

Panic clutched my chest and I cursed myself. This was the conversation I hadn't wanted—had actively avoided—for the past year. Stopping our dance, I backed away, but William slid his hand down my arm and pulled me to his chest again.

"Calli," he said, his eyes searching mine, "stop hiding. Please."

Sweat forming on my temple, an unbearable heat rising under my arms, I looked away. "I hired you to sail me to Gorgona, and that's all this is."

He let me go, his smile gone. I staggered backwards. Catching myself on the railing, I couldn't seem to move, his eyes holding me in place.

"Will," I whispered, like I was begging him for something, but I wasn't sure what.

"You know, your father knows countless sailors in New York City," he said, throat bobbing.

"He does," I admitted.

Thunder rumbled in the distance, a crack of lightning streaking across the sky.

"That's funny," he said, "because you made it sound like I was your only choice, like you were burdened to hire me. So, let's not pretend like this was only ever a 'business transaction'."

I shook my head, hugging my arms close to my chest. "What else could this possibly be? I'm paying you, not asking for some charity work."

"I never wanted your money," he said, running his hand through his hair. "Do you know what's been like for me since you showed up at my shop the other day? All the questions and theories and worries I've had?"

"Worries?" I whispered.

"Yes, Calliope, I *worry* about you. Ever since you pushed me away a year ago, you've refused to speak with me: at your home, in your precious museums, or wherever else you bury yourself nowadays. Then, all of sudden, you just show up and need me so you can get some fake algae for your mother's exhibit?"

A thick wave crashed into the side of the boat, splashing water on the deck. A deep well of anger bloomed inside my stomach, flickering in my veins. After all this time, he refused to respect my mother's work; refused to understand my love and belief in her.

"If you think my mother's research is fake, then why bother to take me in the first place?" I questioned.

A harsh wind whipped through William's red hair. He turned around, hands over his head, and he laughed into the now-cloudy sky.

He turned back and spread his arms. "Because I'm a fool."

"Glad you can finally admit it," I sneered.

Will approached me with a ferocity that had me arching my back on the railing. He stopped in front of me, fresh and heavy raindrops falling on our skin.

"I loved you," he whispered, a scowl creasing on his mouth and tears forming in his eyes. "Before we'd met, my life was a mundane circle run by fishing rods and sailing canvases. You breathed life and color into my empty spaces, and in my foolish love for you, I waited, hoping you'd climb back out of whatever hole you'd buried yourself in. But I see now it's impossible to wait for someone who refuses to let go of their pain."

Thwack.

Another wave hit the boat, the force so strong it reverberated through my legs until I fell on my knees. Will caught himself on the railing. The boat tipped to one side, my knees slipping on the wood. Screaming, I reached out my hand. Will caught it, his other hand gripping the rail.

He shouted something at me, but I couldn't hear him over the waves and sudden downpour of rain. The ship finally tilted back, landing on another wave with a crack. Will clutched me into his chest.

"Get below deck, *now,*" he ordered.

He let me go and raced to the mast and extra sails. Winds screaming and waves crashing, I stumbled across the boat, vision blurred and mind reeling from every single one of William's words.

I'd known I'd been a mess this past year—a *wreck*—but to hear Will call out everything I'd been hiding so deep within myself, like he saw right through me, it felt like a harpoon had pierced my stomach.

A wave crashed against me, and I slammed onto the floor. Mouth bleeding, I couldn't stop crying as I dug my fingers into the wooden boards, dragging myself towards the stairwell. Salt water stung my nose and mouth as memories of a life I'd dreamed with Will passed through my vision:

Drinking wine at newly opened restaurants and dancing in oil-lamp clubs; getting married in a glass-stained church and taking our children to art museums during rainy afternoons; fishing on wind-swept Saturdays and eating ice cream on balmy Sundays.

In my grief, I'd boxed myself into my mother's research and left behind a life filled with happiness.

A life with Will.

Despite my wobbly knees, I managed to stand. Turning around, one of the masts had broken off the boat—hurdling straight for me.

"*No.*" Will screamed.

Closing my eyes, I didn't fight the inevitable, the pain heading towards me that would break my body and mirror my heart.

But the pain never came.

Strong hands grabbed my arms and shoved me next to the stairwell. Eyes wide, I watched as the mast slammed into Will, blood spurting from his mouth while the wind wrapped the mast's loose canvas around his body. Then, he was hurled into the sea.

"*WILL!*"

Slipping and sliding on the deck, I caught myself on the railing, the waves beneath the boat churning in agitation. Will struggled against the canvas, but to no avail.

I screamed his name.

He sank into the waves.

"No, no, *no*," I shrieked, hands shaking and nerves lighting up as frantically as the lightning sliced through the sky.

I could barely swim, but if I didn't jump now, Will would be gone—forever.

Dead. Just like my mother.

Ripping off my hat, I ignored every part of my mind and body screaming for me to stay on the boat. I hit the surf with a crash, ice cold water engulfing me. Salt burned my throat while waves pummeled my face. I screamed Will's name, taking a full breath then diving under the water. A flash of lightning illuminated the darkness, Will's silhouette outlined in the canvas sail.

Swimming fast, I grabbed the tip of the sail and pulled on it. Another flash of lightning ripped across the sky as I wrestled Will out of the canvas, his body limp. My lungs squeezed and dark spots popped in my vision. Grabbing his hand, I tried to tug us up, but he was too heavy.

If I let Will go, he would drown. If I stayed, we would both die.

My throat closed. Vision blurring.

This was all my fault. Leaving Will a year ago, clinging to my mother's research like it was the only way to keep her alive, seeking out this algae like it could bring her back, believing in the sea's mysteries—

The sea isn't entitled to give us answers, Calli. Its ways are mysterious and ever-changing, deeper than any text could explain. That's what makes it so fathomless.

If the sea could harbor souls, could I give it mine in exchange for Will's life?

I closed my eyes and thought of every happy memory I'd ever experienced with Will—the hot dogs in Jersey, his weekly visits to fix my fishing rod, walks by the rivers during the spring, star gazing in the hot summers.

I thought of everything, and then with my last breath, I made my plea to the sea.

Chapter 3

A bone crunched in between my teeth, a shard piercing into my gums. Pain threaded through my mouth. I screamed. It'd been weeks. Maybe years. I wasn't too sure anymore, only that time had passed and all I had to feed myself were old bones that cut into my gums and made me scream. Bubbles escaped my lips and popped on the cavern's ceiling, the algae glowing brighter the louder I screamed. I liked how its color turned from soft purple to bright pink, so I screamed louder.

Louder.

Louder.

Pink shifted into red.

My favorite color.

Red gave way to purple, and I picked the bone out of my gums, sucking in the taste of metal down my throat. It reminded me of what I wanted—*needed.*

Meat and bones.

A sudden rumble sent waves through my cave, a current whipping my brown hair into a pool of ink around my face and the gold locket brushing my lips. Heart racing, I dug my pointed fingernails into the coral lining the walls, broken pieces floating to the floor, colliding with my horde of spoon-shaped lures.

I could smell it through the current, the stench causing my stomach to clench and gills to tense.

Humans.

Men.

Blood pumping hard through my veins, I surged out of my cave, the surface's expanse shimmering with blue light. A cave within a cave, my refuge to protect as designated by the sea herself. Or at least, that's what I'd remembered—waking up in the middle of a storm only to be called to this cave.

A shadow rippled down the way, the ship slowly approaching, and with it, my meat and bones.

Do it now.

Do it now—

No.

Last time my impatience ruined me, my stomach becoming the victim of my foolishness. Attacking too soon supplied them an escape route, the sunlight too glaring for my eyes and too oppressive for my senses. The cave, with its slick walls and glowing algae, guaranteed my success.

Sucking water into my gills, I closed my eyes and focused on the smell. A singular scent—one human. Fresh and savory, like a meal waiting to be sliced in ribbons. There was something else in this scent, something familiar, like a dream oozing through the algae and dripping down the walls.

Cotton dresses, broken fishing rods, a skeleton suspended in glass . . .

Stomach grumbling, I raked my nails across my abdomen, my iridescent blood mingling with the water. Hunger continued to rule my thoughts and dreams. One human wouldn't be enough to satiate me, but no human would be enough to kill me.

Flicking my tail, I made sure no light reflected off my red scales. Coral and urchins decorated a thin portion of the east wall, working its way up to a small pocket where ships were too large to pass through. Hidden, small, and *mine*.

Scrambling up the coral while swishing my tail, I stopped myself before breaking the surface. With a boat entering the cave, I would have to withstand the grimy air filled with black powder, thick oil, and overripe fruit.

Disgusting.

If only humans carried cargo that smelled as good as their flesh.

As I broke through the surface, a frigid wind pricked my skin. Gills clamping on my neck, I fought the shiver slithering down my stomach, the putrid air causing my gut to revolt. It was more than powder and oil and fruit swirling in the cavern. I smelled fire and steel.

Armor.

The human was wearing protection. Chattering my teeth, I scraped a nail along the cave wall. *Damn them*. Still, it would be no different than mussels clinging to their rocks; the gulls picking and picking until they ripped off their shells and slurped their flesh. As long as I trapped them, drowned them, and crushed them, I'd have my meat and bones.

Picking algae off the wall and coating it along my arm, I hummed a soft melody. The cave's glow dimmed. Patiently. Slowly. Soon, it would be too dark for human eyes, like gray clouds knitting themselves over the moon and stars. Saliva forming in my mouth, I watched as the small wood ship passed the point of no return.

Now.

Hissing, I slammed my algae covered arm against the wall. With a bright pulse, a rainfall of rocks fell at the entrance of the cave, sealing itself shut. Warm blood trickled down my wrist. I submerged into the cold waters.

Meat and bones.

With no escape for the human and their boat, my patience was no longer a necessity. Darting through the darkness, the human's scent guiding me, I reached out and was met with smooth wood. Excitement rolled through me, an uncontrollable shriek leaving my lips. The algae flared a bright red.

Clawing onto the railing, my nails scraping on the wood and metal, I found an empty boat. But that couldn't be right—the human's smell was all over this ship. Decadent, hearty, and something curious . . .

Tobacco and leather.

"Who are you?" A deep voice called.

Humming low, I called the algae to glow a soft purple. There was no human in sight, which meant they were somewhere in the ship's belly.

"I asked you a question," the deep voice called again, this time louder and rougher, "*Who are you?*"

Humans and their games. I never cared for them, my stomach growling louder and my mouth salivating more while they wasted their time and, more importantly, mine. Yet, if he was wearing armor while in the ship's belly and I dared to overtake him, I'd more than likely stumble into a trap that ended with a spear in my heart.

Damn him.

"Nucesuan lompen comius," I hissed.

A mermaid of the sea.

The man cursed. "I don't understand you."

"Linsyen nue mesan."

And you delay my hunger.

"I know I'm right about this," the man said, his tone soft. "*I have to be.*"

Snarling, I let go of the railing and fell into the waters. If the confused human wouldn't come out of the belly, then I would use it to drown him. Sharp pain crawling through my hands, I tensed until my bones elongated, claws shooting out of my fingertips. They glimmered in the algae light, long as the steel weapons humans tried to kill me with.

But my claws were sharper.

Swimming underneath the boat, I located the center—where the human's scent was strongest—and I struck.

Wood cracked against my claws. The human's scent shifted from savory to sickly.

Fear.

Smiling, I struck again. My claws went deeper into the wood, the thick structure one hit away from meeting its watery death. Yanking my claws out of the splintered frame, I aimed for my final strike—

Wood gave way to metal, snapping my claws in half. Everything turned red. Heavy pressure crushed through my hand, up my arm, and into my head. The human hadn't been wearing armor. It was the ship.

I shrieked, my fingers bent every which way, my mind growing hazy, the water cold and distant.

"Let me help with that," a deep voice said.

"I'll be alright. It's just a small splinter," I laughed.

"But you're bleeding, Ms. Windsor," the man said again.

Smiling, I let him rip a piece of his cotton shirt and wrap it around my finger, the blood staining the white fabric.

"I didn't know a fishing rod could be so dangerous," I remarked.

"Frankly, I didn't know either," he laughed, his fingers softly grazing mine.

I hitched a breath, his hazel eyes locking on me. A warmth rushed through my cheeks as I looked away and smiled.

"Try to take better care of this, alright, Ms. Windsor?" The man said, the playful smile on his mouth saying something entirely different.

Grinning back, I replied, "Will do, William Bate."

Shrieking, I jolted awake.

What was that? Those words, those feelings? Before I could answer, pain shot into my hand. Heart racing, I gripped my broken fingers. Hunger grumbled through my stomach, raking through my insides and clawing at my organs, more painful than my hand.

Meat and bones.

That's what I needed.

Fresh meat. Fresh bones.

Flicking my tail, I ignored the pain and broke the water's surface. Purple algae cast the human in a silhouette as he leaned against the railing. He had a strong and tall build, but I'd been right: no armor. Not even a weapon in his hand or strapped to his back.

Sucking in water through my gills, I circled my fin in the water, readying myself for a leap far enough to reach him. Then, I'd sink my teeth into his juicy neck and finally be fed.

"Your mother's locket," the man gasped, his voice echoing off the cave walls. "I knew it was you."

Meat and bones.

I flicked my tail harder.

So hungry.

My body was ready for the leap.

So . . . lonely.

"Calliope, stop. Please, it's me, William."

I gasped. The algae shifted from soft purple to bright blue. The man's face was bathed in light. A pale face decorated with freckles, red hair reaching his chest, and brown leather suspenders strapped over a white shirt.

"W-W-Willia—" I whispered.

His eyes widened.

Haziness blurred my vision, my body going numb as the man and the ship grew brighter and brighter and brighter . . .

He laughed, pulling his hair away from his face, its color burning bright in the sunlight, like autumn leaves when they fell from their trees, floating in ponds, laying in grass, or resting in my palm.

"Good thing I bought you that new organdy dress this morning," William smiled.

"I wouldn't have needed it if we hadn't had those forsaken hot dogs," I remarked, gently pushing into his shoulder.

"It's an important experience, you know? Surviving your first encounter with questionable street food," he said, extending his arm.

Rolling my eyes, I wrapped my arm around his. "My books would never betray me like this."

Laughing, Will squeezed my hand. "How about tomorrow you show me that library of yours and I can survive my first encounter with rigorous academics?"

Heart fluttering in my chest, I smiled. "You want to see me again tomorrow?"

He stopped us on the boardwalk, running his hand up my neck and cupping my jaw. "I want to see you every day, Calliope Windsor."

Glancing from his eyes to his mouth, I met his lips with mine.

Hunger pulled at my stomach, aching in every crevice. I submerged myself, forcing the haze out of my body. This is what I got for allowing those humans to escape last time. My hunger was insatiable and this human was somehow filling my head with unnatural visions. If I waited much longer, I might not have the strength to kill this man. I'd die in this cave and float to the bottom and become a pile of bones.

No.

I whipped my tail and leaped out of the water. It was too much. I hadn't given myself a chance to aim as I flung towards a different part of the ship. A hard thud had my teeth clatter. Between my broken fingers and a bleeding mouth, I was turning into the prey instead of the predator.

"I'm not going to fight you," the man said, his shadow casting over me as he stood at a fair distance.

Growling, I replied, "Miensuan vectorem lonus, mun pheluera."

Fighting is survival, you wretched man.

Before he could speak again, I beat my tail on the wood deck and leapt onto him. Despite his height and sturdiness, I was more powerful, and we slammed onto the floor. Ignoring the sharp pain in my broken hand, I sliced with my other across his chest. He rolled, and I missed his heart but broke his flesh.

His blood.

Savory and sweet. Intoxicating. I could already taste it down my throat, the way it would drip and I'd drink as much as I wanted. Saliva falling from my mouth, I swiped again, but he dodged. Turning, he grabbed and crushed my injured hand.

I screamed so loud the algae flared into a harsh red. Sharp and unrelenting pain overwhelmed my senses, my screams growing louder, louder, louder . . .

"Calliope!" a deep voice yelled into my ear.

I gasped, sitting upright so quickly I hit something hard with my head.

"Ow," he mumbled, and we both gripped our foreheads.

He chuckled. I shook my head.

"Will," I breathed, gasping for air, "I didn't mean to wake you."

"It's alright, I was already up," he looped his arm around my back, "did you want to talk about it?"

Rubbing the gold locket around my neck, I leaned forward, leaving his warm skin. The nightmare had felt so real—my mother's round eyes and gaping mouth, the blood covering her sailing outfit and the leg missing from a sea creature that took it.

"I need to go prep for my mother's museum exhibit," I whispered, tears blurring my eyes.

He brushed his hand along my back. I flinched away.

"Calli?" he whispered. "It's past midnight, darling. Let's try and get back to sleep—

"I need to work on my mother's exhibit entry."

Sitting upright, Will said, "Calliope, you've been working on this exhibit nonstop. You need to slow down."

I turned to him, anger billowing in my chest. "Just because you don't believe in her research doesn't mean you get to tell me what I can and can't do. If you can't understand that, then get out of my house."

"Calliope."

"Get out."

"Hold on, let's just talk about this–"

"JUST TAKE YOUR DAMN RING AND GET OUT."

Brow furrowed, he sat in silence. Unable to stop myself, I slipped the newly gifted diamond ring off my finger and handed it to him. His hands trembled with it in his palm.

He waited a few moments. "I've tried letting you work through all of this at whatever pace you needed, Calli, but if being together isn't what you want, then I'll let you be."

"Then please, Will, let me be."

Averting his gaze, he got out of the covers, changed into his khakis and white shirt, and walked out with the engagement ring. I waited until he was gone until I left my bed and locked myself in my mother's library. Tears threatened to fall on my cheeks, but I kept them at bay. I slammed book after book on my desk and reorganized my mother's memorial exhibition for three days straight.

I didn't see Will again.

"Licynea shumua?" I screamed.

What magic is this?

Slashing my claws across his face, the man yelled and released my broken hand. I rolled off of him. Before he could recover, I whipped my tail with such force I sent him into the railing. He slammed against the wood and steel, choking up blood onto the deck.

Blood dripped down his face, pooling in front of him, decadent and heady. Stomach seizing into itself, I raked my nails into the deck and steadied myself. His face was the same one from whatever visions he was filling my head with, and I wouldn't stand it any longer. I needed to feed.

Now.

He spat more blood on the floor. "Calliope, I'm sorry for never believing you. Your mother was right about everything. The sea harboring souls, the algae, mermaids, all of it."

Gills shriveling on my neck, I couldn't breathe. Everything spun: the glowing algae, the urchins, the coral, the ship, this man.

"You need to eat the algae," he continued, voice shaking. "I think it might be the only way to regain your soul and become human again."

"What if I don't want it back?" I whispered.

"Please, Calliope," he cried. "Just because you needed to let go of the past doesn't mean you should ever forget it."

Harsh ringing pierced my ears. I covered them, but it wasn't coming from the cave; something inside me was screaming—clawing to get out. It hurt, burning my insides and flaring into my heart, my lungs, my growling stomach.

Hunger.

Meat and bones.

"*I'm going to kill you!*" I screamed.

"Even if you decide to kill me, I'm not going to hurt you."

I stilled. "*Why?*"

His hazel eyes settled on mine. Countless cuts were scattered along his face, chest, arms, and legs, some so deep he would need to be sewn up to stop the bleeding.

He smiled, tears streaming down his face. "How could I hurt the one who holds my heart?"

Arms and tail shaking, tears sprung to my eyes.

He gasped, but I didn't give him time to speak another word. Enduring the pain of my broken hand, I rushed towards him and unlocked my jaw. Terror laced in his eyes as I lunged for his shoulder.

Stop. A familiar, distant voice cried in my body. *Don't hurt him.*

I widened my eyes. It was *my* voice calling out from the depths. The cave walls spun around me. I twisted my body. Warm blood met my lips, tender skin caught in between my teeth—and something else; slimy and chewy.

I stared at the skin I'd torn through–it wasn't William.

It was my arm, covered in algae.

Pain ripped through my body, carving into my stomach and down my legs, like a fire was burning through me and turning my body to ash. The algae glowed a bright, harsh red, blinding my eyes.

Broken fishing rods. Spoon-shaped lures. Hot dogs in Jersey. My mother's boating accident. The museum exhibition. William wrapped up in a sailing canvas and sinking to the bottom of the ocean, my mother's research notes in my hands, and a deal made to the sea.

Everything—*I remembered everything.*

Chapter 4

Soft fabric slid along my skin as I stretched my aching joints. Criss-cross wood beams stretched along a high ceiling. A small chime sounded, the song it played was a familiar comfort. I pressed my hands into the soft mattress and sat up.

I removed the covers. Tears filled my vision, the red-scaled mermaid tail gone. I moved my toes and bent my knees, a harsh sob working its way up my throat. It'd felt like a nightmare, jumping into the water to save Will, selling my soul to the sea, becoming a monster who feasted on human flesh.

My heart jumped in my throat.

Where was Will?

"Calli?"

I turned. Will lounged in a high-back chair next to my bed. His freckled face paired with stitches in his cheeks and chin, one of his brown leather suspenders crumpled at his hip, his white shirt shrugging off his shoulder and exposing more stitches.

"Will?" I asked, my voice scratched and parched.

"*Calli,*" he rasped, rushing to my bedside. His rough hand brushing flyaways from my eyes. "You're awake."

Cupping his face in my hands, I didn't hold back the tears spilling down my face.

"I hurt you," I whispered, "Will, I'm so sorry—"

Wrapping me in an embrace so tight my lungs squeezed, Will cried into my neck. Emotions rumbling to the surface and spilling out of my chest, I laced my fingers in his hair and sobbed.

"I'm the one who should be sorry for never believing you," Will said. "If I'd just listened, if I'd just stayed by your side, none of this would've happened."

We pulled away from each other, Will's hazel eyes red from sleepless nights.

"How did you figure it out? That I needed to eat the algae to regain my soul?" I asked.

He swept another flyaway behind my ear. "In your mother's work, she always talked about an emptiness when the soul's no longer in the body. It's always made me think of a shark without any fish to eat, roaming the waters desperate for a whiff of blood."

I leaned back. "You've read her work?"

"I think I could recite it at this point."

More tears stung my eyes as I laughed.

He laughed with me, his hands moving to my waist. "You'd been around the algae for weeks yet your soul was still absent. And when you kept talking about how hungry you were, I figured you needed to eat the algae for it to work."

"You figured?"

"I'm a man run by my intuition, Calli."

"You're a lucky man, William Bate."

"Oh, I'm well aware," he grinned.

I smiled back, only for it to fall. "I turned into a monster and almost killed you."

His grip tightened. "You traded your soul to save my life."

"And yet I nearly took it away"

"But you didn't," his eyes searched my face. "You could've killed me, but you chose to eat the algae instead."

Mouth trembling, I ran my fingers along his chest. "It was foolish of you to come back for me."

He leaned in, brushing his nose along mine. I tasted his lips—warm and soft, a familiarity that made my heart squeeze.

"A mistake I'd already made once," he whispered, "and I wasn't going to make it again."

Warm tears ran down my cheeks. I wrapped my arms around him tighter than before, and this time I wouldn't let go.

Smoothing out my organdy dress, I slipped my hand through Will's arm and handed the algae to Ms. Day.

"Here it is," I said. "The algae my mother claims to be able to restore a soul."

Running it along her gloved hand, Ms. Day gave us a quizzical look. "I believe you told me, Ms. Windsor, you'd bring back evidence. A piece of algae is just a piece of algae."

Before I could speak, Will stepped forward. "Ms. Day, with all due respect, I saw it work with my own eyes. It does what Mrs. Windsor claimed."

"One eyewitness from a sailor doesn't offer enough proof, Mr. Bate."

"Now just hold on a moment—"

As Will and Ms. Day argued about what counted as evidence for my mother's research, I took in the exhibit I'd curated for her. The bits of cave rock, the large tome she'd written about sea adventures, the glass case holding the mermaid skeleton. A shudder ran down my back. This had never been an exhibit—it had been a sanctuary of my grief. And seeing Will stand by my side and believe in my mother with me, created a bloom of warmth in my chest that felt light and free.

I couldn't help but smile.

"I think my mother would quite enjoy having her exhibit featured in the myths and legends department." I interrupted.

Will's eyes widened. "What?"

Turning to Will, I smiled. "Someone once told me that, just because I need to let go of the past doesn't mean I need to forget it. And if being able to remember my mother's research means having her in the myths and legends department, then I'll accept this exhibit's fate." I turned to Ms. Day. "May I add one more item to the collection before it's moved?"

Brows raised to her hairline, Ms. Day agreed to the request.

Unclipping my gold locket from my neck, I placed it gently atop the algae. Will's shocked face hadn't changed even by the time we stepped out of the museum and into the sunlight and bustling streets of New York City.

"I don't understand," Will finally said, placing the back of his hand on my forehead.

Laughing, I laced my fingers through his ran my thumb along his chin. "I thought I wanted my mother's work to be believed by everyone, like it would somehow keep her alive in my heart. But I think all I really wanted was for the person I loved most to believe in her with me."

Eyes softening, Will cupped my jaw. "That's beautiful, Calli, especially the part where we almost died."

Scrunching my nose, I said, "I suppose we could've done without that bit, hm?"

Yellow light shimmered on the museum steps as William and I kissed, and the wind whispered with the myths and legends that brought us together.

Chapter 1

The ocean breaks against the jagged cliff below as I stare blankly at the grey horizon from my home's porch. Cold wind whips through my hair, sending it flying around me, but I don't bother pulling it back like I normally do—too lost in the thoughts plaguing me. Warmth prickles across my back, as if the beautiful seal pelt I wear senses my mind's turbulence and wishes to ease my discomfort. Curiosity and fear war in my mind as I run a hand over the silky spotted fur, my eyes wandering to the edge of it hanging off my shoulder. Just what was this thing? It was no normal seal skin.

A nearly silent rustle behind me breaks my train of thought, and is the only warning I have before a steely voice hisses, "Where did you get that pelt?"

I whip around to face whoever managed to sneak up on me, my hands automatically coming up in protective fists. Threats to get off my property bubble in my throat, but only a cough leaves my mouth as I take in the beautiful woman standing before me.

I register first the spear pointed in my direction, tipped in a massive shark tooth, then the fact that she is completely naked save for a seal pelt draped over her back and shoulders. Instinctively, I touch my own pelt keeping me warm over my simple clothes, and she follows the movement with sharp eyes.

"I will not ask again, human, how do you possess a selkie coat?" She seethes, angling her spear closer, and I don't miss the way she says *human*, as if disgusted at having to utter it.

But I don't focus long on her tone as her question fully sinks in. *Selkie*. My impossible theories that have swirled endlessly in my mind since finding the pelt settle—could the myths actually be true?

"Selkies are nothing more than myth and legend," I stutter, still disbelieving that the tales spoken along these shores could hold truth.

Some of the animosity leaves her eyes as her lips pull into a cunning smile. "Do I look like a myth to you?"

I cock my head to the side, taking the opportunity to study her. Brown eyes so dark they are nearly black stare back at me, and for a moment it's as if I'm looking into the heart of the ocean itself. Long silky black hair covers much of her chest and breasts, still wet as if she just leapt from the sea. Her slate grey seal pelt contrasts with her pale skin, and I can't help the flutter in my chest as I trace her body with my eyes—each curve and dip of her belly and thighs on full tantalizing display.

My own lips quirk into a smile, echoing hers, as I draw my eyes back to her stormy gaze. "No, I suppose you don't." She opens her mouth to speak, but I don't give her the opportunity, blurting out, "I found it. The pelt, I mean."

She bares her teeth, and something wild flashes in her eyes as she steps forward. I inhale sharply as a bead of blood trickles down my neck from the tip of her spear suddenly pressing into my throat. "Stole it, you mean. That's all humans ever do is steal," she hisses.

Not wanting to enrage her further, I keep my voice even and speak slowly, "It's true. It washed up on the beach and I—"

She narrows her eyes at me, snapping, "You what?"

I swallow, finally saying aloud what has occupied my every thought since I put on the strange pelt three days ago. "It called to me. I can't explain it, but it was as if I was drawn to it unconsciously and *needed* to wear it. I haven't been able to make myself take it off since."

Her lips part, brows lifting as her grip on the spear loosens. "Impossible," she breathes.

"What is going on? Who are you?" I press, my voice insistent. "My body has changed. I don't know how and I don't know why, but I can do things now that I couldn't before. My vision is better, my hearing more acute. I feel stronger and faster—and not only that, but the ocean *calls* to me." I glance to my right, once again hearing the siren song of its salty depths as it begs me to dive into it and never look back.

She steps back, slowly lowering her spear. Her eyes shift from surprise, to curiosity, to something akin to horror. "The pelt bonded with you."

"What does that mean?"

She spins around, shouting something in a lyrical language I don't know, before turning back to me, her face set with whatever decision she just made. "My name is Oura, and I am a selkie and that's all you need to know about me. That—" she points to the light grey pelt slung over my shoulders, "is a selkie coat. We bond to our coats as soon as we are born, the pelts passed down from our ancestors and kept safe. It is what makes us selkies, and it gives us enhanced abilities."

She pauses, as if loathe to speak the next part, "If this pelt called to you, it is our law that I may not interfere. To take it from you would be the very worst of crimes."

Her words slowly sink in, the impossibility of them rewriting everything I thought I knew of the world. And yet, it feels right, and if there was one thing I've learned since living on this isolated coast, there were some things that could not be explained.

"So, I'm a selkie," I muse, the word sounding strange on my tongue.

She raises her spear again, her eyes lighting with rage, "No, you are not. You are human."

My own hackles raise as I step toward her in challenge, "What do you have against humans? Why come to shore and question me if we are so horrible?"

"You are all monsters," she spits, "and I was sent here to find the very worst of you—a human who is trapping and murdering selkies."

My heart thunders in my chest, and I hope she can't hear it as a flash of a memory invades my mind. Of just two weeks ago, when I'd stumbled upon a mangled body partly covered in a seal pelt a few miles up the coast from here. The local police had come to investigate, but by the time I'd led them to the location, the body was gone.

I had no doubt she was right, but I was not the killer she was looking for.

"I am no monster," I growl.

She steps back, her body relaxed even as her eyes spear me in place, "That remains to be seen."

Chapter 2

The door creaks as I enter the house and Oura lifts her head—her brows furrowing at my reemergence as if she hoped the sea had swallowed me whole. A week of tense stares and her constant disapproving shadow have built up to create an unbearable tension. It's as if she's been waiting for me to prove I was the killer all along, and it's left me nothing short of prickly and frustrated.

"Amelia," she greets tersely, averting her gaze and feigning disinterest while brushing a hand through her silky hair. A purposeful ruse to make me think she doesn't constantly know exactly what I'm doing or where I am.

I grit my teeth, rolling my eyes and peel off the jacket I wore over my seal pelt. "Look, you can be cold to me all you want but it's not going to change the fact that according to you, this pelt has bonded to me. And for all intents and purposes—according to the laws you stated when we met, might I add—I am now considered a selkie."

"You are *not* a selkie," she snaps, focusing that razor sharp stare back on me.

I turn my back to her and sigh, needing a moment from her intense gaze, and choose instead to stare out my kitchen window. The ocean yawns before me, its grey depths stretching for eternity, and churning with unyielding strength. It's never frightened me like it does in this moment.

A selkie.

How had this spiraled into myths and magic from a simple seal pelt found on an isolated rocky beach? How was it possible that someone like me ended up in a fairytale with an iron-hearted selkie at my doorstep? I suppose though, if it was a fairytale, it was a dark one. One with cruel humor, and filled with the ugly brutality only humans know how to commit.

A rustle of fabric pulls my attention back to the present, and my skin prickles as Oura approaches behind me. Slowly, I turn around and catch as she slinks across the room, her dark eyes alighting with something hungry and feral.

"You are no selkie—will never be one of us. Humans don't belong in our world," she growls low.

Despite the harsh words, my heart races, my breath catching in my throat. She's mesmerizing—wild in a way that awakens something long dormant in my chest, igniting it with a blazing heat that spreads throughout my entire body.

It's pure instinct that makes me reach out an arm to pull her closer, and I hum in satisfaction as our bodies align. Every decadent curve of her that I've wished to explore since she threatened me on my balcony press against me and I shiver. Depthless eyes as alluring as the ocean itself look up at me, and for the first time I realize that I wouldn't mind if I let the sea take me. But in the next moment, she's gone, pulling from my embrace as if burned. Though the inquisitive look she wore for a split-second after gives me hope that she doesn't think I'm wholly evil, just unsure of my intentions.

And perhaps a bit intrigued herself.

I busy myself with filling my kettle and pouring us steaming mugs of tea as she returns to pouting in a chair and pretending to ignore me. A twisted sort of satisfaction ripples in my chest as I recognize the oversized shirt I gave her underneath the pelt draped across her shoulders. I've since found other clothes for her, and yet this shirt seems to be what she favors. The strange sensation from before echoes in the lifeless husk of my chest, once again igniting something I haven't felt in years. I've only known her for a week—and had been furiously arguing with her for most of that—but I couldn't help the thrilling spark at seeing her wearing my clothes and sitting in my chair. Even if she watched me with suspicion and mistrust while doing so.

I place a mug in front of her as a sort of peace offering and continue our previous conversation in a softer tone, hoping to lull her into a truce so she stops snapping at everything I say. "I didn't intend for any of this to happen, and I don't know what it means. But if what you say is true, this pelt bonding to me is the least of your worries with a murderer on the loose. Don't you think it would be smart to have a local that could help you search? Someone who knows the people and the town and could help you traverse Verdigris Cove without raising suspicion?"

She glances at me out of the corner of her eye and I smirk. She's listening, but perhaps I could make things more interesting for both of us. I place both palms on the table and lean forward, my skin heating as I stop mere inches from her. My voice pitches low, seductive, as I drop my eyes to her full lips, "And perhaps I could even find some way to prove I'm not a threat." Her eyes flit to mine and I shiver at the wildness in them. "You are welcome to use my knowledge, and," I pause, reveling in her undivided attention, "*other* abilities however you'd like."

I smile as she narrows her eyes and crosses her arms over her chest, huffing softly and leaning away from me. She breaks from my stare to gaze longingly at the dark waves crashing outside the window, her eyes shifting between so many emotions so quickly, I can hardly pinpoint each one.

Sorrow? Frustration? Reluctance? Curiosity? Desire?

She's been difficult to read—an incredible puzzle that I have taken far too much joy in attempting to unravel since she barged her way into my cliffside house. I imagine it would take many years to fully unravel each look, gesture, and inflection. And I'm startled as I continue staring at her beautiful face, realizing that I wouldn't mind at all trading my solitary existence to memorize her every sigh and bask in her alluring presence.

She twirls an errant lock of midnight hair and my hand twitches at the sight—wanting desperately to run my own fingers through it. She cocks her head to the side, chewing on the inside of her cheek before finally saying, "Finding the murderer is my primary mission." She pauses, the air heavy between us as she looks me over slowly, and I inwardly curse my traitorous body for reacting to the appraisal. Gooseflesh erupts along my arms, and I'm thankful my shirt covers it.

She nods as if coming to a decision. "I will accept your aid in discovering them for now."

She sounds reluctant at best, but I'll take it. Perhaps this will be the start to us working together instead of her watching my every move.

I nod, sipping my tea and flick my eyes to her as she does the same. "We'll start searching for clues along the coast. There's a series of caves hidden for part of the day due to the tides. Folks dump things there all the time, though they're not supposed to."

"Filthy humans," she spits, her eyes steely.

I huff, not disagreeing with her. "Not saying it isn't abhorrent to dump trash into the ocean, but it could be a good spot to check for anything someone wouldn't want to risk being found."

She rises from her chair suddenly, making her way swiftly to the door. "Let's go then."

I smirk and take another sip of tea, not bothering to move from my spot in the kitchen. "Don't you think you should wear a jacket?"

She scoffs, "I am a selkie, the cold does nothing to me as long as I have my pelt."

"That may be so. But considering we're hunting a *selkie killer*, it would be smart to conceal your pelt in case someone sees us, don't you think? Seeing as how you will not go without it."

I raise a brow and she narrows hers, grumbling words I don't understand and reluctantly removes her hand from the door before walking back to the chair and plopping down.

I chuckle and get up to search for more suitable clothes for her to wear outside. I toss a heavy maroon jacket, a scarf, and black water-resistant pants that should hopefully fit her shorter frame. Even if she won't be cold, the jacket will do more than hide her seal pelt, it will also cover the outline of her breasts in the thin shirt I'd given her. A practical move on my part, to distance myself from the tempting sight and keep my mind clear.

She scowls at the clothes and I smother another laugh, attempting to keep my face and voice neutral. "Put these on, and then we'll get going."

Chapter 3

The drive is relatively short and we are silent for the hour it takes to hike through the dense forest after. Dark cliffs plunge before us as we leave the lush greenery, and a long set of stairs cut into the stone leads down to the caves peppered along the beach. It's normally a tricky descent, the slippery stone and narrow steps lined with only a thin rope railing, but we both have little trouble, and I once again marvel at how much easier things are when wearing the seal pelt.

"I could do so many things with this pelt," I muse aloud.

She whips her head around, cutting me with a seething glare. "Don't," she warns. "Do not presume to know anything about our sacred coats."

She stalks away and my heart sinks as she disappears into the first of the shallow caves carved into the cliff. The tide recedes and I watch it go as I let out a cleansing breath, trying to tamp down my irritation. Part of me wishes I could follow the waves and be done with this constant back and forth with her. She refuses to leave me alone, and yet she can hardly say a nice thing to me at all—what was the point? Was me possessing this pelt really that awful?

The cliff looms above me, sturdy and impenetrable, its dark grey stone still wet from the morning mists. I groan loudly and glance at the cave she disappeared into, finally reaching my limit of black-handed stares and quiet anger. Especially after the relative truce I thought we'd come to this morning. Gritting my teeth, and decision made, I stalk after her, indignation simmering in my blood.

"Why do you hate me?" I demand as I enter the cave and spot her crouching near the wall.

She stands abruptly, pointing an accusing finger at me. "You are human," she spits, "you should never have picked up that pelt, let alone worn it." Her eyes are hard and I bristle at the statement.

"I am not the one at fault here. I didn't know such things existed, and it *called* to me remember? Something I'm sure you know intimately well," I say through gritted teeth and step forward, forcing her to retreat until her back is pressed firmly into the rough damp stone of the cave.

"Would you prefer someone else had found it?" I challenge. "Someone who would have sold it, or used it against you like I'm sure the maniac we're chasing would have had they been the one to find it instead?"

Her brow pinches and some of the fury leaves her eyes, but she doesn't speak. I press further, wanting to prove I'm not the monster she believes all humans to be.

My voice pitches low, and I brush a wayward strand of her raven hair from her face. She sucks in a breath as my fingers graze her soft cheek, and warmth pools low in my stomach at the sound.

"I don't know why the pelt bonded to me, or what compelled me to pick it up in the first place. But what I do know is this: that's not where your animosity is coming from." Slowly, I lean in, stopping a hairs breadth from her face and tilting my forehead to rest softly against hers.

She's still as a statue, but she doesn't push me away. And I have no doubt she could—I'm certain her strength far surpasses mine.

"I'm not the monster you're looking for. The selkie killer is, and if I need to help you find them to prove it, I will," I promise.

Her voice is breathy as she whispers, "And what if I am beginning to reconsider my initial thoughts. What if I didn't believe you are a monster?"

My mouth quirks in the smallest of smiles and I cup her cheek with my hand, nearly gasping aloud as she tilts her head to lean into my touch. How does she command me so? Make me forget the world around me until she's all I can see? All I could possibly need?

The heat in my stomach ignites into a roaring blaze and travels down, pulsing low in my core and making me breathless.

"Oura," I breathe, her name like a prayer on my lips.

She pulls away slightly and I immediately give her space, removing my hand from her face and distancing myself to look down at her.

Fathomless black eyes stare back at me, like pools of liquid night, or the sea on a stormy evening, and it's all I can do to not lose myself in them. I ache to step forward and capture her mouth with mine, but I will not do so unless she wants it as well.

Oh, how I hope she wants this.

Her eyes search mine, her cheeks reddening at the molten desire I'm certain she must see in them. She reaches out a tentative hand, tracing my cheek down to my collarbone, and it takes all of my willpower to remain motionless as she continues her appraisal. I shiver as she delicately parts my button-down shirt, using a sharp nail to oh so gently drag down my skin—igniting gooseflesh and further stoking the fire blazing inside me. I'm about to get on my knees and beg her to do more, when she flicks her nail and a button comes undone, exposing the top of my breasts.

Her eyes are hungry as she takes in the soft skin there, before flicking them back up to mine. "Kiss me," she demands.

That's all I need to hear before I'm crashing into her like a wave on a rocky shore.

She moans as my lips capture hers, a siren song that pulses in my chest and has me pulling her closer. I grip her hips, digging my fingers into her plush curves, as she sighs in pleasure. My thigh comes up between us and she groans at the pressure pushed firmly against her core. I slip a hand beneath her shirt, just enough to graze her skin and smile at the gasp it elicits from her. I ache to touch her everywhere—to feel her softness and run my hands along her entire body, and as our kiss deepens, one hand travels to her full breast, while the other pauses at the waistband of her pants.

I pinch her nipple between my fingers and she lets out a breathy moan. My other hand traces the curve of her belly, pulling myself from our kiss to ask, "What would you like, Oura?"

Her eyes are fierce, hungry, as she breathes, "More. I want more."

"I am at your mercy," I smile as my hand dives beneath the waistband and dips to her slick core.

Peppering kisses along her neck, I smirk and whisper in her ear, "So wet for me."

She grinds her hips against my hand, a low whine escaping her when I refuse to move my fingers and give her the release she craves. "And so impatient," I tease.

I dip my head to capture her lips once more, but she stops me with a firm hand that grips my jaw. Her previously pleasure-laden eyes now look like a predator stalking prey, and my heart flutters in my chest at the shift. My body stills as she takes control, some long-buried instinct alerting me to danger, but it only heightens every sensation. She dips her head, running agonizingly soft kisses up my neck, and a low groan falls from my lips.

She taps my chest. "Your heartbeat was this fast when we met too," she whispers against the shell of my ear, "But not in fear. No, you liked it when I pricked you with my spear, just like you like the hint of danger now," she purrs.

I shudder, inhaling sharply as she touches the sensitive spot on my neck with a sharp nail. Heat floods my core, but I'm not about to let her wrestle full control from me.

"That's enough talking for now," I smirk, and she pulls her face from my neck, pouting slightly. I don't give her a chance to retort as I plunge two fingers inside her. Satisfaction pulses through me as she throws her head back, moaning loudly into the cave.

"That's it, sing for me, Oura," I murmur.

I curl my fingers inside her and smile as she moans again, pleased at her response and the way she tightens around me. I kiss her again, our movements frenzied and hungry. I'm lost in the way she feels grinding against my hand, and the softness of her skin as I pinch her nipple hard. I swallow her moan as she explores my body—running featherlight hands over my waist and digging her sharp nails into my hips.

I hiss at the pain, but it only heightens my pleasure further and I slide my fingers from her to circle her clit. As my pace increases, her release reaches its crescendo. I bite down on the soft flesh of her neck, licking the skin to soothe the ache as she tumbles over the edge, loosing a cry that fills the entire cave—a breathy exhale of my name the final note in her beautiful song. She grips my face suddenly, her fingers tousling my loose hair and crashes back into me. Her tongue tangles with mine and she growls low—a predatory and claiming sound that pulsates down to my core, making me slick with need, and I moan against her soft lips.

I'm about to abandon my plan of not going any further, when my feet shift and sink in the sand and I realize the tide has begun its slow creep inward. We won't have long to search the caves like we planned if we continue. I'd be lying if I said there wasn't a part of me that wanted to damn this search to hell and drop to my knees and pull from her more of that wondrous melody.

My heart screams in protest as I pull away, breathing heavily, and something about the wild look in her eyes has me nearly coming undone. She's so achingly beautiful. Like a wave bashing into a cliff-side that you can't help but stare in awe at, knowing the sheer strength could kill you in a heartbeat. She is as unyielding and captivating as the ocean itself—wrapped in wild beauty and a fierceness that brings me to my knees. I can't help but feel entranced.

Her smile is downright vicious as she says, "You kiss well, for a human."

I smirk, licking her wetness from my fingers and whispering in her ear, "You kiss well, for a selkie."

She shudders, her eyes half-lidded and her mouth spread in a wide smile. The first true smile I think I've seen from her, and something like hope blooms in my chest. Her gaze lingers on mine for one long heated moment before she turns and surveys the cave. I force my eyes from her back and leave the cave to catch my breath. Luckily, the wind is chill enough that it saps the heat from our encounter in no time.

When I re-enter the cave, I peek behind jagged rocks, finding discarded cans and bottles, along with something that looks concern-ingly like a condom.

My nose crinkles. *Disgusting.*

"What are we looking for?" Oura calls over her shoulder, no traces of the pleasure I'd just wrung from her present in her voice.

I frown. I'll have to try harder next time until she bears the evidence of our encounters for far longer.

Next time. I shiver in delight at the thought.

Clearing my throat, I force the returning desire from my voice and shrug, kneeling down to peer behind another craggy boulder covered in barnacles. "Anything I suppose. It's a long shot that we'll even find any—"

My heart drops as my eyes catch on a glint of rusted metal lying in a shallow pool of seawater. I glance around, looking for something to pull the object out, and find a thin piece of driftwood.

"I found something," I say, my voice echoing hollowly off the rough walls. The ocean's waves continue their relentless creep, pushing further and further into the cave, but my concern for the cave flooding is momentarily abandoned as I realize what the object is.

The silver manacles are dented, but still intact, and they are unmistakable. Oura approaches from behind, and my chest fractures at her pained intake of breath as she notices what coats the manacles. Dark patches stick to them, appearing almost like black paint, but I'm certain it's something far worse. I think back to the body I'd seen miles down the beach from my home, and how the blood had been black, not red.

If this was selkie blood coating the manacles, how had it not washed away already? Oura drops low to carefully examine them as I hold them in the air while surveying the cave again with sharp eyes. The low tide here only lasts for six or perhaps eight hours, and we are nearing the tail end of that time, so there's no way these could have been engulfed by water and still have traces of selkie blood if they were discarded yesterday or before that. This was recent. Mere hours ago.

My blood runs cold and I set the manacles on the ground before swiftly leaving the cave to stare up and down the beach until I'm certain we are alone.

I tear my eyes from the beach, walking purposefully back to Oura's side in the cave. "We need to leave. Someone deposited those not long ago and could still be close. We can take them with us, but we should be careful not to touch them. Use your scarf to grab and wrap them up."

She hesitates, not yet wanting to leave.

"Now," I grit out.

She scowls at the command, but spins around, slipping off her scarf with jerky movements and bundling the entire thing under her jacket. She stands, her eyes flicking to mine, and my heart breaks at the pained sorrow in her eyes.

"These selkies that have been killed..." I trail off, unsure of exactly how to ask such a personal question. "Did you know them?"

She looks away, but not before I catch the tears filling her eyes. "Yes. One is a dear friend, and the other my younger sister."

My heart aches for her, and I instinctively pull her into my arms. She doesn't fight me, instead she buries herself into my jacket as if I'm the only thing holding her upright. I kiss the top of her head, my anger flaring at the cruelty of this murderer to take such important people from her.

"We will find who is doing this," I vow.

She nods, eyes shining but face resolute. "Yes, we will."

I lead us from the cave, the tide nipping at our heels, and we climb the stairs back up the cliff. Once safely inside the expansive canopy of the forest, I breathe a sigh of relief.

"Just another hour or two and we'll be back—" I start, my words cutting off abruptly as Oura races into the underbrush of the trees.

She's incredibly fast and runs at a breakneck pace that I can hardly keep up with. I'm just barely able to keep her in my sight until I nearly crash into her when she stops suddenly behind a wide tree.

"What's going on?" I gasp between breaths.

She doesn't respond, but her face pinches in poorly contained rage. Her nose twitches like she's smelled something foul, and I follow her gaze to see a dilapidated cabin engulfed in moss and sprouting ferns. It blends perfectly into the forest floor, looking as if it grew from the forest itself, and it would have been difficult for me to notice had Oura not found it first.

She hisses softly, and carefully approaches the structure. I grab her arm to pull her back, but she gives me a look that stops me cold and I reluctantly let her go.

"This is a bad place," she snarls. "Selkies have died here."

I scrutinize the cabin more carefully. It doesn't appear to be anything but a rundown rotten house in the forest, but I know better than to doubt Oura. If she's determined to investigate this place, then I will just have to go with her.

We approach a cracked window and peer inside the small cabin. It's not currently inhabited, but a lamp sits on a wooden table and a plate with remnants of food rests on the edge of a small basin nearby. The house only has one level, and from what I can tell through the window, there is one main room with basic living necessities, and a door in the back wall leading to a single room, latched with a heavy lock.

Something about the door makes my stomach drop and I dart a wary glance around us, the forest strangely silent.

"Let's go around and see if there's a window into the back room," I whisper, but Oura is no longer beside me. A creak snaps my attention back to the house and I curse under my breath as Oura creeps into the empty cabin.

I survey the forest carefully one more time, certain this is a bad idea, but reluctantly follow her inside.

The house is dark when I cross the threshold, the only light filtering from the small windows scattered around the main room. Oura hovers above the single table, sniffing at a glove that sits on it. She growls, snatching the glove and shoving it into her jacket.

"Be careful touching potential evidence," I hiss but she ignores me, charging straight for the locked door.

Oura yanks on it, pulling hard, but it doesn't budge. She snarls in frustration, pacing and staring at the lock as if doing so will force it to open. I rack my brain for a solution, but without a key or bolt cutters, I don't think there's any way through it.

I jump when Oura suddenly rams herself into the door, my body on edge as I stare out the windows for any movement in the forest.

"Oura! Stop!" I yell as loud as I dare. "We need to be quiet. Just because someone isn't here right now, doesn't mean they couldn't come later if they hear a commotion and they're still in the area."

"I don't care! I smell blood and I must get in," she hisses, the sound entirely inhuman and sending a shiver down my spine.

"Oura, we don't have anything to open this lock or tear down this door. We can go back home and figure out a plan to return."

She screams, the sound tearing from her throat in a guttural roar as she throws herself into the door again. A sudden gunshot rings out and my blood freezes. Shock holds me in place until another shot rings out, and I drop to the floor as glass rains down from a window, the shards skittering across the floor and stopping just before reaching us. I snatch Oura to my chest, pulling her into a crouch with me.

"Shit," I breathe into her hair. "*Shit.*"

"What was that?" She asks, wriggling in my grasp.

"Don't move. That was an incredibly dangerous weapon. I need you to stay close to me and we need to get out of here immediately or we're both dead."

Silence greets me and my patience snaps, the fear of our current situation making my voice vicious, "Do you *understand*?"

"Yes. I will follow," she grits out.

"Okay, wait here."

I creep along the dirty floor, keeping my body low, and slowly peer out the window at the front of the house. Trees and ferns greet me, the forest looking as innocuous as it did when we arrived. I crawl to check the broken window and see the tip of a rifle poking from behind a tree in the distance. From this angle, I can't see who's wielding the weapon, but it's enough to know we likely only have one chance to escape. The assailant is blocking our exit out of this forest, so we will have no choice but to race for the cliffs and into the ocean.

My heart pounds in my chest, threatening to climb up my throat and leave my body entirely. I'll have to use the seal pelt. There's no chance I could survive a fall and swim like that in my human form—likely something still risky even with the pelt—but we have no other options.

I crawl toward the front door, careful to avoid the bits of jagged glass, and nod to Oura to follow. "The person is blocking us from getting through the forest. We'll need to make a run for the cliffs and dive into the ocean. From there, we can swim home."

She frowns, no doubt annoyed at the thought of me using the pelt in such a big capacity, but she nods, accepting this is our only chance.

Slowly, I stand, forcing a purposeful breath in and out as I prepare to throw the door wide and sprint toward the cliffs.

"Ready?" I ask her.

She places her hand in mine, and despite the gravity of our situation, I can't help but feel comforted by the small action.

"Yes."

A shot rings out as we barrel out of the cabin and through the dense underbrush, swiping blindly at low branches and jumping over sprawling roots to clear our path. We don't stop our relentless pace until we see the grey depths of the ocean churning with a gathering storm. Another shot sounds behind us, narrowly missing my shoulder as it collides instead with a nearby tree.

I don't have the time or the breath to yell in alarm as we continue our rapid pace. We slow as we near the edge to peer over the cliff. Waves crash across the dark sand beach, but there's not nearly enough water for us to dive into. I curse, quickly pivoting and leading us further along the cliff to find a deeper section.

Oura is breathless as she says, "I recognize these cliffs and there's an inlet not far that will be safe for us."

My lungs ache as we keep running, and a garbled laugh escapes me. Safe? There's nothing safe about leaping into the ocean, but I force my legs to run faster anyway.

Heavy steps pound behind us, but I don't look back, too fearful of losing our momentum. At least our assailant is only chasing us and no longer shooting, but I know it's only a matter of time before they do.

A grunt and then a loud curse from a deep voice echo behind us, and my heart sighs in relief as we pull away from the attacker—hopefully it will give us enough time to get away.

"The pelts will only transform us if we are completely naked underneath, so we will need to strip once we get to the inlet," Oura gasps as we push through the final length of forest to our destination.

Oura pulls me to a stop, and we peer over the rocky cliff to see frothy waves crashing against pointed rocks below. Not at all inviting, but at least it's enough water to dive into. Assuming we avoid the rocks, of course.

She yanks off her jacket and clothes, pulling her beautiful black and grey spotted pelt over her bare skin. Her steady presence feels as if it's the only thing keeping me grounded from the knowledge I'm about to jump over the literal edge. She peers at me in silent insistence, and I quickly follow her lead—pulling each article of clothing off in a rush. I shiver as I slip the pelt across my back. It feels even silkier across my bare shoulders than under my hands.

"What about the manacles and the glove?" I ask.

"We can each hold one item in our mouths as we swim. I will take the manacles since I am a better swimmer," Oura says, grimacing as she bites down on the chain holding the manacles together.

I nod, unable to speak as my stomach roils with anxiety and I approach the edge of the cliff with her. My toned bare legs peek from the spotted skin, and I shudder as I picture leaping into the rough water below naked and with nothing but a magic skin to protect me.

"The pelt will mold to you once you hit the water. It is bonded to you, trust that it will protect you," Oura says, her voice surprisingly gentle.

I suck in a breath, look to the sky and shove the glove in my mouth before I have the chance to talk myself out of it. I reach out a hand to her, desperate for reassurance, and she takes it without hesitation.

With nothing else holding us back, we leap from the cliff and fall into the onyx waves. One final shot rings out from behind us and Oura cries out in pain. Dark blood smatters my cheek as we fall, but

I have little time to register what happened as I hit the water and am immediately separated from her, lost in the darkness of the ocean.

My lungs seize and my throat aches, but soon warmth rushes through my body. Glowing blue light encompasses me, and for a moment it blocks out the murky water entirely. The feeling of prickling needles starts in my feet and travels up my legs until it envelops my entire body—the sensation slightly uncomfortable but entirely unnerving. The fiery ache in my chest eases as I sink further into the water, my arms and legs squeezing from an immense pressure. Soon the light clears and I stop sinking, only to find a grey seal in front of me.

I kick my legs on instinct to swim to the surface, but find instead that I'm propelled by a single flipper. Alarm courses through me until the seal bumps against me, her snout beside mine and the manacles hanging between her sharp teeth.

Oura.

She hovers in the water in front of me until I get my bearings, and I focus on her instead of spiraling into the realization that I'm no longer in my human body. A thin trail of black blood leaks from her side, and I bump my snout into her, demanding to get a better look. She pushes me away and swims forward instead, urging us to move on.

I seethe, the anger propelling me forward so fast that I catch up to her quickly. That bastard must have gotten her with the last bullet they managed to shoot off. Increased urgency spurs me, and I swim with everything I have—we need to get back to my house as soon as possible so I can tend to her wound.

Despite my determination though, it doesn't take long for my body to tire and my lungs to scream for air with our relentless pace. Oura keeps a close watch on me and leads us to the surface a few times so I can catch my breath before we dive beneath the choppy waves once more. The blood from her wound slows from a stream to a trickle, though I'm far too exhausted and focused on swimming to wonder at the change. Not to mention, my enhanced senses are overwhelming in this body and make it nearly impossible to think. New scents assault my nose whenever we surface, and the incessant call of the ocean is like a drum pounding deep in my chest—the instinct to turn from shore pulling at me fiercely. It's all I can do to focus on Oura's sleek form, and it doesn't take long to realize I'm entirely dependent on her to guide us home.

When we approach shore, my pelt begins to peel away as if sensing we are nearing land. My hands dig into the grey sand and I breathe in great lungfuls of air as I morph back into my human body. That strange blue glow encompasses me again, followed by the same prickling feeling as my legs split apart, and suddenly the pelt is simply draped across my back and I'm crawling up the beach.

I stand on wobbly feet and pull the glove from my mouth. Oura appears next to me, her good arm holding the manacles with a vicelike grip. I grab her as I spot the black blood dribbling down her shoulder and the ashen look on her face.

We don't say a word as I help her to my house, and I sigh in relief when we are finally within the warm confines of safety. I waste no time in leading Oura up to my room and sitting her atop my bed before pulling my emergency supplies from a cabinet. Fishing and crabbing can lead to all sorts of injuries, and I've learned over the years to tend to just about anything.

She brushes me away though as I attempt to get a closer look at her injury. "I'm fine, just a little dizzy from the blood loss."

I grumble, already shoving my way behind her with bandages in hand, when I see that the wound has mostly healed.

"How?"

My question comes out in a breathy exhale and she chuckles. "My body will heal itself in time, especially if I can take a longer swim tomorrow. Besides, I was only grazed by that evil human weapon."

I gape at her. "Really? Being in the ocean helps that much?"

She nods. "It is our lifeblood, thus it heals."

"That's incredible." I dart my eyes away, busying myself by placing a small bandage over her shoulder anyway to cover the healing wound. "What else can selkies do?" I ask as nonchalantly as I can.

She watches me carefully, her eyes getting that guarded expression that says I pushed too far, but she surprises me by saying, "A great many things. The greatest of which when we are in our seal forms. We can control water to some extent and can call to each other across long distances."

"Control water? Can you show me?" I ask, awe heavy in my voice.

She smiles softly, "Perhaps, but only once I am healed. We cannot use our other abilities when injured."

"Well, I would be honored if you would show me when you are healed." I smirk, getting a sudden wicked idea and tilt her chin up with my finger, my lips brushing featherlight against hers. "I'll take it as the sign I'm no longer your monster, but your muse," I purr.

She hums, flicking her eyes down to my bare chest. That's when I realize we are still only wearing our seal pelts and are currently sitting naked on my bed. Liquid desire pulses through my entire body, and I stand quickly to retrieve new clothes for us both before I follow my tempting thoughts and lay her out before me to continue what we started in the cave.

She smirks as if knowing exactly what I'm thinking, but doesn't protest when I toss her the clothes and pulls them on.

I haphazardly pull clothes on as well, turning away for a few minutes to pack up my medical supplies, and by the time I face her once more, she's asleep. A small smile tugs at my lips as I watch her peaceful form in my bed—something about the moment so precious and delicate that I want to imprint it into my memory forever to relive again and again.

As quietly as I can, I pull the blankets around her and light a nearby candle before turning out the main light overhead. I pull my chair to the side of the bed and snag a blanket from the end, preparing to settle myself to rest as well. I'm about to drift off into sleep when a shadow and a glint of silver catches my attention outside the window. I sit up to peer out more carefully, but rain from the ongoing storm obscures my view of the forest outside.

My heart thumps loudly in my chest as I stare into the darkness with razor sharp focus—I could have sworn I saw something move in the trees. I watch for what feels like hours, my eyes constantly roving the woods as my hands grow numb from gripping the armrests. I mentally flit through options to fight or flee, ready at a moment's notice to protect myself and Oura, but no mysterious shadows appear again.

"There's nothing in the woods," I whisper to myself, and clutch Oura's hand. She mumbles something incoherent in her sleep, but my smile is strained as my words ring hollowly in the quiet room. My body sags with exhaustion as the night wears on, but I don't stop my diligent watch until the sun rises and casts its warm light over the room—banishing even the most stubborn of shadows.

I take in Oura's peaceful face, so at odds with her usual scowl. I know I would be lying if I said I wouldn't do whatever is necessary to protect her. The promise settles in my chest, the feeling strangely comforting. I stare out at the rosy sky, my face reflected in the window a picture of pure determination. It's a new day, and we will face whatever is to come together.

Chapter 1

I hide, they seek.

Sounds simple enough. Like a game I played a hundred times in my youthful days.

But I'm no longer a child, and this isn't a game full of giggles, thrilling heartbeats, and tucking myself behind my mother's clothes in her closet. This is a wicked ploy, full of hungry monsters and fueled by my own twisted torment of indecision.

I made myself prey, and they took my bait without the slightest hesitation.

And if they find me, I'm theirs in every way a person can belong to another.

Mind, soul, and body.

Theirs to own, theirs to obey, theirs to spread open any time they ask me to.

I should be angry that this has become my fate. Livid that as the only highborn women of my court I had no choice in the selection of who hunts me. But oddly, as I run on tender toes through the foamy ocean tide to a nearby cave, my heart doesn't patter from disgust or fear but with enthusiastic energy. Because in this moment, I feel more myself than I ever have before.

Once I'm merely a foot away from the rocky area that will be my hiding space, my clumsy pixie feet stumble and I fall with a loud splash onto all fours. With a stifled gasp, my wings flutter furiously, trying to shake the wet droplets of frothy liquid off them, and I look around. Worried that I've already ended this intriguingly fun game of 'monster come find me.'

Once I realize no one is around, I crawl the rest of the way into the nearby watery crevice as quickly as a crab and gain steady control over my heavy breathing.

As I squeeze my upper half through the naturally carved opening, a tingle of claustrophobic jolts down my spine. Shit, I might not fit. I've miscalculated the measurements of the doorway. My wings scrape against the rocky edges, and it's barely big enough for my hips to fit through. With a little coercion, it'll work though. I gaslight myself thinking positively…I'll just need to shimmy my way inside or get stuck trying.

As I wiggle the final section of my lower half through, a grainy section of the entryway rubs against my bottom…and my needy core betrays me.

It warms and tingles with filthy intentions.

Lustrous thoughts of large hands catching my thighs in a tight hold and dragging me across the sandy shore floods my mind. For less than a second, I shutter and stop, dreaming that fantasy to life. I think of my seeker taking me in the open, raw and deep, under the fading light of day until both of us are too exhausted to move. The raunchy thought boggles my intention of staying hidden and letting the game play out as long as possible. But my mind doesn't stay lost in heady thoughts for long. With mindful intent to play this ploy out as long as possible until the perfect male finds me—one whose need to find me knows no bounds and would cross all the lines to lick the salt from my lips—I push the last of my body into the small cave and circle myself around to face the opening.

As my feet sneak their way into the damp, moss-dense entryway, I flatten my back against the rocky, slick walls, shaking any lingering sexual thoughts from my brainwaves.

That's not the sort of image a pixie princess from the reputable twilight court should invite into her unblemished imagination at a time like this. My mind should be dutiful, wifely and filled with ideals of my wedding dress and vows...not the way my husband to be will feel touching me for the first time. The longer I'm left alone, though, listening to nothing but the rhythmic patterns of the waves as they subtly churn and crash into the rocks surrounding me, the more penetrated with dastardly naughty ideas my mind becomes.

Under pinched eyelids, each head of the mighty Hydra, the five Keeper Kings of the unruly Oceans, cascades through my tight vision like the dancing shadow pictures of a zoetrope against a canvas tent. And with every passing image something new, something I've never had the chance to let in before, begins to form under my clothes, and I welcome it with everything I have.

It's hot, impulsive, and needy.

Lux, Keeper of the Pacific, his image forms first behind my closed lids. He bites his opulent bottom lip as if he's starved and wishes to devour my body like the hungry great whites that lurk beneath his unforgiving prussian blue waves. His piercing black eyes penetrate so deep into my soul, it feels as if he's here within this cave, and innocently I gasp at the thought. Clenching my legs tightly together, I whisper,...what if Lux was here? Out of all the Hydra Heads, he and I never had the chance to have a proper conversation, so he's the truest mystery to me. So, I wonder, would those eyes and those lips ravish me without a word? Or would he ask for permission before touching me?

A crushing wave against my hiding spot startles my heart and shatters his image from my darkened vision before I have the chance to decide the type of lover he would be. What I do know is, inside my soul, I don't believe he's the one I truly care to call my husband.

Just as one devilish image begins to fade, a new one appears. This new face is similar to Lux's in shape, but his features and the hues of his eyes are quite individual. His deep bronze skin gives off a naturally slippery appearance, like he's recently bathed himself in coconut oil, and immediately the rich tropical scent swims through my senses. Just as slippery as his skin, his name slides off my tongue...Calvix. The boisterous Keeper of the humid and colorful Indian Ocean. Just as bustling and vibrant as his waters can be, he is loud, intimidating, and his gorgeous outline screams for me to touch him. Many times he's cornered me into a winded conversation I barely speak in and I already know if he finds me first, there will be no asking. Without a doubt, he'd make me his before I had the chance to utter, you found me.

Gods, that thought has my stomach twisting, and my pale cheeks blushing a deep, penetrable red. As his image blurs and a new hydra head forms, I wonder, would I enjoy such a formidable lover? Or would his own love for himself dry me out and render me forgettable before our first year of marriage is over?

I yank my knees into my chest and instinctively cower away from that idea when Noxxin, the Keeper of the turbulent Southern Ocean and quietest of all the Hydra Heads, flickers into my fantasy and a soft, needy smile lifts upon my lips. His features are sharper than the two before.

Dangerous and mystifying.

His thinly toned limbs are long, and in the fictitious image he studies me like I'm the rarest gemstone plucked from the deepest corners of his mysterious ocean. The corners of his cold mouth tick upward. Not necessarily in a smile or smirk, but in a mesmerisingly attentive way that makes me swallow as if I'm starving for water. He's a monster who would know what he likes, teach me how to please him, and take the time to understand what I need.

But his downfall...he's never alone. Each Hydra Head is kin, brothers born to the same water nymph, but Noxxin and his Arctic brother Finnix were born under the same moon, on the same night, and are twins. Slowly, like a ghostly shadow, Finnix's image appears beside Noxxin's, and I'm quickly reminded of the words he spoke before this little game started...

When we catch you, we keep you. When we keep you, we fuck you.

They whispered the words so delicately into each of my ears that it left goosebumps across my skin. The kind that rise with intrigue and haughty delight, and beyond the humidity in the air, I can still feel them. Then, the way a wispy winter night wind might. Then the two of them, Noxxin and Finnix, simultaneously disappeared from my side as quietly as snowflakes melting over warm flesh.

The two of their faces linger in my mind longer than any of the others until my core aches with needy desire, and my fingers slide mindlessly down my inner thigh. Studiously, the tips stop a centimeter from my panty line, wondering if they should continue their exploration or wait to be found. Humid heat fumes from underneath the pink sheer fabric of my panties, urging my fingers to rub back and forth against my tender walls, and a small whimper escapes my mouth.

When they whispered the word, *we*, did they mean it figuratively or literally? The rules of this game state that I can marry only one Hydra Head. But dare I dream about the two of them, the keepers of the coldest waters in our realm, claiming me as theirs in tandem?

My legs drop open at the possibility, and two of my fingers find themselves beneath my sheer panty line. In unrestrained circles, the pads of my fingers rub my clit. I'm so wet, it's hard to keep rhythm, but as the heat in my belly rises, the voices of Noxxin and Finnix become clearer.

We keep you, we fuck you.

Suddenly my haughty imagination clears of all the other possible brothers, knowing one never even got the chance to bloom into my thoughts, and I know one thing for certain as I messily attempt to bring myself to a swift climax.

I wish Noxxin or Finnix to find me. I want them both to call me theirs, and I desire to have them in sweet, sultry tandem until the end of time.

Before my orgasm can reach its peak, a gentle caress of something unfamiliar tickles against the side of my foot.

The sensation surprises me and causes my eyes to fling open. I instantly move my hands to a more appropriate placement, and my heart thunders in my chest, waiting for a mystery hand to wrap around my electrified ankle. Hidden in such tight quarters, it's hard to see. There's only a sliver of sunset light shining in, but under its orange shimmer, I can make out the tiny shell of a small blue crab as it scuttles along the rocky, water-drenched floor.

Not the hands of my seeker come to ravish me.

Softly, I chuckle, but my heart sinks at the realization I've not been caught. Not by Lux, Calvix, the frigid twins, or their final brother. And I am alone, unsatisfied, unclaimed, hiding in rising saltwater that I am utterly unfamiliar with.

Suddenly, the fear that should have evoked itself earlier, finds its grasp on me.

I can't fucking swim and the tide waves are growing larger, entering my cave one dreaded spill over at a time.

Chapter 2

I'm a pixie with iridescent wings that take me as high as the clouds and beyond, where the stars play. They can carry me to a kingdom in the sky, made of clouds and moondust. Up there we don't have oceans or waterfalls. Just clouds filled with rain, ready to fill up the lakes on Earth. I don't get into the water unless it's to bathe.

Why in the heavens would I know how to swim? And why on earth did I not fucking think about that ahead of time?

Faster than I could have imagined, the salty tide has reached my waistline, and I want to scream. I could. There aren't any rules against my making noise. The men's heightened hydra senses would latch a hold of my terror so quickly the game would be over in less than a thunderous heartbeat, but that's not how I want my future husband to earn me.

Claiming me out of default isn't romantic or sexy...

...though neither is drowning.

Still, I want the man who calls me queen to hunt me down and find me with his own wits and skills. Deep within my soul, I long for a love that's sent from the universe. A person who feels me within the patterns of the waves, and blindly knows the sound of my breathing within a crowded room. I desire a man who will rock my world for eternity. Not because he's forced out of duty to bed me and make an heir, but because every inch of us is made to be touched by the other.

That's what I wanted when I called to play this game. So I keep my mouth shut and continue to stay hidden.

Wet, nervous, and high on adrenaline, my head lulls back against the rocks, and I think about how I came to this moment.

I am a pixie born from starlight and moon dust, one of the future Keepers of the Night and a voice for all the creatures who come alive under the beams of midnight light. This marriage pact between one of the ocean's keepers and the princess of the stars will be the first merging of water and sky in the history of our realm. My chosen husband and I will be an unbreakable alliance with a turpitude of unstoppable power. One that will keep our world safe from the attacks of our outer-realm enemies once and for all.

But like the indecisive, flighty female I am, I couldn't just point to one male subject and choose him as my husband. No, of course not. That would have been too easy. Instead, I had to act sheepish and overthink, and make a damn game out of it.

Surrounded by thousands of eyes, the words fell from my mouth like vomit.

The one who finds me gets my hand in marriage.

My coyly impulsive decision pleased their cryptic court well enough. They're always looking for new ways to entertain themselves when our lands are welcoming a rare moment of peace. My family, on the other hand, was not pleased in the slightest. Their sour faces told me everything I needed to know.

Disappointed.

But that's nothing new.

Since the day I came out of my mother, a wailing, too small baby girl, I've always been a disappointment. But after today, no longer will I have to look at their miserable, snooty faces. I'll belong to someone or someone's who will worship me.

One of the five Keepers of the Ocean.

The Hydra of the seas.

By themselves in human form they are manageable, or at least that's what I've let myself believe, but as one giant beast they are the waves that destroy mountains and the swirling storms that carve new landscape across every league of land their depths touch. I'll be his wife through promised vows, but in hushed truth I'll be bound to them all. When they are the mighty hydra, one dragon like monster with five heads, they share thoughts in the same way a hive mind would. The thought of that is equally as terrifying as it is titillating.

Breaking me away from my internal thoughts, a giant wave thrashes against the outer rocks, sending a multitude of formidable vibrations through the inner walls. I muffle a startled yelp as a gush of frothy water pours into the cavern. Like the banks of a flooding river, there is no way to stop it. Within the span of three heartbeats, my entire body is swarmed by churning ocean water, and I grapple for higher ground. Digging my sharp nails into the crevasses of hard earth, I pull my bottom out of the water and, catching my breath, I rest on a small plateau. But before I have a single moment of peace, another outside wave pummels the barrier beyond me, and I have to keep moving upward.

Soon, there's nothing but jagged ceiling above me, and thick falling water droplets. But to my left, I notice a small pocket of airflow. It grazes against my shoulder like a soft summer's kiss, and I rush towards the small opening.

Could that be a sign to safer ground?

Without more thought, I pick away at the rocky section. Miraculously small pebbles crumble into the pooling water beneath me, and when another crashing wave pummels the outer walls, a sharp piece of panic settles into my stomach.

What happens if I get myself out of this cavern and am surrounded by nothing but angry waves waiting to drag me down to their depths?

It doesn't matter, outside of this damn place, my wings can dry off and flutter above everything to another hiding spot. Plus, I'd rather risk the waves taking me under because I chose to fight for freedom and the future I want, than sit and die waiting for someone else to rescue me.

Under the rush of desperation and growing anger, picking soon turns into clawing. Before too long there's a hole big enough for my head to fit through. As frothy white rapids rush higher and threaten to consume my body up to my breasts, I've no time to wait. I poke my head outside and hold my breath, expecting to be pummeled by the oncoming fits of raging waves. But the crashing of oncoming rising water never comes.

Instead, what I see is even more stimulatingly treacherous.

Four eyes shimmering with the glint of a champion and two sultry mouths grinning mischievously at me.

"Hello, wife."

Chapter 3

The twins hover over me like towering glaciers, mighty and dangerously wicked, and in mesmerizing rapture I freeze. Noxxin, with his lanky arms, wields the taunting waves away from us. His commanding magic creates a bowl-like shape surrounding the three of us. It towers and rumbles around us, but never breaks the barrier created by him.

As waves collide against it like a glass wall, Fennix kneels beside my chin and with a single press of his forefinger to the rocks trapping me in, he dissolves them into tiny grains of sand. And I am free.

Well, free from drowning but not from matters of the heart.

Fennix, still kneeling before me, reaches his opposite hand for me to take. "I'm so glad to finally hold you in my hand. For far too long we could sense you but we couldn't find you. My dear brother was beginning to get frustrated."

"But you found your way to us. How entertaining." Noxxin muses, in his low whispery tone.

The sound of his voice causes my skin to rise in lustful goosebumps. "Must be fate." I lightly tease, trying my best to sound securely seductive but knowing the tremble in my words gives my over zealous desire to be touched away.

Fennix pulls me up and then into his chest. "Let us take you somewhere more relaxing. These waves are far too turbulent for a flighty pixie as yourself.

Behind me Noxxin's lips penetrate my ear. "There is a warm cove not too far, full of soft ferns and pillowy sand instead of jagged rocks."

"Would you like that? Us to take you there...together?" Fennix spurs, licking his lips as he ends his sentence.

"Yes." I exclaim, swallowing down dryly the nerves of what it means once we get to the cove.

I become theirs.

I look at each twin and bite my lip, holding back a smile as I remind myself...that's what I want...both of them touching me. Wanting me. Pleasing me.

Through parted waves the three of us walk in silence. With every footstep my heart beats louder and louder until it overwhelms my senses entirely. But my mind is as clear as the waves we've put behind us. Standing on this beach shoreline I know I'm with the one, or the ones who will marry me.

There is no doubt in my mind that this is what fate wanted for me.

Each of them takes one of my hands and welcomes me into a stunning cove. It's humid but not hot, the perfect temperature. The lush greenery that grows from the ground makes a natural earthy bed and once I've found myself at the center of the cove, I take a seat. Letting my legs drop open before them both.

Noxxin with his blue-black serpent-like tongue teases the nape of my neck and simultaneously tugs the thin left strap of my dress downward.

I shimmy my shoulder out of it, letting him partially undress me.

There's no hesitation or worry for me to stop him. It feels right, natural, and even deeper through my core it feels like a flurry of emotionally driven energy I desperately want to explore further.

As the string falls under my elbow, he kisses my collarbone with tender lips that feel like frosted rose petals upon my fire-laced skin and asks. "You remember what we told you before this little hunt started?"

Fennix strides to my other side and removes the remaining strap from its perch on my right shoulder, a little more eagerly than Noxxin. It falls, and suppressing a moan, I nod slowly. "Yes."

The rhythm of my nodding causes the light bodice of my floral dress to slip downward. Revealing my peaked pink nipples to the warm air and the glacial, hungry gawking of the men who can't wait to each suckle at their leisure. Blotches of blush flood my cheeks and blooms down my chest as I study them.

One question fills my lustful intoxication...I'm still unsure if they plan to have me in unison or whether one will simply be an observant?

A cold, addictive grin forms across Finnix's face. As Noxxin licks his lips, revealing once again a forked tongue that has my core tightening to know what it would feel like inside me. As my mind fogs with filthy thoughts, Fennix repeats their words. Slow, hot, and awakening.

"We find you, we keep you..." Eagerly my mouth parts with desire.

Then, on my other side comes the wispy winter voice of Noxxin. "...We keep you, we f—."

Before he can finish the last word. Noxxin is cut off by the squelching sound of metal cutting through solid flesh. Instinctively I buck backwards away from incoming danger. Something hot and sticky splatters across my face, and I watch in absolute horror as Noxxin's head swivels across the ground.

"No!" Finnix yells, getting to his feet. He doesn't fight the thing that took his brother's head, but, instead, runs for the cove opening.

It's too late though, a curved sapphire-tinted sword, still bearing the remains of Noxxin's blood, cuts evenly through Finnix's neck. Sending a frozen, furrowed look upon his face hurtling into the night air and away from me. The head lands somewhere in the distance with a splash I can hear but I can't see.

I scream and crawl backwards as fast as I can until my back hits the closest fern-covered wall. Then out of the dusky shadows come eyes that swirl like morning mist over the Atlantic shores, and I know the man in an instant.

"Axxis..." I utter, barely above a stilted breath.

Chapter 4

Cleaning the fresh crimson from his blade, he looms over me more monstrously than all the other hydra heads combined. "The one and only, here to claim his future bride."

"I was already found, and you killed him...or them." I stutter. Glancing quickly at the still bodies on the ground, then reluctantly back to the monster who caused the slaughter.

With the brightest grin, he smoothly retorts my statement. "That's not what I saw. I saw you clawing out of fright at the wall of your hiding hole. I ran to help you, but was too late. My frigid brothers blocked you in, but they didn't help as the panic of survival sank into your veins." I watch his muscles tense out of stilted anger. "Using my emotive power, I could sense your fear, and *they did nothing*. For that alone, they deserve to lose their heads today."

My brows pinch together. "They stopped the waves from continuously crashing against me. They broke the barrier that locked me into that cavern. Together they freed me, while you, apparently, stood and watched it all."

He chuckles. "Tell yourself that if it makes you feel better. Truth is, they did not find you. They happened to be in the right spot at the wrong time."

"And you think chopping off their heads seems a fair thing?" I say, my eyes wide with blundering astonishment at his conceited confidence.

He shrugs and tucks his sword into its hold. "They will grow back. It's part of our Hydra charm."

I tighten my gaping lips and think about that for a second. Glancing again at the horror laid before me, I remember the tales of the mighty water-ruling Hydra. He's right. In monster form, their heads will grow back double until they have defeated their nemesis, but in human form their heads grow back as normal.

Lifting my chin to the man standing above me, I fold my arms and stubbornly grunt. "Still, they were the ones I belonged with. Or one of them was, anyway, and I loved them."

Axxis kneels down in the sand before me and begins to wash the splatters of red from my skin. "Then you, my sweet and innocent Delphi, have no idea what love is."

I should move away. Continue to act upon my stubborn will, but a curious feeling of comfort takes over my mulish behavior. As he takes care of me, my eyes rove along the shape of his dark hair, and oddly, I feel a sense of home within its vast midnight hues.

After a silent minute, he's finished and sits back on his thick thighs. "There is no one you belong with more than me. You and I, Delphi, are a match written within the elemental powers around us. You and your sky have owned the depths of my soul since the moment I was created and bound to the sea that is my essence. My ocean waters come alive more vibrantly under your starlight than any other. The creatures beneath the Atlantic waves hunt and sway to the call of your summer storms, viciously and vibrantly. Free to be themselves under your starlight power, and my tides grow strong and regal by the pull of your commanding moon."

Axxis tucks a piece of loose hair behind my ear and smiles. "We are a match made by the heavens and a love that will be feared by the hells."

I'm lost for what to say back, but a stunted laugh that I can't control escapes my lips. "You're cockier than I expected you'd be."

He licks his luscious lips and leans in so close I can breathe in every particle of his thick, solid body. Iron-rich seaweed, turbulent winds, and suffocating citrus attack my senses in a way I find impossible to control, and I can't help but reach out and grab a handful of his well-fitted shirt.

He notes my sudden grasp to anchor him to me and muses in my ear. "And you are much needier than I expected. So ready to spread those dainty legs wide and welcome the cock that will claim you. It's absolutely addictive."

Axxis brushes his bottom lip against the start of my jawline. "You were even ready to take two cocks at once, should my tundra brothers have asked that of you, weren't you?"

I say nothing, but a hearty moan spills from my partially parted lips, releasing my inner thoughts with a single wanton breath against the nape of his neck. He pulls away and grins wider than before, all teeth and watery sin. "Mmm, you are a promiscuous pixie, aren't you, Delphi? Good on the outside, absolutely ruthless on the inside." A deep groan rumbles from his chest, and the sultry vibrations have my back arching to hear more. "Good thing I like to share almost as much as I like this drenched pussy of yours."

He says, running the tips of his pointer finger and middle finger over my soaked panty line. That simple touch sends tidal waves of pleasurable sensations through every part of my body, and I grind for a deeper touch. "Would you like that? Me watching you while my brothers take their turn with you?"

Sharing.

That wasn't something I'd thought any of them would be into, except maybe the twins. I knew each of their minds was connected, and that eventually all of them would likely know my deepest desires and filthiest thoughts before long.

But sharing?

Physically and intimately being with all of them?

It seems outrageous...but yet...I bite my lip and grind into the palm of his large hand.

"You would watch and not grow jealous?" I say, voice full of airy desire. Axxis moans and snaps the thin lining of my sheer panties in two. Then, he presses two thick fingers inside my core, and a kaleido-scope of atmospheric colors bursts within my eyes.

Gods, I've never been touched like this and, fuck, if it feels this incredible just with his fingers, I dare to imagine what it will feel like with his penis. "What's there to be jealous of? The blue-green sapphire ring you'll wear on your wedding finger will say that you belong to the Atlantic and you're mine. At social events, you'll be draped in the finest clothing, showing off my ocean's colors of rich indigo, dreamy granite, and lustrous teal."

An image forms behind my vision, and I picture all the heads turn-ing, including my own stuffy family's, in absolute awe of the two of us hand in hand. And I ride his fingers with more fervor and elation.

He meets my elation with demanding affection. And his other hand gently trails the clothing, left side of my collarbone and then traces downward. The deep grooves built into the pads of his palms add heightened tension to the growing sensation under my skin as he presses his hand across my left breast. He doesn't squeeze or rub, but waits, as if he's searching for something. My heart flutters, and his searching stops at the erratic beating within my chest.

He smiles widely. "Even this pixie heart of yours will, in time, belong to me. So what does it matter if in the secret moments behind closed doors you have a little fun with other men? I will get just as much pleasure watching you come undone for them as I am watching you unfold for me now." His fingers curve inside me and hit that small spongelike area I've found pleasurable when touching myself, and I bite his shoulder to stop from yelling out in pleasure.

He grunts and moves his fingers faster.

"That's it, Delphi, come for me. Show me how needy you truly are by coating my fingers in your wetness." Axxis demands. His voice is gruff and just as full of lustful eagerness as I am. Two more pulses of his fingers against that electric spot within my pussy and I'm writhing against him. Shockwave after shockwave consumes me until I'm entirely spent, and I'm so sensitive I push him away.

He pulls out of me and accepts my need for space, then utters so smoothly that deep rosy blush crosses my cheeks. "You are pure perfection."

Chapter 5

Shyly, yet filled with a euphoric happiness I never want to forget, I put myself back together piece by messy piece. I tuck the straps of my dress back to their original placement and then yank the edges of my skirt to a more appropriate position. Then, half embarrassed, half impressed, I bawl up my disheveled underwear in my fist and hold it close to my stomach.

Axxis gets to his feet and then helps me to mine.

For a moment, we stare at each other. Saying nothing but taking in everything that has happened between us. My mind boggles with all the words he said, and frustrates with all the words still left unspoken, then with as much fire as a bursting volcano my eyes gaze into his. A raging sense of unjust pride thrums up my spine, and before I can calculate my thoughts properly, my tongue lashes out the words burning my spine. "And do you plan to be with other people while we are married?"

Axxis laughs in that deep, addictive way I'm learning I adore, and steps towards me, then kisses the bridge of my nose. "No," he says, moving his kisses to the right corner of my mouth. "There is no one else I want but you, Delphi Starfall, Princess of the Night, and future Queen of the Atlantic Waves."

I pull away.

Confused.

Searching his face for a trap. "That seems one-sided and unfair."

He raises his hands in the air. Like a prisoner showing they are unarmed, then, his face grows slackened with earnestness. "I speak nothing but the truth. I've spent a lifetime serving the Gods, doing other people's bidding time and time again, and wishing for a Queen to come home to when those adventures are done. Now that I have you, I want only you."

I lift an eyebrow. "I feel like there is a 'but' behind that statement."

He drops his hands and gives me a half-frown. "But…"

A frown of my own follows his. "I knew it…"

"All I demand of you is that we marry before we fuck. That way I can take my time with you. To learn you. How you taste, how you move, and everything in between. Then, after that, when you are ready, together, we will unlock all the secret pleasures within your pixie soul. Including letting these two headless imbeciles have their way with you if that's what you want." Axxis nuzzles his nose against mine, then moves away. His misty eyes hint with honesty, but his stance tells me he's waiting for me to say something snarky.

I let out an airy giggle and lean into his arms. Pressing my chin against his chest, and look up in the sarcastic way he's waiting for. "Is that all?"

He laughs and wraps me in a snug embrace. The gesture feels tranquil. Peaceful and exactly right. Like fate knew just what they were doing all along.

"That's all." He says.

"Well then, how soon can we marry?" I say, nipping at the bottom of his chin. "I'm ready for my proper claiming right now."

He groans and a seductive grin touches the corners of his mouth. "Hmm, pure perfection indeed. My promiscuous pixie." Then with rough, playful fingers he unfolds my curled hand pressed between us, and swiftly snatches the ruined pink fabric. I try to reach out for them, but he's too swift. Without a word, he places it in his pocket.

"Those are mine." I tease.

Lowly, he laughs. "Looks like they are mine now."

I fold my hands in annoyance. His face softens and he rubs a finger along my collarbone. The small touch sends a wave of soothing adoration through my body and my arms unbind, instinctively reaching out for him. With ease my hand finds his as they slow their dance along my sensitive skin. As soon as they touch, he fists his large fingers through mine, and mutters with sheer boldness. "We will hang them above our shared bed frame, so every brother of mine is reminded which Hydra Head was the winner of the seeking game and touched you first."

I can't help but lift an eyebrow in his direction. "Wait, is that a tone of jealousy?"

"Never. But it is a tone of cockiness from a very lucky male." He assures me. Then runs his large fingers through my wet hair, lightly tugging at the ends. It's a small prick of an action but it has my head bending upward and with a groan of adoration Axxis presses his luscious lips against mine.

And I drown in his assertive fidelity to me.

His soon to be bride.

His Queen.

Tucked away between the boarded-up Tarot shop and a 24-hour pharmacy that never seems to be open anymore, sits The Mermaid Museum. The façade is rundown, sun-bleached paint peeled away in soft pastel strips, littering the dark wood planks below. A large, faded sign still advertises *Wonders of the Deep* behind dirty windows, their salt-crusted panes turned into cloudy mosaics. Despite the dirt and grime, silhouettes of transparent tanks can still be seen inside. I press a hand against the glass, the years of dirt sliding against my skin. I know she's not in there, hasn't been for ages. The night I freed her, she made me promise I'd never come looking for her again. And I've kept my promise, but all the same, I'd love to see her one last time…

Chapter 1

July, 2005

The Boardwalk

The summer breeze was alive with the sweet scent of cotton candy as I passed by Mrs. Davis's Confectionary Delights, making my way towards the arcade booths, looking for Alana. She'd said to meet her by the corner with the Skee-balls, but she wasn't there. Neither were Josh and Travis for that matter, and I felt like such a tool standing there, my brand-new, pink, knock-off COACH baguette dangling from my arm as I furiously smashed the phone buttons in a desperate text to her.

It felt like an age before my phone chimed and vibrated with the notification of the text I so desperately waited on. I flipped open my phone, annoyed at seeing a message from my mom asking if pastrami sandwiches were okay for dinner.

Sure idc, I replied, defeated. Summer break was off to a rotten start, and it was barely the end of the first week.

I decided the best course of action was to do a lap around the boardwalk. If I didn't get a text back, then maybe I could find them. This was an important mission. After spending the better part of my freshman year being a nobody, I was about to erupt on the social scene as part of the popular crowd. I needed Alana and her group to like me.

I wove in and out of the crowds, blue eyes scanning every face for a trace of Alana. The whole boardwalk buzzed with that easy, sun-soaked energy only found in a California coastal town. My stomach swelled in excitement when I thought I saw her and Josh standing in line for the Ferris wheel, but it was just another couple that looked like them. I checked my phone again, holding it up closer to the sky, despite the visible four bars, hoping it was just a signal issue and not that I'd made a horrible miscalculation in how much Alana actually liked me.

On my third round of the boardwalk, during which I'd stopped off for a churro, my phone finally buzzed with the golden text. But, when I opened it, I felt the hot sting of tears pool in my eyes as I read the words, *Srry! We left. HMU 2morrow lu!*

They'd left. Without so much as an afterthought. No doubt doing something way cooler than hanging out with me. I knew it. Chloe Berghlin was destined to remain a nobody. The downfall of being a teen with a secret in a small coastal town. The pit in my stomach widened, and I needed to get out of the sun.

The brightness of the day and general merriment of strangers around me was making me feel sick. Tossing my half-eaten churro in the nearest trashcan, I searched for an escape. I was at the furthest end of the boardwalk and didn't really feel like calling my mom for a ride home while I baked under the sun beside the parking lot. I glanced around, weighing my options. There was Madam Obscura's Tarot Shop. Dark, yes. But it would involve me having to talk to a person, which wasn't ideal. Besides, I was in no mood to have my fortune told, I already knew what bleakness the future held. The front beside it caught my eye though. The Mermaid Museum.

I walked closer, the sign in the window reading, *Wonders of the Deep*. On it, a pale, beautiful girl was sitting on a rock, winking. I peered inside through the darkened windows, not sure what to expect. "WELCOME!"

I jumped, a little yelp escaping my lips as the door flew open to reveal a short, balding man in his fifties dressed like a circus ring master. He smiled, the widened grin on his face revealing a missing bicuspid.

"Didn't mean to scare you," the man introduced himself. "I'm Lenny, curator of this fine little establishment, and who might you be?"

"Chloe?" I hesitated, realizing too late that I would've been smarter to give a fake name. "You don't sound like you're sure," Lenny teased, winking before widening the door and gesturing for me to enter. "Come in and see our live mermaid!"

I laughed. "You don't actually have real mermaids in there."

He stepped closer, "But we do, and you'll be the first person of the public to meet her." All the hairs on my body were begging me to run, but there was something enchanting about the inside of the museum. I wanted to step in and see for myself.

"That'll be $5," Lenny held out a hand.

I paid, and he quickly ushered me inside, treating me like a VIP as he led me towards the back, past the little display in the front detailing the history of mermaids.

"You can read all that later if you want. You're here, for her." He said, parking me in front of a large tank. It looked like any other giant display at an aquarium. Only, there were no fish or anything inside. The tank was dim, lit only by a wavering blue glow as the water slid over glass. "It's empty," I scoffed, sure that I'd just paid into another boardwalk scam.

But then, a quick flash of silver caught my eye. I stepped closer, pressing my hands to the glass as I peered into the shadowy water. My heart pounded, not sure what to expect, bracing for a jump-scare any second.

Slowly, she appeared – a mermaid – suspended in shadow. My breath stalled as I watched her float forward, observing every careful movement of her body. I studied the way her blue and silver scales shimmered like starlight in the darkened tank. As her gaze reached up through the glass, there was something magnetic about those pale grey eyes staring back at me. It created an awareness in the pit of my stomach, and despite the warning label on the glass, *DO NOT TAP. Monster of the Deep*, I felt pulled to get closer.

"Is this real?" I turned, but Lenny had disappeared.

There was no one around, just me and mermaid in the tank. She swam closer, pressing delicate limbs against the glass – staring. We scrutinized one another, each as equally curious about the being beyond the glass.

"Who are you?" I wondered aloud.

The creature's mouth opened, a beautiful tune moving through the water as she answered with an ethereal, "Syrena."

"Syrena," I repeated. A warm fuzzy feeling settled in my chest as I watched her move through the water, showing off graceful movements.

She sang a lyrical tune as she twirled in the water, while a while school of fish erupted from the shadows, their silver scales flashing in the dim lights of the tank. They swam around her, undulating in a magical display. The way she commanded them with her voice left me awestruck.

Syrena swam up close to the glass once more, silver hair spread out like a halo as she floated before me, staring. Our faces were inches from the glass, she was so close I could make out the light teal shimmer under her cheeks. She was so beautiful, so mesmerizing, the light in her eyes made me feel seen. "Why are you sad?" The question, while posed in a flirtatious manner, brought me back to the stark reality that I had no friends.

"I'm not sad," I replied, refusing to discuss my life with a half-fish girl.

A coy smile spread across her face. She flipped in the water, beckoning me to follow her. I found my feet propelling me further into the museum, following the aquatic tank as it wrapped around the corner. I hesitated, seeing the Employee's Only door.

She pointed, bringing a finger up to her lip in a hush. Steeling my nerves, I pushed the door open just enough for me to slip through, letting it click softly behind. It was dim, the hallway smelling faintly of salt. The low hum of the aquarium grew stronger. Pipes lined the ceiling, dripping occasionally. I looked to my left, seeing her resting her arms against the edge of the opened tank.

Half out of the water, she looked different. Her head was small, her long, wet hair trailed down her back like a thin sheet of metal. Her skin wasn't as glossy as it appeared in the water. Still, she carried the same, enchanting energy. Despite what her tank had labeled her, I couldn't help but approach her when she beckoned.

Standing before her, I was close enough to count the water droplets that clung to her lashes. My breath was caught in my throat, suspended as we looked at one another.

In a hushed tone, she asked, "Now, will you tell me why you're so sad?"

I swallowed the lump in my throat, "I'm not sad."

She laughed, a high melodic sound that echoed in the small space. It was infectious, filling me with a sense of calm, and I found myself spilling my guts.

"I want this girl at school to like me. And if she likes me, my life will finally be perfect. I'll have popular friends, probably a boyfriend. It'll just be...perfect."

"But this girl doesn't like you?" The scales around her brow raise slightly. "And that's why you're sad." I felt my cheeks blush. "I don't think so," I admitted, feelings of defeat settling in my chest. "But you don't just want her to be a friend, right?"

The heat was unbearable. I couldn't believe that I was standing in a back room in some random boardwalk business, getting called out by an actual mermaid over my deepest, darkest secret. I scoffed. "I have no idea what you're talking about."

"I think you do," her eyes narrowed, like she was x-raying my soul. Her voice had lost some of its lightness when she said, "if what you want is a perfect life, then I don't think it's a good idea to hide who you are."

I let out a dry laugh, folding my arms. "You think it's that easy?"

Her gaze didn't soften, it sharpened. "You're good at pretending."

I snorted.

"No, it's true. You're in denial about everything that you are."

Something in my chest tightened. "And you're good at pretending you know anything about me." "But I do," she said, quietly, voice less melodic when she was above water. "I know things."

The words hit harder than I expected. I looked away. For a moment, all I could hear was the dull hum of the water filtration running through the pipes, muffled by walls that suddenly felt too thin, like they couldn't hold the truth about myself pressing in from all sides.

"Hey!"

I jumped, turning around to see Lenny standing in the open doorway, a cross expression darkening his face.

"You're not supposed to be back here."

I picked up my little pink bag from the ground, rushing out as a small, "I'm so sorry," squeaked from my lips.

He sighed, momentarily forgetting his anger.

"It's not your fault, kid. I should've known those creatures can't exist out here with us. But don't let me catch you back here again," he growled as he shooed me away, before returning to the employee door. It clicked with finality behind him, and I felt a sense of dread wash over me when I thought about Syrena, still back there. Then, I heard a melodic shriek that made me run.

Outside, the boardwalk was warm, the late afternoon sun still bearing down hard. I rushed through the crowd, my bejeweled pink Razr shook in my hand as I flipped it open, hurriedly calling Mom. When I got in the car twenty minutes later, she could sense the mixed emotions radiating off me, but she didn't say anything on the ride home. Instead, she quietly pulled into the Dairy Queen drive thru and ordered us a banana split to share.

Chapter 2

The next morning, I was awake before the sun. I couldn't sleep, anxious to get back to the museum. I'd spent the whole night rationalizing what I saw. Syrena. A real mermaid. Besides the awe of seeing a real mermaid, I wanted to make sure she was okay. I left in such a rush, a bit of guilt rooted itself in my chest as I worried that I was the cause. I had to get there.

"You're in a rush this morning." Mom had reluctantly agreed to drive me the 25 minutes on her way to her part-time job at a florist, surprised that I was once again interested in the amusements of the boardwalk.

"I thought they were lame and for babies," she teased as she started the car.

"No, they're not. Plus, Alana seems to hang out there a lot," I fitted myself into the seatbelt. "Well, if this Alana girl says so," Mom snorted.

I wanted to retort but I bit my tongue. I needed the ride and didn't want to depend on the bus. I hadn't even thought about Alana that morning until my phone vibrated in my shorts pocket, disturbing my power walk from the parking lot towards the mermaid museum.

I answered. "Hello?"

"Why are you walking so fast?

I turned to see Alana and the boys posted by the start of the boardwalk beside the stairs leading down to the beach. She looked so cool, dressed in low-rise jeans and a cropped yellow tank top, arms casually stretched out while she watched the local skateboarders that were doing tricks along the railing. The yellow of her top caught the mid-morning sun, and she looked brighter than everything around her – the dull wood of the boardwalk, the bleached railings, even the brilliant blue ocean behind her. I tried not to stare, but it was impossible not to. She was just so cool, the way she leaned her weight on one hip, smiling without fully committing, like she was in on a secret no one else around her knew. I watched as she pulled her white rimmed sunglasses down the bridge of her nose as she looked in my direction asking, "Are you just going to stand there, or are you coming over here?"

"Coming," I said a little too enthusiastically, as my feet rushed towards her.

One of the skaters landed a trick nearby with a sharp crack of his wheels against the pavement, startling me. Alana let out a soft, impressed laugh. I tried not to feel like an idiot.

She pushed herself off the railing, falling into step beside me. "We're cool after yesterday, yeah?" The statement lacked in sincerity, but I nodded anyways. Anything to get back on her good side again. Maybe today would be better. But first, I had to get to the museum.

"I'll be right back," I gestured towards the boardwalk.

"Seriously?" Alana's voice was laced with annoyance. "What is with you?"

I looked down, staring at my bubblegum pink toes. They popped against the white of my flip flops. I took in a sigh, deciding the best course of action was truth.

"There's something you need to see. It's incredible."

Alana's thin eyebrow raised in curiosity. "Is it going to explain why you're acting all weird all of a sudden?"

"I'm not acting weird," the sentence lost its steam as the words left my lips. I felt small and stupid in front of Alana and the guys. I still needed all three of them to like me, to accept me into the wider network of cool people at school. I needed their cover so no one on the dance team would ever again question who I'm into.

"So, what is this thing we need to see?" Alana's disinterest was apparent by the way she admired the raspberry-blue polish chipping away from her nails.

It was time to come clean. Maybe if Syrena saw my new friends she'd get it. Or better yet, if Alana saw Syrena, she'd think I was so awesome for discovering a real mermaid's existence. The blood pounded in my ears as I finally answered, "A mermaid."

Chapter 3

We entered, the museum buzzing with the *oohs* and *ahhs* of a large crowd gathered in front of the aquarium tank. But as I approached, something wasn't right. Rather than Syrena, the water in the tank was playing host to a woman in a bright pink tail. She waved at the people, smiling through a breathing tube as she flipped and glided in the water. Compared to Syrena, her movements were rigid, labored, nothing like a natural mermaid. A splash from above gave me hope, but it turned out to be another woman in a fake green mermaid tail, coming to relieve the previous underwater performer.

"I...I don't know what happened," I stammered, embarrassed by the judgmental looks passing between Alana and the guys. "I swear yesterday there was a mermaid, a real one!"

"Oh my god, Chloe." Alana scoffed, "Do you still believe in the Easter Bunny, too?"

Josh and Travis laughed. Redness stung the middle of my cheeks.

"No, I..." my voice trailed off, weak and pitiful as I took their tormenting.

"Hey," Travis said, slipping an arm over Alana's shoulder and pulling her towards him. "Maybe, Chloe really is a lesbian. That's why she's so obsessed with those chicks with fake tails." Alana and Josh burst out laughing, their heads rolling back as they gasped for air once they clocked the look of shame spreading across my face.

I felt so small, so exposed, watching them laugh at my darkest secret like my pain was some kind of punchline. At first, I did what I always did. I froze. I let it happen. If I stayed quiet, if I smiled it off, maybe it could pass. But it didn't. Syrena's words from the day before echoed in my head. *Don't hide yourself.*

"You know what?" I interrupted their moment. "I'm done."

"Come on, don't be so sensitive," Josh dismissed.

"I'm not," I stood up taller. "You can keep laughing. But I'm done hiding."

I left them in front of the display tank, mouths still agape, while I went in search of Lenny. He wasn't as hard to find as I thought, having posted himself just outside the interactive kids' display, where neon sea creatures pulsed under glass and little hands smacked against the tanks.

"Where is she?" I demanded.

Lenny turned, a plastic smile already halfway across his face until he saw me. "Where's who?" "Syrena," I said.

His smile slipped, jaw tightening. "I don't know who you're talking about. You must be confused." "Where is she?"

I didn't get my answer, Lenny very quickly having called security to come escort me out amid the curious stares of the others in the museum. I needed to get back to the Employees Only section, but that required some planning.

I was normally quite good, Mom never needing to question what I was doing or who I was hanging out with. So I felt quite bad that evening when I called, lying that I'd be staying over at Alana's. "Just call me when you need me to pick you up in the morning," her voice carried a hint of annoyance and concern as we hung up the phone.

I sat on a solo bench at the far end of the pier, watching as the sun slowly crept towards the horizon. The sky stretched in layers of molten gold, peach, and soft lavender, while out over the water, light scattered in ripples across the waves. The wooden planks of the bench still held the day's heat, warm against my skin. The breeze picked up, carrying the lingering scents of salt, sunscreen, and fried food.

Seagulls whirled overhead, their cries sharp in the distance. Somewhere behind me, music still drifted from an open arcade, while shadows stretched long and thin as the crowds slowly dwindled. Once I was sure most of the business fronts were closed, I made my move. The side door wasn't supposed to be unlocked, but thankfully it was propped open with a dented yellow bucket as the cleaning crew started their evening clean of the facilities.

I waited in the growing shadows as the cleaning crew hauled out black bags, calculating the moment when they were most distracted to slip through the door. The museum felt completely different after dark – emptier, colder, like all the wonder had been packed away with the last of the visitors. The tanks glowed faintly in the dark, soft blues and greens of water tanks flickered in the hall lights.

My footsteps were silent against the tiles as I made my way towards the very back where I'd last seen her. Every sound felt amplified – the hum of filtration systems, drips of water, the pounding of my own heart in my ears.

The door opened with a click, leading me into a darkened room. And there she was, silver tail curled up at the bottom of a shallow tank. She was barely in any water, her skin having turned very ashen and scaly overnight. The bright, grey eyes I remembered being enchanted by, were sunken and glazed, like a fish on ice at a market. For a moment, I feared that she was dead, but then she stirred when I called her name.

"You came," she breathed, raspy and muffled through the glass.

"Of course," I tried to hide the unease in my voice as I got closer, noting the thick, metal chains wrapped around her hands and torso.

She caught me staring, a dry chuckle escaped her lips. "They've been cutting into me all day." She raised an arm, showing me the dark, navy-colored flesh wounds forming on her skin. "Why'd they do this to you?"

"According to Lenny, I'm a monster. I lured you to me, so I could attack you."

"But that can't be true."

She shook her head. "You're the only human who doesn't see me as a monster." "Because you're not," I found myself reaching into the tank to offer some comfort in the form of my hand caressing her cheek. "You just wanted to help me yesterday because I looked sad to you." She nodded.

"Well, I'm going to return the favor," I said, looking around for something that could help me get the chains off of her. "I'm going to get you out of here."

A low, grinding sound echoed through the room, followed by the rattling of steel. I'd managed to find a pair of rusted bolt cutters, but it was tough going getting them to cut through the heavy links of Syrena's imprisonment.

"Come on," I grunted, trying to lift her out of the tank. But she was quite solid. I stopped for a moment, wiping my brow.

"Any chance you can turn your tail into legs?" I asked.

She looked at me with a hesitation in her eyes. "A human can help a mermaid temporarily transform if…"

"If what?" I persisted, not wanting to waste any more time potentially getting caught. "If they were to kiss."

My heart beat faster. "That's the only way?"

She nodded. The silence stretched for a moment before I made my move. I leaned in, catching her lips, which were warm and tender against mine. For a heartbeat, the world stilled, and when I pulled away, I felt all lingers doubts that I was into girls, vanish.

Chapter 4

Present Day

The Boardwalk

I have lived twenty lives since that summer, but I often think about it. But more accurately, I think about her. The way she freed me in the span of a couple days. I stand on the pier, watching the last shreds of the marmalade sunset sink into the horizon as the indigo night moves in. A breeze picks up, bringing with it a haunting tune.

"Chloe…Chloe…"

Could it be? I haven't heard that voice say my name in years. I peer over the edge of the railing into the dark waters below. A streak of a silver flipper catches my eye. Syrena. I turn, racing the length of the pier towards the sand. My sneakers are unsteady over the cold, splintering planks, each step a sharp echo. The wind claws at my jacket, salt air stinging my lips with every breath. The boards shudder beneath me, like the whole pier might give way. A loose nail snags at my sole, and I stumble, catching myself.

"Chloe…"

The voice is growing closer. I reach the end of the pier, trudging across thick blankets of sand into the surf. The cold bites instantly, needling through my shoes, my jeans, my skin. Still, I keep wading out into the sea, the tide pulling at me.

"Chloe…"

"I'm here!" My voice cracks, carried off by the wind.

The water climbs past my ankles to my knees, then up to my thighs until I'm waist-deep in the sea. The horizon has nearly swallowed the last of the light now, and everything feels suspended between worlds. Momentarily, I wonder if I've imagined it all. If this is just another distant echo of a girl who never really existed outside of that summer.

Then the surface breaks.

Slowly, she rises. First a face, then her shoulders. The silver of her tail flickers in the light of the rising moon. She's exactly as I remember.

"Syrena," I whisper, afraid that if I say her name too loudly, I'll shatter the magic of the moment. "You're here," I say, reaching out a hand as we bob together in the surf.

"I felt your presence," she says, a sad undertone to her lyrical voice.

"I've missed you," I admit, the sandpaper touch of scales under the palm of my hand as I cup her face.

She leans into my touch, pressing her lips against mine. I can taste the brine in our kiss, and I feel like I'm fifteen all over again.

"I wish I could follow you," I say when we break apart, echoing the same words from that night I set her free.

Syrena smiles, a melodic giggle escaping her lips. "You don't mean that." "I do."

Syrena's eyes sparkle in the lowlight, her pale skin glowing even lighter in the darkening waters. She lets out a light sigh, the tune getting carried off by the wind.

"I belong to the sea, and you to the land."

"I know," I try to mask the morose sense, but she catches it.

"You have a life to live."

I know she's right, but the last twenty years have been an ebb and flow of self-discoveries that have left me yearning for the past.

"I think I've loved you all my life," I confess, momentarily afraid my words were lost to the crashing of the waves. But she smiles.

"And I will love you for all of mine. Even when the tide forgets my name," she murmurs, her voice barely more than the hush.

She brushes her fingers along my cheek, cool and weightless, like a passing current. "I used to think I dreamed you," I confess quietly. "That I made you up to survive everything else." Her smile softens, touched with something close to sadness. "Maybe you did," she says. "Maybe I dreamed you, too."

A wave swells between us, rising gently, and when it falls away, she's drifting back, like the sea is reclaiming what was never mine to keep.

"Goodbye, Syrena." I call, the word catching in my throat.

She doesn't say it back. Instead, she sinks beneath the surface, the water smoothing over as if she was never there at all. Only the rhythm of the tide remains.

When I finally turn back toward the shore, my clothes are heavy, my shoes full of sand, my hair damp with salt. I walk up the beach, leaving a trail of footprints the tide will soon erase. And this time, I don't look back.

Acknowledgements

Hey readers, friends and fellow writers, it's **Stevi Lynn** here :) I want to personally thank a few vert important people!!

First and foremost, I want to thank **Anastasia** for taking one of my many wild ideas and running with it wholeheartedly! It was one year from the publishing month that I mentioned an idea about creating an ocean themed anthology, and she was immediately on board! No questions asked just, "I'm in!" Her only stipulation...that it releases during the month that celebrated mermaids! Well here we are friend! And this is just the beginning...next up October. From there the world and the future is ours to manifest.

Next, I have to thank the wonderful group of authors that came together and created absolute magic!

Taylor, girl, I'm forever grateful that bookstagram brought us together all those years ago! From buddy reads, to podcasts, to writing sprints, to publishing the same year, to now, you have always been there! Never...ever...lose that go with the flow and count me in attitude!

Sareya, you freaking did it lady!! You have a piece out in the world, for readers to find and fall in love with, and I am so proud of you. Even more so I am blessed to have you on this whimsy anthology journey with me! Can't wait for our next adventure!

AJ, you literally saved this anthology in more ways than one! Without you the stunning cover would not exist. Without you my anxiety would have likely gotten the better of me, and without you I wouldn't have finally pushed myself to get a book on Ingram. You are such a lovely human, and I am now so thankful to call you friend!

Emily, I appreciate you for bringing pirates into this ocean themed book! Honestly, it would have felt strange without them. haha You know how to pump out five star reads and do it quickly. Thank you for always saying yes when I throw random ideas and projects your way...from this anthology, to the podcast, and writing groups you are a part of it all!

Jennifer, at this point we have been booksta friends for so long, I can't remember a time when we didn't talk daily! I'm forever grateful that you joined this anthology and that our names are written in print together. You're promptness, in depth emails, and expansive creativity truly brought a level of enchantment to the book that only you could have generated. Thank you!...Onto our next book together now ;)

I also have to give huge thanks to the artistic genius behind our cover! **@spiritofebullience** your creative magic is untouchable. You took a few images, a jumble of thoughts and made absolute perfection! Thank you a million and one times over!

Lastly, **our readers**. Thank you immensely for all of your support! From the beginning we have felt the interest, the enthusiasm, and the love because of your comments, likes, and sideline cheering!! Thank you for loving mermaids, mythology, and monsters the way we do! Though these are short stories, we hope you found characters that will stick in your heart for a lifetime. Because you and your reviews, support, and late-night shouting in our messages keep us going and will stick with us until the sky falls into the ocean.

About The Author(s)

Anastasia Arellano is originally from California but now lives in Dublin, Ireland. She is a graduate of Trinity College Dublin with a Master's in Creative Writing. She's had short stories published in The Honest Ulsterman, Honey + Lime, The Hellebore, Anti-Heroin Chic, Dragon Soul Press, and Dark Winter Lit Magazine, among others, as well as some poetry published in Smithereen's Press. She's completed several YA novels, two of which are now making the querying rounds, while her debut "Between the Shadows" is coming from Rowan Prose Publishing in April 2027. When she's not writing, she's cooking, plastering her bedroom walls in storyboards, or seeking inspiration from the Irish landscape. You can follow her on **Instagram and TikTok @writeranastasia26 and Twitter @aarellanowriter**

Stevi Lynn is a writer of lush world building, addictive banter, twists you won't see coming, and high-tension spice that will leave you panting. Often you can find her scribbling in a fresh new notebook or sitting on her deck typing away, lost in her own creations but in the moments when she is not writing she's usually hanging or searching for new adventures with her family. She is a wife obsessed with her husband and a loving mother of three humorous and busy boys. She is also a strong believer that all her problems can be fixed by walking barefoot in her garden or sitting at the beach near a body of water. Find her on social media **@stevilynn_author on instagram or @authorstevilynn on tiktok.**

Read her other stories on KU.

Violent Delights Under Crimson Skies – A multi POV epic romantasy

Yours To Take – Dark romance with a paranormal twist

S.B. Barrett is a writer and mother who enjoys tucking in her children with a made-up bedtime story. These are the seeds that spawn and grow darker and deeper once the little ones are asleep, and she writes into the evening. No longer will they bring sweet dreams once they are ready for you. She is often lost in the forest amongst the trees when she's not at home crafting up dark tales. Follow her writing journey on social media **@sareya_writes on both tiktok and instgram**

Jennifer L. Linn writes stories where magic is dangerous and love is devastating. A lifelong storyteller and unapologetic book hoarder, she fell headfirst into fantasy and never looked back—because reality simply doesn't come with enough magic (or morally gray love interests). She spends her days riding and competing in dressage with her two horses, Taylor and Theodore, and her nights escaping into fictional worlds and snuggling with her cat, Caper. She is also a freelance writer with published articles in outlets like *Horse Illustrated* and the voice behind an award-winning equestrian lifestyle blog. She is currently working on her debut fantasy novel. If you love stories with sharp edges, characters who ruin your emotional stability and just enough chaos to keep you turning pages well past your bedtime, you're in the right place.

Follow her on social media **@jl_books** or visit her website to step into her world. **https://www.JLLinn.com**

<u>Emily R. Bellas</u> writes contemporary romance with a pulse (and the occasional dark-ish fantasy short story when she's feeling feisty). She's published five romance novels over the past five years, along with *Little Stowaway*. When she's not writing, she's reading, drinking coffee, or pretending she'll only have one glass of wine. She lives in Brooklyn with her husband and their dog. Check out her website for more info: **emilyrbellas.com or follow @authoremilyrbellas on tiktok, instagram and bluesky**
Stand-Alone Novels:
Stuck, He Found Her, Expecting Stars
Campus Love Series:
Ink & Ambition, Data & Deception

<u>A.J. Braun</u> is a licensed therapist and a romantic fantasy author of their debut novel, *Of Blood & Stone*. With a master's degree in social work, A.J. enjoys writing stories that explore how systems impact people's views of themselves, each other, and their worlds. When they aren't in the session room or working on a manuscript, A.J. can be found playing D&D, cuddling with their black cats, or playing in local recreation leagues. Follow them on **IG @ajbraunauthor** for more!

When not writing, **<u>Taylor Lust</u>** can be found collecting books, watching trash tv with her husband & pets, thrifting, hiking, and line dancing with the girls or playing Stardew Valley on the weekends! Her debut, The Cave of Swords, is a passion project born from a love of writing from a young age and the desire to create a cozy found family that rivals her own. She's an advocate for mental health, and made it a priority to not shy from the difficulties of anxiety with her main character, Laira. Taylor has many more stories coming, including finishing The Cave of Swords trilogy, a spicy monster romantasy short story, a gothic fantasy series, and a standalone that will channel all of her inner feminine rage. And if you loved Oura & Amelia's story, do not fret, as Taylor plans to turn it into a full book someday!

You can follow along with her writing progress through her website, **www.authortaylorlust.com or on her Instagram and Tik-Tok @authortaylorlust**